THE BIG INDIAN

TRUE LOVE IN A FALSE WAR

SAIGON, VIETNAM; 1968

By Norma June "Juni" Allen

Table of Contents

Chapter 1 1
Chapter 2 13
Chapter 3 25
Chapter 4 39
Chapter 5 56
Chapter 6 73
Chapter 7 87
Chapter 8 103
Chapter 9 122
Chapter 10 137
Chapter 11 160
Chapter 12 176
Chapter 13 188
Chapter 14 198
Chapter 15 208
Chapter 16 229
Chapter 17 241
Chapter 18 262
Chapter 19 283
Chapter 20 295
Chapter 21 309
Chapter 22 327
Chapter 23 338

PREFACE

In Loving Memory

This book unfolds as a genuine love story, a heartfelt tribute to Norma June "Juni" Allen, my beloved momma. Originally penned in the early 1980s, it beautifully captures the essence of her enduring love for Douglas Eugene "The Big Indian" Allen, my father.

The journey of this book remained hidden for over four decades, residing as a stack of typewriter paper on my shelves. Crafted by my cousin "Aunt Karen" Shefford ("Aunt" to me), the manuscript silently waited until, one day, I was drawn to its pages. From the moment I started reading, I found myself captivated, unable to put it down until I reached the poignant conclusion.

The narrative opened a portal to the past, transporting me to my 9-year-old self in Saigon, Vietnam, during the Tet Offensive of 1968. Each word resonated, and memories flooded back, creating an unbreakable connection with the profound tale within.

ACKNOWLEDGMENT

Published by me, Stephen D. Allen, the middle son of three children born to Juni. Within the pages, you'll also encounter my younger brother Jeff Allen and my older sister Cindee McDaniel.

In the spirit of gratitude, I extend a heartfelt acknowledgment to my momma and daddy, expressing an eternal love that transcends time. May both of you rest in peace forever and a day; you deserve nothing less.

With enduring love,

Stephen D. Allen and Family

Chapter 1

In 1967, I was striving to raise our three children alone, as my estranged husband, Doug Allen, was employed under a government contract for civilian construction and installation of telephony and communication engineering at the Tan Son Nhut Air Base in Saigon, South Vietnam. The years without him were difficult, to say the least; they were long years, as he had been overseas since 1964. The endless nights were hard to endure, and sleep did not come easily, especially after watching the evening news and learning of the thousands of deaths, the prisoners, the plastic charges being used to devastate the city of Saigon, the rockets, the mortar attacks, the napalm spraying of the vegetation up country, the evacuation of the wounded and the dead, the suffering of little children and the starvation of the old…all these horrors of war left the pit of my stomach green. And my man was somewhere in the middle of it. The kids would scoot a little closer to me on the couch, seeking comfort from this mother/father person, and the question would be asked each evening, "mommy, when is daddy coming home?" or "Do you think daddy is OK?" or "When was our last letter from daddy?" It became more difficult to answer them truthfully because I did not know the truth….

it appeared our government did not know the truth, and it turns out no one knew the truth. Just years of unanswered waiting since he was flown to Saigon to fulfill a government contract on Tan Son Nhut Airbase. Only he knows why we waited.

I was trying hard to get in the spirit of Christmas but found it difficult knowing we would be alone without the Big Indian, and it wasn't because of his height that he was called that; let's just say that God gave him plenty to "work" with….Thinking of my Cherokee wasn't like having him at home. It was snowing, wet, thick snow, dragging the branches down to the ground, its weight overpowering the strength of the brittle limb as it gave way. I was already numb from the sub-zero temperatures, my strength was fading like the hours in the day, and loneliness crept inside for winter warmth as I tried to sleep. The nights were long and lonely. I had a never-ending job of nightly baths, shampoos, shopping, homework, don't forget to put the cat out and the dog too at bedtime type chores, gas the car, endless dirty dishes, laundry, up at 4:30 a.m. in a Midwestern blizzard to drive Steve and Jeff's paper route so they wouldn't freeze stiff like the snowman on the neighbor's lawn, the occasional 75 miles-per-hour trips to the emergency room after some childish accident, take the car to the garage to see what the funny noise is, more dirty laundry, the teachers conferences, my job, and Cindi's never-ending demand for clothes. Oh, how I dreaded those shopping trips! It was a rough, yet not totally a thankless chore, being both mother and father to the kids as they, too, were suffering unbearable hurt from the absence of their dad. They often told me how much more fun it was when daddy was home, and they reminisced about the many hours spent with him when he was laboring over race cars or barbequing with our friends, floating on the Platt or 102 River in welded Buick hoods….fishing and frying our catch on a sandbar. He was a big man in their eyes, and mine too. We all loved him and missed him awfully; we talked about the past well into the nights passed, many a winter evening remembering our favorite pastime!! Life was better before he took the overseas job. We worried about him 24 hours a day and feared for his safety.

Doug returned to Missouri twice a year for 30-day Rest and Recuperation leave….we treasured these visits from the early '60s until we decided to move to Asia in early 1968. But, too, there were rumors he had been seen in Las Vegas when I had no idea he was even in the States. So, this was the murky situation we lived with, knowing his love for us was indeed "there" but lacking full strength in his dedication to the children and me. He would not have accepted the overseas position in the first place if ours had been the perfect union. It was not. It was an on-again, off-again marriage, a storm of passion, love and hate we both weathered. We actually needed this separation. Although we found it hard to forget one another and the tender moments we had shared in the past. I called him my pet name, "My Big Indian," and continued to do so for years to come. He was rarely "Doug" to me but "daddy" to the three children who admired and loved him so very much. Memories of the past were filling my mind as I watched it snow on this bitterly cold night as the blizzard winds howled around the house. I found myself lonelier than usual, longing for the passion and companionship only a man can bring. Too, the pains of Christmas were grabbing at me harder than other months, as it's a difficult time of the year for a woman alone. Holiday purchases had to be made, gifts wrapped, decorations hung, family get-togethers planned, festive parties at school and the office….so shedding tears seemed easy at this point in early December. I was not as strong as I should have been, but I did wait till the children were in bed sleeping before I would have my nightly cry. Life was miserable, especially having to front it at the office the following day. Happiness was all around me during this holiday season, but not within me.

I was thinking of our twelve years of disrupted marriage, how we had gone through pure hell, our common law relationship at the beginning, our marriage and divorce, our off-again togetherness and the causes and reasons. The marriage was endured only through an accommodation that left both partners much free time to pursue their own interests. It had its closeness, yet its distance was that of a marathon at times. There were the normal reasons, the usual another woman (or was it women?), his numerous nights away from home, the impulsive gambling at poker, pool and golf, the fusses, fights and tears that led to impulsive statements flung hurriedly in hate and jealousy. But there were the good memories, too, and there were the children: three lovely innocent siblings born of love. Somehow, that love still bound us and was encasing us and desperately pleading with our hearts to shorten the vast distance that kept us apart. We were no longer man and wife, having gone through the proper divorce, yet when I spoke of him, it was of "my husband," and we both knew we would soon remarry. There could be no life on this earth for either of us unless it was with the other. It was just a matter of time, and we discussed it fully and in great detail, we belonged to each other forever, and we would go through another ceremony. We were divorced, yet in our eyes, it had never happened…. we did have a future together. Just a matter of time because I missed him as the heavens would miss the moon and stars. Meanwhile, the schools were being closed for the holidays, and the children and I were still trying to get in the Christmas mood. A "Northern" had blown in, a Midwest blizzard that closed roads and caused power failures. Temperatures dropped. Falling rain mixed with the snow and was freezing on contact with the trees and bushes; everything glistened in God's Icelandic fashion.

Midnight in Missouri and noon the next day in Vietnam when the telephone broke the silence, and

I heard his voice. The connection from Vietnam was bad, but I heard the words, "Honey, I'll be there in time for Christmas." I gently cried and let the tears fall down my cheeks….I could hardly talk. I was thanking God for the happiness I felt at that very moment. This was the call that was bringing him back to us, and I was too speechless to relate my feelings to him. I can't even recall whether I said anything other than, "Oh honey, it's wonderful," then the line went dead. But I had the message, and I was thrilled….the warm feeling within my heart extended throughout my entire body, leaving a happy sensation of tingling satisfaction. The telephone connection had been so poor, and the balance of the conversation was lost in the miles between us, but I knew, and I believed, and I was elated. I ran to awaken each child, telling them the happy news, "Your daddy will be here for Christmas." Their tears of happiness rolled down their little faces, and their eyes soon reddened, yet smiling through it all. Our tears dampened each other as we hugged one another. Soon, silence fell on the room. God had answered our prayers; daddy was coming home. Then I realized I did not have an arrival date or time, but we knew for sure he was coming, and that's what was important. The next few days, we anticipated, laughed, planned and talked, knowing it would be "any day."

Four days before Christmas, on December 21st, 1967, the Big Indian called, saying he had landed at KCI airport. I heard anticipation in his voice, the longing to be with us again. I felt tension welling up within me at the thought of what the night ahead would hold. I knew I would soon be in his arms, have his body and his love. Just touching him again made me quiver at the thought. I would give wholly and completely of myself tonight….God, help me make it through the night, that is, if it has to end at all. Good thoughts pleasured my body with longing desires of hunger for my Big Indian. Yes, yes, we would watch the cab bringing him the last 35 miles of his long journey from halfway around the world. "Merry Christmas, kids! This is going to be a great Christmas!" There were last-minute things to be done, and we scurried around with final preparations for his visit. We would treasure these 30 days as though they were 300 instead, nothing was to go wrong, and everything had to be "just perfect." He arrived late in the evening, and I can well remember how he looked as he approached the top step at the end of the long, curved brick walkway that led from the boulevard to our home. The neighborhood was a winter wonderland of glistening snow, and it was still coming down. He must be thinking the snow is his homecoming gift from the Lord. What excitement to walk through newly fallen powder….it's as though you are in another world. It was just that, another world after the steaming jungle of Vietnam. It had to appear pure and clean to him after the blood of the Vietnam War. His wavy, silverish hair roofing his tribal dark skin and high cheekbones were a sight amidst the blizzard….he looked so out of place. I thought I saw another figure, I strained to see through the heavy snow.

There was someone with him, a slightly dark body giggling and sliding everywhere, unsure of his footing on the slick walkway. Doug approached with a big smile on his face, a look of total happiness, followed closely by his small person having the time of his life sliding toward the house. Doug hugged me tightly and whispered, "I love you." There wasn't really anything to say as we both knew what was in the other's heart…. total happiness! He then introduced his house guest as Teddy Adawag, his most trusted employee "shotgun riding" from Tan Son Nhut Air Base in Saigon. Teddy was cute with his wind-whipped, curly black hair. His eyes danced when he spotted the children, and they fell in love with him the moment they met. Teddy was a Filipino and enjoyed telling stories of his land, showing the kids his native dances and speaking in his native tongue….they found him adorable, to say the least. I found him an absolute delight the remainder of the evening as the house rang with laughter and the wine warmed the weary travelers. Soon, Teddy was in the middle of the floor, scuffling with the boys and teaching them karate self-defense. Our friendship was firmly established, and we officially welcomed Teddy to the United States of America on his very first visit. He had witnessed his first snow….and before we knew it, he was outside in sub-zero temperatures, removing his shoes and socks and venturing down the sidewalk, kicking snow as he went. Flurries were swept to the left, then to the right, as his feet worked their way towards the boulevard. He was having the time of his life, playing like a 6-year-old and sweeping the sidewalk clean. The kids were glued to the window and giggling as they observed his antics….they thought this was quite a feat and worried about his bare feet getting frostbitten! More wine, good conversation, kids tucked into their beds, it was a wonderful evening…. my Big Indian was home at last.

The next day, Doug called his mother in Little Rock, inviting her and her husband to join us for the holidays. She flew in, and we decided we should have his brother and wife and daughter from Texas with us also….another call and they, too, arrived for a big Christmas. It was a wonderful holiday, but memory tells me Doug's sister could not be there to complete the family. The time went fast as we danced, entertained and visited. We went out on the town the following evening, followed by a midnight feast and pots of hot black coffee. Our kitchen table overflowed with love and laughter till the wee hours of the morning. We talked of everything we could think of….including America, Vietnam, the war, and my sister-in-law's home in Caracas, Venezuela. We drew pictures as we sat around the big round kitchen table one-night, grown-up pictures that resembled the artistry of a kindergartner! How we laughed at the results….we drew pictures of Connie's home in Caracas, of her old boyfriend. She drew him with big ears and skinny legs and said it looked just like him, we drew pictures of the enemy "gooks" in Vietnam and what we thought they looked like, complete with full battle gear, slant-eyes and huge teeth. But the results got better (or was it worse) as the spirits poured and the night lengthened.

It was one of the most fun evenings we had as laughter rang from the walls and the house shook with humorous convulsions. I remember I drew the Big Indian with his broken nose, headband and feathers and completed my work of art with the hangings of a horse. Connie and I cracked up over this one, and to this day, I treasure this piece of innocent art. We laughed till we were almost sick….Just good, clean, fun and visiting, all together for the first time. Outside, the snow continued falling as though God had ordered NW Missouri fresh and clean for the Big Indian's visit. Pure, white and without sin….a deft description of the weather and of our holidays. Soon, our guests drifted off one by one, and Doug and I retired. The wine warmed our bodies, and we embraced in each other's arms and not of shame. We belonged with each other, and we knew it. Knowing the Big Indian was coming home, we had waited to let him purchase our Christmas tree. He always got the darned thing to stand straighter and taller than I did….I wasn't too good at the "bucket and the sand" bit and not much better at nailing the crossed-wood base into the bottom of the trunk. In fact, I detested the chore simply because I couldn't do it like he did. During past holidays, I had managed somehow to get it up but was never too proud of it as I watched it lean to the east when everyone knows a Christmas tree should point straight north! Some years later, my dad came to the rescue. We figured the trees would be picked over, and Doug would come home from the local Sertoma Tree Lot with a 3-foot-high skinny, scrawny little burger, but he managed to find a lovely tree. It was 9' feet tall, and we laughed, thinking that we were lucky to live in an elegant old home with high ceilings. It was bulging with branches, and its fullness delighted the kids. It was just about the most perfect tree we had ever had!

We enjoyed the evening, and by the time the children had decorated it, and daddy put the final star on the top, we stood back in amazement, and it was grand in its splendor! We were proud of The Big Indian; he had outdone himself. Gifts went underneath, and as the snow kept coming down and the wind whistled around the house, we were in the full spirit of Christmas….The next morning, a delivery truck drove up bringing a new refrigerator and a big console color TV. The Big Indian's gift to the house. Carvings, hand-tied bedspreads from the Philippine Islands, wooden toy tops for the children to spin, China from the far East, Asian silks and satins, tea sets, boomerangs hand carved by the Aboriginal tribesman of Australia's bush country, Ivory and lots of love for us….all in the same suitcase. He had surely enjoyed buying gifts to bring home, and he delighted us with his story of the little lady in Manilla with whom he bargained over the price of the crocheted bedspread. I think he outdid himself when it came to bartering because he always came out ahead! He said that he gave her a piece of jade and $10.00, whereas she had an asking price of $150.00, so he did well. The bedspread is lovely, and to this day, I am immensely proud of it.

Glorious, wonderful holidays, so perfect. But it all ended so soon, and with tears and pleadings on The Big Indian's part…wanting us to get back together. He must have been off guard when he asked me to join him in Saigon, to bring the children and live in the middle of the Vietnam War. I laughed; he couldn't possibly be serious. This was the most absurd thing I had ever heard. I couldn't even believe he said this, yet he let us know he really meant it by the sternness of his voice and by repeating the offer a second and a third time. He went into great detail during our last evening together, he convinced me it would be good to be together again, to raise our children and make up for them. The family environment that we had robbed them of. I told him I would think about it, but it would take a hell of a lot of thinking. You just don't pick up and travel halfway around the world without serious thought and a lot of consideration for the children's safety and their education. He told me he still loves me dearly and wanted me at his side, he assured me that the children would be safe….

Chapter 2

Doug had been overseas since 1964, and I longed to join him. Several years without your husband is too long….but it seemed the war had escalated each month, and the months turned to years, and I wondered if going to Asia was really the thing to do. We had talked it over several times, and the longing to be with him was always there, yet I was fairly content on the boulevard, me and the damned Persimmons tree. I had so many things going for me. Like my good friends and my parents and relatives were all in the Heartland….gee, could I get along without them? It would be difficult to say goodbye, and there was my realtor, my dentist, my attorney and my doctor, all my best friends and my political buddies.

Urgent missives and mysterious phone calls cut his R&R short, and he returned to Kansas City Airport. It was a tearful goodbye, yet I knew in my heart that I would see him again soon. I had not actually made a decision to join him in Vietnam at that time, but he called often after he returned to Saigon. With over a dozen hours difference in our time zones, his calls usually came in the middle of the night. It became more difficult to sleep; I tossed and turned, just thinking to myself, "Halfway around the world to a war-ravaged country?" I needed time to contemplate. I couldn't concentrate on my job at the office. I needed more than anything else to "talk it over with myself…. just me and God." The Big Indian was interfering pleasantly with my lifestyle. I had a lot of thinking to do, and I had to do it fast, for there was not much time to prepare for such a detailed move just in case my final decision was to move to Saigon. He had set the target date as early as February 1968, and he called often….15 or 20 times during January. He was happy when I told him we were coming. He sounded calm yet anxious and said our tickets would be in the mail. Not to worry, he would book us on a non-stop MAC flight out of San Francisco so that it would be easier to travel with three children. The thought of it scared me….it was one hell of a giant step from the harsh mid-west winters of Missouri to the death and destruction of war in the stifling jungle.

Follow-up calls and letters advised me to bring extra tennis shoes and Levis in graduated sizes for the kids because we could not buy American clothing in Saigon. He was happy and looking forward to our arrival. We were happy; excitement was the order of the day every day in our house. Withdrawals had to be made from school textbooks and teachers' manuals acquired from the school board, China and linens packed for storage, rent the house and sell the car. I had to figure out how to fill eight large pieces of American Tourister luggage and stay within the 40 pounds per bag limit. I soon learned to step on the scale, weigh myself and have

Cid hand me a piece of luggage. If we could squeeze just one more pair of shorts in it, we did! It was like packing for a family of 15, only there were just 4 of us!

I couldn't and didn't sleep. I was so excited. I gave notice at my job, sold the car, leased the big place on Ashland Avenue and proceeded with all the necessary paperwork. I wondered why I had let him convince me this trip was the right thing to do, and if we still had enough going for us, maybe we could get back together as man and wife. I thought how much easier it would have been to have stayed in my old routine, getting up early to help the boys throw the paper route, shoveling our own snow, digging the car out of deep snow drifts…. and just letting the world go by seemed simpler to me at this time. But I managed to buckle down. I packed the photographs and family heirlooms carefully in storage barrels. Clothes and toys were sorted and given away; we had a new life ahead of us and had to concentrate on everyday survival items. Department stores would be unheard of, so we had to be sensible as to whether the article in question was "chic" or just plain "wearable" and "bearable" in the jungle heat.

I still had to tell my parents. It took days just to get up the courage because I knew it would be heartbreaking news to them. Somehow, I told them, and they were devastated….as I knew they would be. They were concerned for my happiness with a man with whom I had not been totally happy before, and for the children's safety within the limits of the war. Those poor people were hurting at the thought of us leaving the confines of the good old U.S.A. and looking back on it. I can understand just exactly how deeply they were hurting. First, they were hit full force….then silence fell, and their hearts were broken. They were not prepared to lose the baby daughter they loved so much. That meant "no more poppin' in for a surprise visit" and no more "quick lunches with them." The daily calls would cease, those days would be gone forever. From here on, it would be newscasts of the war and letters telling them of death and destruction in a far-off land of napalm and monsoon rains, Agent Orange, choppers and naked Asian children….

The next few days were so hectic; I would pack a bit, shop a bit, curse a bit, then think a lot. My thinking consisted mainly of his unfairness in requesting the children, and I travel halfway around the world to the jungles of Asia….I wanted to call him and tell him it was off. He could quit his position and return to us, and it sure would have been a lot easier! But no, I was going….to Southeast Asia and to the Big Indian that I loved and longed for. A new life awaited me, another chance to make a good marriage with him. The thought of him living in this tiny country for the past four years, doing his part in the war made me proud. I knew it was our place to go to him if this was what he wanted. His loneliness in hell was over; we would soon be on our way, and he would have his children once more under his roof as a family.

It was January, 1968, and a short time before we were due to land in Saigon when the "Tet" Offensive occurred. The North Vietnamese attacked Saigon with all they had: 106-millimeter recoilless antitank guns, artillery, howitzers and sneaky communists armed with their A-K 47's; the strongest army in all of Asia. Thousands were killed in this epic battle, a battle of blood and torture that saddened the entire world. I was fully aware this should have been a New Year's celebration of laughter and gifts, instead of blood.... and right in downtown Saigon. This was the closest the war had ever come to my husband, and I was moving there! The Tan Son Nhut airbase had been badly bombed and overran temporarily; newsreels showed death and destruction everywhere, and the city was one of chaos. This was soon to be my home. Fear gripped me, but I kept on packing. I wasn't one to back down from a difficult decision once it had been made, and my decision to fly to the Far East held. It seemed there were a thousand calls to be made in these final days before our departure. I contacted the banks, the charge accounts, the utility companies, the attorney, doctors and dentists, friends, schools and neighbors. I utilized lists upon lists....constant reminders of what not to forget. There would be no corner drugstore in Saigon, so I had to remember to take it from America.

Our tickets arrived, $3,000.00 and something worth….one-way for the four of us from Kansas City International via San Francisco and on to Saigon, South Vietnam; the once beautiful city of Southeast Asia. The tickets were impressive, and I read: Mrs. Norma June Allen, Cynthia Lynnette McDaniel, Stephen Douglas Allen and Jeffrey Lee Allen; Kansas City, Missouri, to Saigon, South Vietnam. Both Cindy and Jeff resemble their grandfather's family, as they had the "Jeffers" look. Steve, on the other hand, was "Little Doug," as everyone called him, the spitting image of the Big Indian. Respectively, they were ages 11, 9 and 7….very tender ages to be dragging them halfway around the world and into the fears of the frights of a war. I re-read the tickets again. My heart pounded when I carefully spelled it out: "S.A.I.G.O.N., S.O.U.T.H. V.I.E.T.N.A.M." Everything was official now, and the pounding hastened as a lump swelled in my throat. Could I go through with the plans? Should I actually risk the children's safety by moving to a war zone? Was I being totally fair with their future and well-being? Would they have fresh milk and healthy food? Would they be allowed to be themselves, to grow and gain wisdom during their formative years? Or would they be prisoners in their own villa, shirking into the corners, all the while the Viet Cong lurked in the streets outside?

Yes, we were going to join the Big Indian. We had gone this far with the plans, and so we were going to board the plane. I had gained new confidence talking it over with myself, as I always have been my best friend. It stems from those long years of loneliness when I would often wake up in the mornings and stare directly into the mirror and say, "Hi Juni, you pretty little thing!" That always started my day off right! I felt I might as well love myself, then I didn't have to worry so much about others loving me….and too, I had my hello for the day. I found this system really worked. I had to keep going, and often that morning, a friend was reflecting back at me and really "made my day." I have to admit though, that this morning ritual with the mirror eventually felt me falling from my high status to a point somewhere between distrust and disgust with myself.

Countless letters, forms and documents were passed back and forth between me and the Vietnamese Consul and Embassy officials. Like any official government business, there were fourteen copies of everything to be filled out, notarized, and returned to Washington, D.C. and then just wait. The waiting was hard to endure, for it appeared they didn't work as fast as I thought they should….didn't they realize I had to know if I was to be allowed to make this journey or not? Then, the form came that shook me. The simple question to be answered was, "Why do you wish to make this trip to South Vietnam?" What where my reasons? Oh God, please help me find the right answer. Truth prevailed 99% of the time, so I answered with a simple "I want to join the children's father, he is a civilian communications engineer on Tan Son Nhut Airbase in Saigon." That must have been good enough, because soon the documentation I needed for the trip were arriving in the form of passports, certifications and very official verifications of other sorts. Visas were soon to follow….and the four of us were almost on our way. It was time to start the painful inoculations for plague, yellow jaundice, tetanus, malaria, typhoid, yellow fever and etc.…

One quick call to our friend and physician, Dr. Lawrence Piefer, assured us he could acquire all necessary vaccines. However, he could not give the children so many shots at once, so we set up a shot schedule for what little time was left before our departure date. He said, "Come on in, and let's get started." He was such a fine person….being ever so gentle with his wiggling charges. He told them in all honesty, the shots may be painful….and so he suggested we all four go into the same examination room together. Doc was so personable, he assured them they would make it because he knew they were tough, and they were! He actually convinced them he had the smallest, sharpest needles in the business…. and he did a super job. I never saw a tear shed during any of the appointments. They were great little kids, and they knew what they were going through was necessary for the trip to be with their daddy. I never heard a complaint. They jumped on the tables, smiled and giggled, and Doc praised them and cajoled them about what the children would be like in Saigon…. their new friends they were about to meet. We went to Doc's office so often that the car knew the way. He reminded me of their doting grandpa, we could group all these great men into one category: TOPS!!!

Each of us had our own yellow Immunization book…Doc filled it in and initialed it and stamped it, so, everything was in order. The pain of shot after shot was something they had been used to, at least pain on the inside from missing their dad, but all four books were a complete and absolute necessity for this faraway country we were going to. A feeling of comfort came over me, knowing they had the protection from the many horrid diseases we seldom heard of here in America. Doc explained we were to locate a Field Hospital within 30 days of landing in the jungle so the children could have their booster shots. Doc was envious of our trip, for he, too, had been a world traveler. But never having gone to a country at war in Southeastern Asia, he envisioned a fantastically interesting trip for us. He frequently flew his plane to Nassau, St. Thomas and the Virgin Islands, and he hunted the northern slopes of Canada and Alaska and fished the cold waters. He was sincerely interested in our trip, and though he was frightened for the children's safety, he was also kind and understanding of my love for the Big Indian.

He knew Doug personally from the golf course. Their paths had crossed often, sometimes betting $50 on their game at the course, and then winding it up with a couple of drinks in the Club House. And though he knew our marriage had not been totally happy and smooth, he had remained a faithful friend and physician to the both of us. Yes, he was genuinely intrigued with our plans for the trip to Vietnam, our trip to war….Doc was indeed a respected man, and his sincere and tender goodbye kiss meant a lot to each of us. He wished us luck from his heart, probably pondering our fate because, by now, the war had escalated and the situation more terrifying. The TV and newscasts, the front pages, all the news everywhere were all screaming headlines of Saigon….they told of death and destruction, of horrendous torturing of prisoners, and of the role the United States played in suppressing Communism. I was scared, I lay awake at night wondering what kind of security we would have over there. Would we have guards? Would the villa be secure? To the tune of $800 a month rent, it should be a fortress! Would the children be allowed to go out and play, or would they be prisoners in a small world within a stucco, stone and tile finish? Was it really fair to them….such a drastic move to a jungle full of uniformed men filled with hatred, the cunning and vicious North Viet Cong? Could I go through with this trip? My mind kept saying, "Don't go," but my heart kept winning the battle over my mind, and hectic preparation continued. We readied ourselves for the long flight. To war. To the Big Indian….

Another call from Doug assured me he had taken all precautions for their safety, the villa would have thick walls topped with concertina barbwire, and a 12' tall locked gate. He told me "Nigh and Teddy" would ride shotgun with us as our personal guards whenever we ventured out. He said he wanted us there and he was awaiting our arrival. Little did he know how long it was to take us to complete a 24-hour flight. The Big Indian had been more than considerate of us in making the reservations for the long trip. He had foresight and realized the numerous problems that could arise if traveling around the world with three young children, so he carefully planned with only two flights involved:

A commercial flight from Kansas City Airport to San Francisco, California, and a Military Air Command (a MAC flight) from San Francisco to Saigon. It sounded so simple…

The mid-western weatherman must not have been informed of my departure date, or he would have cooperated by ordering mild weather and clear skies. Whatever the reason, a misinformed meteorologist or an act of God, and I prefer to think it was the latter, the weather simply did not cooperate. Mom and dad were taking us on the first leg of our round-the-world journey by driving us to Kansas City. They had to shovel six inches of wet snow out of their driveway before they could drive the 5 miles across town to get us. dad then found the streets were ice-coated under the newly fallen snow, and so it was back to the garage for chains. After a hectic trip to our house, my dad was convinced we shouldn't attempt to make the 60-mile trip to the Kansas City downtown airport. God forbid anyone would go out on a day like that, man nor beast. Mom and dad hoped we would delay our departure till better weather, but this was my day! I had planned and anticipated this trip for weeks, and there was no turning back. Besides, the house was leased, and it was too cold to camp out! Come hell or high water, snowplows or tornadoes, we proceeded to load the Ford Country Squire, which was not an easy job. The winding brick walkway from the door to the boulevard below was a rather long walk, and even longer when you inch your way along wrestling with a 40-pound piece of luggage. We had four large and four medium pieces of luggage, four flight bags that weighed 20 pounds each, two shoulder bags, three kids dressed to the hilt for the blizzard, and a tired…. but anxious mother bringing up the rear. I was on my way at last; I appeared to have enough gear with us to manage for a while. We looked like a wagonload of gypsies from Siberia, and if the smiles and tears could be seen around the fur parkas framing the faces, no one said anything. Goodbye, St. Joe, Missouri, this is it. Goodbye, sub-zero temperatures….And hello to the up-and-coming steaming jungles of SE Asia!

Chapter 3

I laughed as I rode down the highway, remembering how much fun we had when we packed and how we tried so hard to stay within the 40-pound-per-bag limit. As little as the kids were, they would grunt and groan, one on each side of a nearly full suitcase, taxing their young muscles to hand it to me for a "final weigh-in" on the scales. I had already weighed myself: a trim 118 for the trip, and added to that should total 158 with a suitcase in hand. We had a lot of fun…. if it weighed in at 153, we would add another pair of jeans and a shirt. If it weighed in at 155, we would add another blouse or shoes. If it was closer to 157, we would squeeze in another bra or a pair of panties, vowing to get our full 40 pounds per piece. But toting them down the ice-covered brick walk, we wished they weighed a mere 20 pounds each. But we made it…. excited and nervous to hit the Interstate that would take us the first leg of the trip by land.

The Interstate was slick, and driving conditions were hazardous. The governor should have declared martial law and ordered everyone to stay in by their fireplaces. No human should have been out on such a night. We slowly made our way towards the airport, praying the snowplow in front of us would not turn off to clean some farm road, but would continue towards K.C. downtown airport, leading the way for us. Soon, the sky lit up, and the lights off in the distance assured us we had made it. I could visualize our plane on the ground, preparing to load the variety of passengers headed to the West Coast. I wondered how many of them could guess we were going to see our Big Indian. I wondered if they could guess we were headed to war, this family of three small children dutifully tagging behind their mother. Thoughts raced through my mind, but the main thought was to arrive before the plane took off without us. I wanted to tell my daddy to "hurry," but I managed to keep my mouth shut the entire trip. I knew I would be saying goodbye to my parents, and I cried….This was only one of many times I shed tears over them, as I missed them terribly from that moment on.

What happened next should not have happened in a thousand years, and never to me; All planes were grounded. The weather was severely rough, and all flights were canceled due to the short runways at the downtown Kansas City Airport. A new terminal was under construction further up I-29, which would provide the runway length necessary for the big jets….but the new International terminal was not yet completed, and all air traffic was still being routed in and out of the downtown Kansas City airport. We sat. We waited. We watched it snow. Soon, the wind picked up, and the snow and sleet mixture were being whipped across the plate glass windows of the passenger terminal like horizontal lines drawn across a piece of paper. It looked bad as take-off time approached. The boys busied themselves with plastic worms and scorpions from their flight bags. These little green bags were private, packed with personal items of their choice. What went into the luggage was my priority, but their little flight bags were very private. If it fits, and they wanted it, it went! The contents of each personal zipper bag were never questioned by the other….this bag was about the only remembrance each had of old friends.

That bag would hug its owner's shoulder of each particular child, the total contents to be revealed only at the end of the flight. Precious things like plastic spiders from their Mattel Fun Factory were in one, along with crossword puzzle books, decks of cards, a rusty pocketknife, a year's supply of Double Bubble, Hot Wheel cars, perfumes, pictures, ponytail ties, lip-gloss and so forth. It was an unwritten law between us: "If you don't ask what's in my flight bag, I won't ask what you have in yours!" And too, orders from headquarters had already been issued stating, "The weight of your individual flight bag is to be minimal enough for your own shoulder to support it….and only your shoulder. Do not ask for assistance from this commander." These cute orders and notices had actually been posted during late January in very conspicuous places like the bathroom mirror, the cookie jar, the TV screen, the Kleenex box and other frequent habitats. The notes had worked….

although the one on the TV screen disappeared during an old Zorro movie, but the posting of "my orders" had been in places where I knew they would be seen and read. This was my way of indoctrinating them into the military world like the one they were headed to. And too, it was to put a little humor into everyday life, days that were filled with doubt as to our safety at the other end of this trip.

Announcements were coming over the loudspeaker; Our flight to San Francisco had been postponed for 30 minutes, and we were advised to listen closely for updated announcements. My heart sank, I wanted desperately to be on my way, yet I was grateful for the extra time with mom and dad. Prolonging the departure by 30 minutes was actually harder on them, they would have been better off if we could have said our goodbyes without the extra tears and anxiety. We discussed the feelings developing deep in the pit of our stomachs, we all felt it, this fear of the weather. The storm was whipping against the glass, and we were wondering if we ever got on the plane, and if it did leave, would we be able to stay up there? The wind seemed like it was around 70 miles an hour by now, but probably more like 35….and the 30-minute delay turned into another one-hour delay, followed by another 30 minutes. All planes were grounded as the density of the storm increased as it churned like Dorothy taking off from neighboring Kansas, blowing with the ill winds of old man winter. I noticed Cid digging into her flight bag. Pretending not to see her, I observed her popping a miniature Hershey Bar into her mouth. I knew then she had dozens more where that one came from. No one asked for candy, knowing full well she had spent her personal travel money on what she wanted, and the rule was "you don't have to tell or share" held fast.

I don't know who was the most upset….Mom and dad are so worried about us flying out in this storm, or my concern about their driving back to St. Joseph? A snow sled would have been safer than dad's big station wagon on icy roads. We visited without discussion of the drive home, yet their fear was felt. We wiped tears, knowing it would be a long, long time before we had this opportunity to hug and hold again. And perhaps never, we still had not forgotten we were going to a war-ravaged country. Headed to war….I still had to pinch myself to be sure it was true. Perhaps not the way a G.I. goes to war, loaded down with full battle gear, but our green shoulder packs were just as big and important to us as his….it was the same war.

Boom! There it was! The announcement we had been waiting for. The voice on the loudspeaker announced the San Francisco Flight would be boarding passengers….but we had to go by bus to the north! God, I couldn't believe this. We were to board the bus and proceed further up Interstate 29 to the new K.C. International Airport. On further explanation they told us this downtown K.C. terminal had short runways, and while the new International was still under construction, the runways were completed. International was not yet in use….but due to a combination of the blowing snow and short runways at the downtown airport, it was impossible for any plane to land during this storm for fear of sliding into the Missouri River. So, all passengers holding boarding passes for San Francisco should board the bus and be transported to the new airport where we would have long, safe runways. Our flight was to land in 15 minutes, and we were told departure would be within 45 minutes.

The storm continued to rage, and from the lounge of the downtown terminal, we could see the sleet mixed with snow being furiously whipped in all directions by even more accelerated winds. The small talk ceased. Mother was crying. It was time to board the bus and say my farewell "I love you" to mom and dad. Am I really going? Will the plane climb out of the storm? How much easier it would be to cancel out and reschedule a later flight than to take chances in this God-awful weather. I thought, "The pilot has to be either awfully brave or really crazy." No, this was really it. We had our goodbyes of tender words, but sadness prevailed. Mom and dad had hoped to see us off and gesture their last silent wave as the plane departed in the distance. They wanted to see their baby daughter and grandchildren off properly with their last wave toward the skies.

Goodbyes to a bus were not quite as dramatic as what any of us had envisioned;

"Bye, grandma."

"Bye, grandpa."

"Bye, mom."

"Bye, dad."

"We will be OK, so don't worry."

"Yes, we love you too."

"Please don't cry."

"God Bless you both." I said as we boarded the bus without them….

We were on our way.

Somewhere out there in the blackness of the night, a plane was landing at the ghost airport….an airport without a terminal or people, the plane we would board for the flight to Frisco. The headlights of the bus cut through what seemed like the blinding snow, and the tires seemed like they were spinning on the ice. We didn't have too much further to go; we must have been within a few miles of the International. I smiled….An amusing thought. I realized we held the distinction of being the first passengers to use the new International Airport, ever….It was still under construction, and here we were, flying out of it!! "Jesus," I thought. "What a distinction!" Soon, I came to my senses and knew we all had to be crazy to hold such a distinction because a sane person would not be on this bus headed to a deserted construction and incomplete airport to catch a flight on a night like this. I wondered what the new International would look like vacant of hangars, a total lack of activity. It was not at all a normal situation, and just the thought of it seemed eerie. An airport with no people was like invading an alien planet.

We drove directly onto the runway….no leather lounges and coffee shops to greet us, only the darkness of the night. Passengers departing the plane boarded our bus through the rear door as we clamored out the front entrance and ascended the steps to the plane. The wet snow was clinging to the handrail, and I was thankful the decision to take off or not take off was not mine, but up to the well-trained pilots. They had a lot of courage; they had to have it to be responsible for so many passengers. I wondered what fears they felt, if any, or if they could fake calmness during a time like this? The wind blasted the snow across my face and stung my cheeks. God, what weather! I prayed for the pilot and co-pilot. Finally, the passenger exchange was completed, and I watched the bus as it rolled down the runway with its new load of passengers. They, no doubt, were very thankful to be on the ground and probably had no idea of the bad highways and the 30-mile drive ahead of them to the terminal at K.C. downtown airport. We boarded the plane and settled down into our seats…. hardly exchanging any conversation between us. I think everyone was busy talking with their own God, praying for a safe take-off.

The flight to San Francisco was uneventful, smooth and relaxing. We climbed high and left the storm behind us…and the coffee soothed my ragged nerves. Jeff was napping, but Cid and Steve sipped their hot chocolate and chattered endlessly. It had already been quite an experience, and they were only one hour into their long trip to South Vietnam. I was thinking of my dad and how he deserved credit for driving the slick roads to get us to the plane. I was so proud of him…. and equally proud of mom and myself for not harping about his driving. I know it was difficult maneuvering the icy highways; not everybody could have kept the wagon on the road, as we had seen many cars in ditches alongside the highway en-route to the airport, and I was wondering if they had arrived home safely. I prayed for them. A saying my father prided himself in came to me, and I joshed it over in my mind. He told me, "Juni, I was driving horses in blizzards before the wheel was ever invented!" I knew better, but I assured myself with that "funny" that they were home, and the wagon was tucked in the garage for the night. I thanked God for getting them home safe and sound. Presumptuous, wasn't I? But I had the vision that they were OK, and it relaxed me. Now, I could settle down and concentrate on my flight and hope for an on-schedule military flight connection out of Frisco.

Next Flight? Here I was, a lady with three small children in San Francisco, fresh out of a mid-western tornado-type blizzard, a survivor of sorts, a lady holding this stupid distinction of having flown out of an unfinished airport. Now lost and bewildered in a strange California air terminal of endless miles of walkways and steps, I felt like yelling "HELP!" Approaching the desk to inquire if we had passage on the MAC military flight, or if we were to use a commercial flight? We were informed both flights had departed prior to our landing because of our late take-off from Kansas City….damned storm! We were assured we would be on standby for the next Military flight to Saigon, and the airline would taxi us to a motel for the night. All we had to do was to return the next morning at 8 a.m., and perhaps we could get out. Needless to say, a motel had not been on our itinerary, and we hadn't packed accordingly, or nowhere near it. All the Levi's went in one suitcase, all the shirts in another, the boys' underwear was in a different suitcase and socks elsewhere. Cid and I had the same problem. We had planned to stay the full 24 or 26 hours in the same clothes on a straight-through flight from Frisco to Saigon. What a dumb traveler I was in those days….never allowing for the unexpected.

We had to unpack all eight large suitcases to find the correct number of pajamas. I think it was midnight when we finally located them and could settle down for some rest. Not sleep….just rest. We had our personal items, combs and toothbrushes in our individual green bags, so we had packed something right after all: our toothbrushes and secrets tucked together and neatly zipped up. Suddenly, realizing I had failed to notify the Big Indian we had missed our plane due to bad weather in Missouri, I locked the children in the room and headed for a phone, making contact with an airline representative. He obliged me with much kindness and assured me he would send a cable to Tan Son Nhut Airbase in Vietnam. The rest of the night was a toss-and-turn kind of night….fearful for what tomorrow might hold, wondering if we would get out or not, or if we would even get a taxi and arrive at the airport by 8 a.m.

The next morning was exciting. No, it was a bitch! We repacked and closed the luggage and called a taxi. If you have ever seen 7 and 9-year-old boys loading luggage of such weight in-and-out of the motel and the taxi, you would realize they have Wheatie strength in those tiny muscles. Cid, too, managed well with her share of the load, though she and I were a bit more prone to occasional cursing as we trotted along lengthy tunnel ways with the unbearable weight. Back to the San Francisco airport….we loaded and unloaded, we approached the counter where we were told there might be a chance of standby on the MAC flight if we would please approach gate #17,982,461 (or so it seemed we walked that far). We thanked the agent, and without a porter in sight, we started the distance. Each of us carried our load, this time two pieces of luggage, each, plus the laden flight bags. Oh, those little green bags…. so cherished at the beginning of the trip, but such a burden, already cutting like razors into our shoulders.

Yet, no whimpering from the younger kids, just Cid and I complaining all the way. At age 11, you could cuss kind of we decided at the last moment, providing the weight was over 60 pounds distributed between two hands and two shoulders. Good thing we had a sense of humor, or we would never have made it. It was the longest mile on earth….we finally found a hard bench, and we sat down there, glad to rest our feet. We sat. We waited. Finally, after 45 minutes or longer, a gentleman walked towards us and told us there were four empty seats to Saigon if the last four men were a "no show," and so far, they were just that! He said we would wait 10 more minutes for them….for us to please stay nearby, and perhaps we could board. It did appear we were getting out of Frisco at last. You guessed it, they showed up.

Back to the longest mile in history, to the same agent, where he politely again wired the Big Indian that we were not on that flight after all….another delay. He advised him to be on "Standby" for the next cable, no idea when we may get out of California. Another taxi, another night at the motel. Another packing and unpacking. At this rate, we would have to buy another suitcase just for the dirty clothes as they were stuffed here and there, and the "here and there" places were filling up fast! We stayed inside with the exception of a short trip to a mediocre restaurant. All other meals were taken in the room close to the motel phone as per instructions from the agent, just in case a cancellation came through on a commercial flight. The next MAC flight was two more days away… either way, he would do his best to get us on our way. Another night at the motel. Three nights now, and we were no closer to Saigon than a slow-flying bird. Hell, as the crow flies, we could have been there two days ago. That night, the kids started to get restless and were deeply saddened by the numerous delays. Saddened? Hell, the real me was coming out now, and irritation was the order of the day! But somehow, I managed to sleep, although I thought I heard the kids up and down during the night, whispering little hope of a flight tomorrow morning. I wondered why they had such little faith in our flight schedule. Ha! Load the luggage one more time, and don't forget the little green bags. Taxi them to the terminal one more time. Checkout at the motel had been rather fun, and the little old man just couldn't understand why we would check in and out daily, we had him totally confused!

Finally, the agent (an old friend by now) called us by our names as we walked towards his counter…. and his smile could only mean one thing. Good news for a change? He happily announced that we were leaving San Francisco. I heaved a sigh of relief, and I hugged him rather than thanked him. He assured me he would wire the Big Indian and make him aware of our flight, but we weren't going to Saigon, only to Hawaii. "Hawaii?" I asked, "But why?" He said that was as far as he could route us, but we shouldn't have any problem getting out of Hawaii and on to Southeast Asia, as there were a lot more flights to Saigon from

Hawaii than from Frisco. Jesus, that long mile again, but we didn't mind too much this time, as we finally had a destination to head to….

Chapter 4

We was on our way, our fourth night would be in Hawaii; not all the way to Vietnam. The Big Indian had routed us for a quick and convenient straight-through flight to S.E. Asia…. he had tried to make the trip easy for us, but it was becoming our own war. Perhaps overnight in Hawaii wouldn't be so bad after all, and we settled down for the flight over the Pacific to the Islands of paradise. Ahh, airborne at last! I sank down in my seat, relaxed and happy to be on another leg of our 24-hour journey to the Far East. At least we were making progress. Goodbye Frisco, goodbye mainland….I observed the kids with tears in their eyes, and I presumed they were thinking of their beloved grandparents left behind.

I decided all I needed now was a Coke and a cigarette….then I could give some serious thought to the Big Indian and the life ahead of us in a steamy new land with old customs, and a new war. I reached into the green bag for a package of cigarettes. The no-smoking light had not yet gone off, but I would be ready when it blinked; I wanted to be the first to light up because my nerves were burned out. But I immediately came up with a handful of messy white stuff….I then realized how I had goofed. In the excitement of getting our flight out of Frisco, I had packed the toothpaste without a cap. I laughed. I had to be the only person over the Pacific Ocean at that particular moment with a handful of goo oozing between my fingers. I said a couple of words I had heard the boys whisper one rainy day, and then the cussing turned back to laughter, and I soon realized this was one of the hazards of flying. I rang for the stewardess to bring a towelette as the "Fasten Your Seatbelt" sign was still on, and I didn't want to chance the trip to the lavatory. Rather than waddling down the aisle and bouncing from seat to seat, I would let her accommodate me and the messy fingers. She wasn't without a sense of humor and found my predicament very funny! I toweled the fingers and pack of cigarettes rather than pay the airline price of $1.00 per pack.... and hope they had my brand.

I was napping over the Pacific when Cid startled me and said she left her robe on the shower hook of the motel door; so we lost a robe to San Francisco. I told her not to worry about it and we would buy her a pretty silk one overseas. It seemed the appropriate answer because the pilot was not going to turn around and let her go get her robe. Now, for a good looking steward with a promise of passion, he may have turned around, but not for a little girl and a fuzzy robe. I could tell this flight was going to be one to remember....everything was going wrong, and we had several hours of flying time ahead of us. I was anxious to land in Hawaii and see what kind of connections and/or MAC flights to Saigon were going to be available. Or so I thought….

The stewardesses appeared shocked and surprised when the two miniature "Howard Cossels" broadcast their unusual destination, although I knew they didn't fear for their safety in Saigon, as they knew nothing about it. Not too many American women and children move to Saigon, Vietnam, if any at all. The city had just been attacked, bombed, strafed, rocketed, and shelled, and thousands and thousands of people had been killed during the Tet Offensive of 1968; it was partially devastated and suffered severe damage to its historical architecture. Those two little guys thought it was really going to be great moving to the jungle, and they wanted to tell the world; anyone who would listen soon found out they were going to join their daddy in Saigon. The stewardesses gave them gentler care after their story….they managed extra goodies, playing cards and coloring books to keep them busy for a while, and enough Cokes to float the Titanic. I think they pocketed enough peanuts into their little grubby green bags to last them throughout the month. They were actually bulging when we landed in Hawaii….I accused them of lifting peanuts from other passengers, but they said no; they had just smiled at the stewardesses and "made a killing." Sometimes I wanted to smack them. They sure do learn young!!

The Hawaiian Islands appeared in the blue waters below. What a beautiful name. Hawaii… and to think they were formerly called the Sandwich Islands. I wanted to kiss the hand of the person responsible for such a lovely new name, so fitting of the tropical beauty before us. My historical recollection was poor, and I had no idea who had been responsible for the change, so I just raised my eyes to the sky and thanked the man above. He was always there, and he had been a close friend indeed, especially on this trip….I thought to myself, "Why couldn't I be here on a second honeymoon with the Big Indian, instead of with three small children, eight American Touristers, four flight bags and two shoulder bags?" The circumstances could have been different….I thought he and I could have enjoyed the warm sun, the mild breezes of the beach and the bronze girls that placed the leis around our necks when we stepped off of the plane. On second thought, I was thankful that The Big Indian was not here; I never could trust him around a pretty girl. Nor an ugly one, for that matter. He stalked all females like a hungry cat. The brown men were easy on the eyes, too, so I decided it was in my best interest to visit Hawaii as a single girl for full appreciation. We were taken to the terminal by a small open-air bus, another thrill for the children. They had already done so many new things and seen so many new sights. Now, they wanted to be with their daddy.

Bad news at the terminal….Just what I had expected; "I'm sorry, Mrs. Allen, we cannot get you out of Hawaii for several days. However, we will put you up in the airport Motel where you will await a MAC flight or a commercial flight on to Saigon." We presumed this would go on for two or three days, as had the San Francisco delay, so we decided to enjoy our stay. We soaked up the sun at the pool, met a lot of interesting world travelers, took our meals when we wanted, bought all the postcards we could find and slept late! It was not a bad mini vacation, yet I was anxious to see my Big Indian. The cablegrams were going out daily to Doug, telling him of our progress (or lack of progress) and of our standby situation. I contacted the counter agent at the terminal and advised him we were taking a day on the town and asked him, "Does it appear we may get out of here today?" He assured me we were there until at least the following day and wished us "Aloha and have a good time."

We took a bus to Waikiki Beach, where we sipped cool drinks and swam alongside the outrigger canoes. The dark-skinned men drew my attention away, and I found it very difficult to keep my eyes on the 3 children in the surf. It was this macho distraction that forced us out of the cool, clear waters and onto the streets of shops, where I managed to spend a good deal of the traveler's checks I had with me. The shopkeepers were more than cordial, making us comfortable as we dipped into our money. Mumu shopping with Cid was no fun….She just had to have "this pink one" and "the Mandarin orange one" and "Oh, Mother, please, this is the most beautiful baby blue I have ever seen. I'll just die if I don't get it. It matches my eyes!" I wanted to tell her to get the high-heat aluminum one and take a stroll on the beach, and then I realized how cruel that sounded, so I gave in to all three.

We left the high-heat, aluminum-colored Mumu there on the rack for some older, hotter lady!! It was not for my little girl!! The boys looked handsome in their wild flowered cabana sets of cherry red, yellow and popsicle orange blended with moss greens on a background of ivory. We purchased a green and white Aloha outfit for The Big Indian….I wondered, "Are these his tribal colors?" He would have killed me if he thought I was joshing such trivia about his Cherokee ancestry. We had been on the road for a week now and really having a great vacation from the snow and ice back in Missouri. We continued to enjoy the warm breezes and visited the miles of warm white sand that stretched the shores. Basking daily in the sun, we soon looked native, and no one could tell we were snowbirds (damned Yankees!) from up north.

I knew the Mid-Westerners were still following the snowplows to get down the lane and to the store. I thought, "We really have it made," and I learned to relax and enjoy this vacation at the airline's expense. We visited different islands, only a short "hop" from one to the other, and marveled at the fern forests, waterfalls and orchids that adorned the islands. What a lovely place, I knew I would be back someday to this "heaven on earth" location…. Mementos of Hawaii include stone images to adorn my coffee table, and myriad carved wooden Gods, poi bowls, and a quilt. Everything is colorful and denotes happiness and beauty in the islands, yet the culture and royal heritage of these islands remain largely unknown to "mainlanders" like us. The native cuisine was delightful. Hawaii will celebrate its 50 years of statehood in 2009….an anniversary I hope to be a part of when they throw the big Luau! The zoo housed caged squirrels, snakes and dogs….I didn't know they don't freely inhabit the Island. We enjoyed a picnic under the palms and viewed the native dances under the moonlight. We saw it all. We spent an afternoon at a museum viewing the thousands of royal heritage items, paintings, books, drawings, maps and historical carvings that truly represented the early Hawaiian Islands.

The bronzed fishermen and sailors were handsome, and the beautiful ladies had long, black hair that had the glossy sheen of a raven. This beautiful chain of islands was to step back a century, a one-time sheltered anchorage for a generation of sailors and fishermen. Maui, Molokai, Lanai, Hawaii and Oahu, among several smaller islands. I could have stayed forever in this Paradise land of foliage, ferns, birds and waters. We utilized room service at the airport motel, and it didn't take the kids long to realize the airline was footing the food and drink….then just sign the food check. They all-of-a-sudden decided chocolate malt would taste just as good in the middle of the night as in the heat of mid-afternoon. The little devils ordered enough malts and shakes to wear out the malt machine bearings in the café near the pool. Funny how they learn so quickly. Or perhaps they thought the malts were the Hawaiian version of Dr. Pepper: 10, 2 and 4, and then again at midnight!! At any rate, they sure put them away. I overheard them at the poolside one day, and Jeff said, "We're getting even with the airline for our delay…. one malt for every hour of delay!" And I think they felt justified, I realized they were abusing their food and drink privilege, and I was forced to put an end to their eating rampage. They were plotting against the airline, and I overheard their schedule for tomorrow consisting of malts, pork chops, chocolate pie, and their determination to "sock it to them really good." I stepped in and ended their fun and games, explaining how inappropriate their thoughts and actions were. The topper was when I caught them ordering from room service after I had gone to bed for the night, I realized they were still plotting. Whoever heard of a bedtime snack consisting of two dozen fried shrimp and dill pickles? Damned kids….

Outside of the motel maid stealing my new blue Star Sapphire and diamond earrings from the top of the bedside table, I really fell totally in love with the Island. "I would love to live here," I thought…. The swaying palm trees and blue water were equally beautiful, rivaling only the beauty of the golden wheat and the stately green corn of the Midwest. But soon we were on our way, the phone call that sent us back to the skies and into the waiting arms of the Big Indian. Eight nights had passed since we departed by bus and told mom and dad goodbye in Kansas City….and finally we were now headed to our final destination: Vietnam. Doug has been advised by cable when to expect us, and I knew he, too, was filled with anticipation. Two weeks later, but "en route at last," we closed our luggage for the last time! Little did I know that at this time, he was busily moving out his mistress "Missy Kim" and her little girl, so I would have been happier without that bit of information which shortly came after we landed at Tan Son Nhut Airport. I know now he shared a roof with her from 1966 until we arrived in early 1968….

We boarded only after struggling with the damned green bags and sacks of purchases on the islands. We were so thankful to be on our way to Saigon. We were quick to realize we held another distinction: That of being the only American woman and American children on the flight, and a long flight it was from the Hawaiian Islands to Saigon. Did you ever try to occupy three kids for 24 hours of straight flying time? It would have been difficult playing kick the can or baseball in the aisle, so that was out. The fascination with the tiny restrooms soon wore on, leaving their devious little minds free to concoct whatever mischief they could think of. But it turned out they were more entertained by other passengers and soldiers as the flight got well underway, for which I was thankful to a lot of strangers….A big relief to me, I was one tired mama! By now, we were accustomed to motel restaurant meals and the home cooking we loved was far behind us. We ate out of boredom. One time, we had breakfast two times when we crossed the International Date Line. I was wondering if it was a joke or what, but there it was; ham, bacon and eggs and biscuits for the second time within a few hours. Were they trying to acclimate my body, or my mind, to the time change? It was the stomach that got the education: "Not big enough in here for two breakfasts," it said. We were all queasy due to eating from boredom. We napped for a while, happy about The Big Indian awaiting us in Saigon….

Cid really grew up on this trip. Her eleven soon sprouted to a "Would you believe I am going to be 16?" type daydream. I blamed her actions on all the G.I.'s on board; they were just more than a young lady should have to bear at the tender age of 11. Men were wonderful. I was the first to agree, but it's a different story when it's your own pre-teen daughter flirting amidst a sea of 18, 19 and 20-year-old soldiers. I ordered her to remove the makeup, but I handled it gently and with the suggestion that "the colors are not really for you; they do nothing." It pleased her to think I had good taste (?) and she accepted the beauty hint at once, whereas I heaved a sigh of relief. God, one young girl already grown up at 11, and all these G.I.'s…I thought, "It's just not fair." It was a monster of a plane, a 747, with hundreds of passengers. Flirting never entered my mind, yet I'll have to admit I wondered what was on the notes she kept passing to the young marine sitting behind her. God help me, and if I could get to Saigon and deliver her to the safety of her daddy, she would have some protection. Confusing, those thoughts are high above the ocean….

I don't know how many she gave her home phone number to….the number back in Missouri. What good would this number be to them in a foxhole, or a rice paddy in Vietnam? It didn't matter; I had already planned to outsmart her by having a silent number assigned as soon as we returned to the States. Then it hit me hard; we were really gone, gone from mom and dad, from niece Karen, our favorite summer sitter and from friends. Gone from the great U.S.A., so never again will we see golden shafts of wheat, the rows of corn, the milk cows, and the amber waves of grain were gone. The endless cheeseburgers of McDonald's were a thing of the past….we were somewhere over a vast body of water, in God's hands from here on. I wept openly. I was frightened and wanted to "get down" to kiss land and to see my Big Indian again. I drifted off into a deep slumber; I remember dreaming I was throwing salt on the icy brick sidewalk that caressed the Persimmon trees on the avenue front lawn. Could I be homesick already? I closed my eyes as snowflakes caressed my face, warmed by my icy thoughts of back home.

The next thing I knew was when I was awakened by the sound of the announcement that we would be approaching Guam to refuel….fasten your seatbelts. We had about one-half an hour there, just long enough to see what there was to see. An American base, white and neat and precise like all government installations. It didn't do a lot for me except make me want to "get this show on the road" to see if the grass could possibly be greener on the other side. The jungle would have to be prettier than Guam, yet it was a welcome chance to walk in the fresh air for a moment and to enjoy the stares of hundreds of men in full battle gear. I had to watch Cid….and found myself wishing I had brought the dog's leash. She loved every minute of this trip, and it scared the hell out of me. The thought crossed my mind to cut her long blond tresses to make her look more like an 11-year-old.

Confusion. Was it day or night in Saigon? Had we lost or gained hours? And I didn't know whether to go to sleep, or to wake up. Jet lag was already upon us, and I didn't know how to fight it. My nerves were giving in to the anticipation that Doug must be getting ready for us, he knew we were finally on this, the last leg of the trip. I remember thinking, "What will he have on? How hot will it be over there? Will he be alone, or will some of his site men be with him?" I was afraid I wouldn't look too good to him after the trip and the naps and the confusion. Bags under the eyes….the mirror told me so, and I reached for the makeup only to find the toothpaste once again. Damn it. That cruddy green bag was nothing but trouble for me, and I vowed to cremate it as soon as I could get to the villa he had leased for us. I had it all figured out….we would make a wake celebration out of it, mix the Martinis, pour, strike the match and have a good cry to celebrate the bag's death and our arrival. Silly thoughts, but they passed the time away. It was a bit bumpier, and the weather was blowing in a total lack of either consideration or cooperation, or both…. The seat belt sign stayed on and this pleased Cindee, who by now was across the aisle and a good dozen seats behind me. So, this gave her the opportunity to bug some poor young marine just a little longer. She couldn't go anywhere, much less back to her mother. Damned kid. I was becoming irritated and amused at the same time, searching my past for a common behavior pattern. Found it, only it was worse, my like years and actions. God forbid….

The boys had passed the time playing cards with the guys, I am certain a good part of them had little brothers at home about their ages, so they were good for each other. They won a few dollars, and I never heard the end of it. They thought they were Pros at the game as they chewed everyone's gum and ate everyone's desserts. They were the life of the party….

and looking back, I can see where they may have been considered the last "fun and smiles" before action by the replacements on board. Dressed in full battle gear and handsome bodies of brawn and muscle, they were soon to take on a full-time job in a steaming jungle. I wondered if the people back home really appreciated these kids, giving of their lives so willingly. Tomorrow was a different day for them; they would check in with units and flush the enemy from the muck and mud and rice paddies. I prayed for their safety with tears in my eyes.

One more stop: Saigon. We began our descent to Tan Son Nhut Airfield, and I caught sight of land. It seemed we sat on the plane for hours, and perhaps we did. The plastic raincoats everyone carried folded across their arms or laps were being held in even more heat. The pilot had announced the tropical rains were falling in Saigon, so everyone was prepared. My umbrella found its way off of my lap and rolled down the wide aisle. I was wishing I had two or three more arms when a G.I. retrieved it for me. Trees, trees and more trees, as though it was a cushion of hunters. I looked out the tiny window of the plane hoping to get a glimpse of Doug. Was he here to meet us? Yes, I knew he would be here, anxious with thoughts of seeing us again and concerned with thoughts of a safe touchdown amid fighter planes taking off and landing, evacuation choppers bringing in wounded and dying, praying for a safe landing in a rocket-bomb crazed area of danger; Tan Son Nhut

Airbase….We landed a short time after the Tet offensive that had torn up Saigon itself, and done devastating damage to the world's busiest air base in this year of the Monkey. Sadness sickened us soon after departure from the giant 747 that had set us down to safety from the skies, but dared us to walk into the new life where we were to struggle for our very survival.

You could feel the war and smell death. The "Tet" of 1968 marked the escalation of the war to new heights, leaving over 3,000 dead in the city of Saigon. We had landed on the heels of "Tet," and in the aftermath, fear showed in the still-frightened people of Saigon. Green for us to land on… and it looked good till I spotted the pillboxes and machine gun turrets and anti-aircraft guns poking through this lush tropical greenery. Then I saw the barbed wire circling the base and the ugly Quonset hut of an airport passenger terminal. How sad to see the green foliage dotted with the unnatural iron and steel weapons of war….No more laughter from the kids or from their new friends. No fanfair, it seemed like it was just silence, but then reality set in. An air of fear gripped the passengers. This was it for the young men headed to war. My God, I felt sorry for them. It was a difficult time for my children, knowing some of these newly made friends would die. I was still sweating… still remembering what I had read about this new country. It was humid and miserable, and it had started raining softly. The heat was almost unbearable as we sat on the plane, slowly acclimating to the temperatures in Saigon. Here we were at last....

Our pilot announced we would remain on board for another 15 minutes or so while the cabin was depressurized, and that was so the heat of the jungle would not be quite so stifling. He said it was unbearable outside....high humidity with high temperature, and rain. So, we sat. Not a word was said. We sweated profusely. My lovely pink and white dotted dress became limp, and I cursed. I had wanted to look decent for the Big Indian, or at least presentable. We were sweltering, and the plane got stuffy. It seemed like I was wringing the palms of my hands together in nervous anticipation....they were actually wet. I felt a trickle of sweat run between my breasts. I was oppressed by the heat and felt sick. My head became light, and I thought, "Please don't let them take me off of here on a stretcher. Get a hold of yourself, Juni." I looked out the window and the fighter jets lined the runway, everywhere the drab colors of the military were evident, very unlike the airport in Kansas City, or San Francisco, or Honolulu for that matter. This was war, and we were here. The heat was melting me and my hairdo....I must have looked like a sick, wet chicken. I decided to think about this new country to take the heat off of my mind, I remembered what I had been reading the past two months about Vietnam, as I was finally here. South Vietnam. It flashed across my mind, and I wondered if I could learn to understand it fully, this country….to respect it as a visitor should, and if the kids and I could endure its suffering of war.

I wondered how many would come back alive, these young men with all limbs still attached. I think they were wondering the same thing. I looked across the aisle to see a red-headed young man loaded with full gear, tears streaming down his face. I knew he would rather have been back home on a tractor or a combine. He was already missing his girlfriend, his mom and dad, the farm and the prized 4-H animals he left behind….he was just out of high school and scared to death. I wanted to take him in my arms as though he were my own son and tell him not to be afraid; but in this war, he was no longer a kid, he was a man, and I had to respect that. He almost cried as he tussled Jeff's hair, shook Steve's hand and patted Cid's shoulder. Turning to me, he simply said, "Bye, Ma'am." A shiver went up my spine as I managed a "Good luck, we'll pray for you….

Chapter 5

rriving early in the afternoon, The Big Indian was there to meet us, shadowed by Nigh, his trusty friend and employee who played bodyguard riding shotgun atop the company van in a specially constructed seat that closely resembled the "shot gun" seat on the old stagecoaches. Nigh and his driver led the way down the ravaged streets of devastation and past starving naked children as we brought up the rear in the family Toyota. We were headed to our new residence, a huge French villa fit for a king….Our talk was small and garbled. The Big Indian wanting to tell of the war and the three maids that awaited us, while all the time we were trying to tell him about our blizzard and tornado in Kansas City and the lay-over in Hawaii. In general, the exuberance felt by all of us at just being together once again was one of total happiness and joy. Everyone was talking at once. So much to see, the sounds of war; this was Saigon at last.

It was wonderful being with Doug. It would take the kids weeks to tell him all they had planned to say on that short 8-mile ride from the airbase to our French villa near downtown Saigon. We melted together as a family and thanked God for the safety we felt with the Big Indian. On the way, we discussed the rudeness of the Vietnamese officials at the airport terminal, the ugliness of the Quonset hut serving as the passenger terminal and the fact that the counter agents could have attempted to speak regular English, rather than delaying me for an hour with their gibberish Vietnamese questions…. which they knew damned well I couldn't understand. They finally solved this matter by allowing Doug to leave his "waiting for passengers" post behind a wire gate and proceed to the head of the line of incoming passengers. He argued, bickered and cussed, waving his hands all the time. The Big Indian really went on the war path for us…but he managed to get an official "O.K." for us to pass through this station of ignorant officials. I wondered what would have happened to the children and I if Doug had not been allowed to leave his waiting area and assist us with the language problems….I presume we would have been there for hours and hours, and maybe not even allowed to proceed to a waiting vehicle. They were giving me a rough time with abusive, toned questions in a language I hardly knew. I couldn't figure out why the passports and visas were not sufficient to just "pass us through" and beyond their incoming passenger counter….Hell, I had the accumulation of a mountain of paperwork between embassies and consulates and passport offices, and the mound of papers I carried should have been enough to have admitted even Ho Chi Minh without any questions.

We headed west down a dusty street toward 331A Vo Than as he told of a large villa of stone, plaster, teakwood, marble and beauty. During the ride, I noticed the tools of war. The road was lined with traffic in both directions, traffic of armed men and armored vehicles. There were men riding and men walking, running alongside vehicles, men with slanted eyes and darkened skin weathered from the sun, and men from America of a broader stature….They were heavily armed and looked at me with an air of uncertainty, just as the agents at the airline counter had. They had been rude back at the terminal and loud shouting had prevailed. This language difficulty began when I entered the Quonset hut at the base, and now the men and armor; I began to get the feeling I didn't belong in this war. We passed a field of barbed wire and gun turrets atop pillboxes, and an edge of fear enveloped me. I thought, "What in hell is an American housewife, who is an Administrative Assistant with adequate smarts, and a mother of three small children, doing in the middle of this war?" It hit me: I had landed in this God-forsaken jungle of war, and there was no turning back. I knew then I had to be a survivor of sorts.

As we rode along, I was totally lost in my thoughts, but those thoughts were soon disrupted by the noises of distant shelling and cracks of rockets. It was like no other town I had ever seen, or even envisioned; war was everywhere, and I felt frightened. I felt sweat when the plane was going through decompression, but it was nothing like this, I was not acclimated to the jungle heat, and my nerves were not yet of iron….a necessity of survival to "make it" in Saigon. "What in the hell am I doing here?" I asked myself. Then I knew: Doug was at my side, and we would soon be turning off of Vo Than and through a huge heavy iron gate swung wide by the eldest of the three maids, and we would be driving down the concrete drive to the red-tiled carport at the rear and side of the villa we would call our home. We were met by 40-year-old Chi Hia, the eldest maid, her daughter Lon, age 23, and Kim, age 12. They bowed and smiled, and I knew then they would be fascinatingly faithful and loving in all ways, a real "Mother" to the children….Doug had made a wise choice in hiring them, and his selection process must have been grueling for the hundreds who vied for the honor or of working for an American household, complete with fair a headed wife and three blond "babysons." Chi Hia knelt at my feet as we entered the villa like she owed me the respect, and Lon rushed to make us our cool drinks. Stingers on the rocks for The Big Indian and me, soda for the kids. "It had been a long trip," I thought as I settled back into a plush, easy chair. My thoughts were interrupted as I felt my shoes being slipped gently off my feet….there was Chi Hia, slipping new red and white oriental sandals onto my feet. She proceeded to do the same for the three kids: a gesture of love and welcome to her land.

We had passed mountains of garbage in the streets, children running naked, and people urinating at the curbside. Men stood unashamedly, and women squatted. I had so much to learn, so much to see, how terribly naïve I was that first day. You must remember, when you reach South Vietnam, you will be in a land with a civilization that predates the birth of Christ, but which, since 1954, has been divided like Korea. North of the 17th parallel, and the Ben Hai River lies Communist north Vietnam, and south was the free Republic of Vietnam. Only half of California would fit into the Republic of Vietnam, a long and narrow country neighboring to the west with Laos, Cambodia, and Thailand. Beyond Communist Vietnam to the north is the vast territory of Red China. South Vietnam's tropical climate has been said to have two seasons: "hot and dry" and "hot and rainy!" The rains fall beginning in late May and continue through the fall, at least through September. Life with the Viet Cong negotiations, along with the Democratic Republic of Vietnam, was begun by the French, and an agreement was reached that should have established an independent Vietnam in March of 1946. Bao Dai was the Chief of State of the newly established State of Vietnam. Formerly an emperor, he lived the classy life of the French Riviera, but he never gained the support and dedication of the Vietnamese. His deposition by President Ngo Dinh Diem followed the establishment of the Republic of Vietnam in the mid 50's

So, the vast war between the French-supported government and the Vietminh continued on, day by day. The Vietminh were given money, guns and equipment by communist China, and the United States supported the French-sponsored State of Vietnam, shipping tons of equipment to the far eastern area of conflict. With the French defeat in 1954 at Dien Bien Phu, the July Geneva Conference produced a truce with the Vietminh, which left the area north of the 17th parallel in the hands of the communist-dominated Democratic Republic of Vietnam….and the southern area in the hands of the weak French oriented State of Vietnam. This separation was blamed on the decline of European imperialism in Southeast Asia and the rise of nationalism and communism. By 1964, American vessels patrolling the Gulf of Tonkin vicinity were attacked by the North Vietnamese P.T. boats. President Johnson retaliated by ordering the bombing of the North Vietnamese navy and bases, and Congress passed a resolution to take all necessary measures to repel any armed attack against the forces of the United States and promised to prevent further aggression.

The Viet Cong's heavy attacks on American troops in South Vietnam in early February, 1965, and the newspaper headlined a visit to the country by Soviet Prime Minister Aleksie Kosygin to Hanoi. Saigon's government was losing control and found itself in a situation of political deterioration. These early 1965 attacks on our troops were retaliated by continuous heavy bombing and air attacks on northern military bases and installations, while the Kosygin was on one of the bases. The Americans became more involved as the war escalated….They were directly involved in the fighting by June of 1965. We had campus rebellion, "walk-ins" and draft card burning. Street fighting broke out as there appeared to be no legal basis for the intervention halfway around the world. American policy was under attack as one party blamed the other, and it appeared they were committed to a long, drawn-out war amidst the steaming jungles. And for what? No one seemed to know. The Christmas Truce of 1966 had failed, producing no kind of compromisable peace hopes, and bombing of the north was soon resumed. The morality and legality of American involvement in Vietnam was questioned, and by early 1967 there were over 500,000 American men fighting this damned war. And for what?

Attitudes in the United States were polled; most Americans felt we should fight to win, or get the hell out, and that we really didn't belong there in the first place. We were in a bitter, bloody war in Asia for the third time in a single generation, and with people who courageously opposed French domination for more than 80 years. Fighting alongside American sand, learning new techniques and firing new equipment…. determined to muster what they had left to guard the safety of independence in South Vietnam. These poor people had always known war and of the cruelties of Ho Chi Minh's soldiers, and of the enforcement of inhuman laws. We didn't get the coverage we should have on this war; our government censored new and distorted intelligence information and selectively only released what they wanted us to hear about this "Police Action." All humanity and justice were laid by the wayside, being two words the Viet Cong had never heard of. The South Vietnamese have been impoverished.... and their lands devastated by Napalm and bodies, blood and guts, cratered holes and lack of growth. Starvation was imminent, taxes were unjustifiable and extreme poverty abounded. Children went to bed hungry because raw materials like rice fields had been taken from them by force; there was nothing left to free enterprise.

The framework of the Viet Cong military units is quite standardized throughout South Vietnam. Control varies from village to village, and from district to district....yet it all falls under forced activity. According to the size of the village, the Viet Cong soldier may or may not be a paid soldier. He may fight with sophisticated weapons such as rifles and submachine guns, land mines and plastic charges, but more common are knives, spears and machetes, all homemade. Some troops received half pay, and others, nothing except knowing they were fighting for the glorious leader. "Ho Chi Minh," or "one who enlightens," was born Nguyen Tat Thanh in the early 1890s. As an early communist, he took the name of a Patriot, and he studied in France. Villagers were totally controlled by the Viet Cong and often forced to serve them….either through kidnapping or threat of death to family members, or rape of their sisters and mothers. Rather than see families annihilated, they marched off to do what they could.

But they soon found the Viet Cong were seizing what they grew and taxed them to the hilt so as to maintain their army. They took tools, women, food and dogs….whatever they needed. They took their sex with great force and collected taxes at gunpoint. Villagers were constantly lectured on the "Glories of Communism." People have been known to be drug out of religious services and made to stand in sweltering sun or torrential rains to hear long, boring lectures about these glories. Villagers shipped in wares and crops to Saigon, and more than once, stories told of the Viet Cong raiding the buses and robbing passengers where many were left bleeding to death with a bullet between their eyes. The military organization's "harder core" type Viet Cong soldier has been trained way more than Ridgeley for soldering….and draws a regular salary. But these types of Viet Cong banded together to make life hell for the peasants of South Vietnam, as they lived in constant fear for their lives. The Viet Cong were effective, usually, because they did not hesitate to use their weapons to get what they needed and wanted, as they knew their job and performed well. Priests, Hamlet Chiefs, sidewalk vendors, school teachers, whores and children alike were targets and fair game for the most brutal forms of coercion that Congs resorted to. Hospitals were attacked, and drugs stolen; many patients were blessed with the bullet as they lay dying on their cots. It was faster now that the Viet Cong had broken into their clinic, as there would be no more sleepless nights, no more suffering.

Police stations, workers, farmers, and sons and daughters of politicians, and even the politicians themselves were beheaded, burnt alive or disemboweled. Many ears were severed through a common practice, and much of this was done as family members were forced to watch in stoned silence. These are the memories that the Vietnam Vets will carry to their deaths. Assassinations were rampant; no one was safe. Tiny children were raped and abused while in the city, people hid in burnt-out buildings, curfews were enforced, and people stayed off the streets; life was miserable for all citizens of the south. Many civilians and officials alike were on a "death" list of wanted people in the eyes of the murderous Viet Cong. It is most difficult to begin to describe the severity of their atrocities. Blinding communism dwelt in them, and being diseased, they declared their undying devotion to Ho Chi Minh. A sick type of people, yet devoted totally to their beliefs. The Viet Cong were condemned, as were the Americans, for being there. And suffering for it were Asians and Americans alike….hiding, and some dying for a freedom they would never know. Entire villages were burnt as the Viet Cong raged sneak attacks during the night….more ears were showing up on captured Viet Congs as the fighting continued. North Vietnam's objective was total conquest, regardless of how painful it was. They were unmerciful….the North Vietnamese were stealing what they could as they snuffed out the lives along the way. They looted after they had kidnapped, tortured, shot, raped and beheaded their enemy. They were a superior force and found they could reduce their dependence on the long supply lines from the North if they could have the instant money and food.…and all for the price of a bullet.

Children saw their fathers taken away; I watched as blood-covered bodies were removed from the gutters of Saigon's streets one morning. One was a very old man; someone's own father, or grandfather, caught up in the middle of a skirmish in the dark of the night. Children wandered the streets, and I wondered if it was their father or grandfather they were searching and crying for. War plays many games and takes on many faces, so I dismissed any feelings I had at that time. The old man could just as well have been a Viet Cong who infiltrated the city via the river or tunnels; I would never know. I never really wanted to know…. Fishermen's boats were sabotaged if they didn't pay them off in the form of taxes, and a sabotaged boat meant no fishing, when translated means no income and no food. War is hell. Viet Cong were well trained in the north; the regular leaders had endured extensive training and indoctrination in socialism and communism, just like they all were. "Imperialists, warmongers and colonialists" and all their puppets were criticized by the Viet Cong, and at the same time, "Charlie" as they were called, was promising freedom for the intellectuals, education for the youth, land for the peasants and safety for women and children. Those were lies, nothing but lies. Children were being blasted from curb to curb, and district chiefs were being killed in cold blood…. just shot in the back. Torturing was common, and suffering was beyond what average Americans in the states could comprehend. A book of torture has now been compiled, but it is said only the strongest can read it; it is so ghastly. Peasants were advised not to take the medication for Malaria; a brutal, painful death followed for many who did. Supposedly, it was "for the glory of the country," and it released the medication for the soldiers, too.

It was the summer of '68 in Missouri, but it appeared to be the first season of the year here in Vietnam, the "hot and dry." My underwear was soaked by now, and perspiration was flowing down the valley between my breasts and trickling down my spine. Again, Cid and I cursed, and I found we were more adept with profanity now than when we first left Kansas City International. She had grown up a lot on this trip….and a lot. I failed to correct her when she was irritated, and it had been an exasperating flight actually, the long trip was hard on all of us. I was guilty of being lax with the recriminations, showing a total lack of parental authority. Manners would come later. In the presence of the Big Indian, everyone would be on his/her best behavior. I recalled his gruntled, deep voice that whispered of law and order, a commanding tone that no one dared to disobey, and eyes that could see the thoughts conjuring in your mind. Then I chuckled as I sat there wet and miserable, remembering that I had disobeyed him on a few occasions and gotten away with it. Naughty but nice thoughts….

I seldom felt guilt of any degree; my parents had brought me up with a solid Christian background, and I was in Sunday school and Church every Sunday, but this was a different matter….a personal matter between the Big Indian and me. I called it marital revenge, something not taught in Sunday School. Maybe someday there will be another book entitled simply "The Life and Love of Juni." I had read a great deal of the country, its culture, its habits and a history of this land where I was to find happiness amidst the war, and bombings, and shellings, and torture, the bugs, the snails and snakes, lizards, mosquitoes, the monkeys and elephants, the coconuts and conical hats, sandals and beer can baseball. These were tiny, thin, dark-eyed people who worshiped the teachings of family love, and respect they learned in their childhood….yet all they knew was war.

God, it was hot. In Asia, it is the beginning of springtime now, the time when the cherry blossoms herald the start of a new hope, and a new year. To the Vietnamese, the New Year means many things. It is a children's celebration, a family celebration, a religious celebration and a chance to commune with the spirits of ancestors. It's a time to honor one's ancestors and relatives who have passed away, and a time to ask the dead to come back to commune with the living. To the Vietnamese, there is not a large psychological gap between life and death that exists in this country. The New Year is also a time when extended families get together, and when children admit to their parents for the bad things they've done during the past year, and how they promise to be better during the coming year. All children….no matter what their age, go to their parents during this time. They pray for God to bless the New Year. Lots of fireworks are set off as a means of chasing away evil spirits. Much like Christmas in America, the Lunar New Year is a children's celebration. Children get toys and goodies and sweets, and it is a time when even poor families spend money they can't afford. Eating the New Year's cake….banh chung, is another means of ensuring prosperity. The cake consists of a combination of sticky rice, pork, and soybeans wrapped in green bamboo or rush leaves and then boiled. I had read that the many mouths of the Mekong River join a dense canal network that fans out across the delta plains to nourish the fertile paddies of a bountiful "rice basket." Rice? I had not eaten rice in Yankee country, but mom ate it occasionally with sugar and cream on it as a breakfast variation from oatmeal or Wheaties. I knew that Southerners ate it with chicken livers in a dish they called "dirty rice dressing," but all the Yankees in northwest Missouri ate it sweet. Little did I know at this time how precious a main meal of rice was to become in the months ahead.

I thought about my new country and what I had read about their Tet Holiday, which marks the beginning of The Lunar New Year, and, by the solar calendar, usually falls toward the end of January or in early February. A general rule is Tet will be celebrated on the first new moon after January 20th. All work usually stops for the first three days, and most shops are closed. Imagine Thanksgiving, Christmas, New Year's Day and the Fourth of July all rolled into one big super holiday. The local Vietnamese residents look upon the beginning of the Lunar New Year in this way; as a holiday made up of many holidays. I had read of Vietnamese tradition and how they attached a great significance to the first visitor of the New Year. This is thought to influence the happiness or well-being of the entire family during the entire year. If a rich man, or one with a lot of children, or one of high social position is the first to cross the threshold, the family's fortunes will be correspondingly affected. A happy man with a good name, like Phouc (happiness), is preferable to a sad man. In fact, some families go out of their way to invite a propitious first guest, and to discourage all others from entering before him.

By now, the North Vietnamese soldiers were secretly wandering through the city asking the people to show them an American, and then they would "show them what they looked like inside." Although….there were many refugees who knew where Americans were hiding, but none seemed to want to view their entrails, and therefore the Americans weren't reported. The answer of the day by the South Vietnamese was "Toi khong biet," i.e. "I don't know." The North Vietnamese were in command of many sectors of the city, and they were going door to door looking for the Americans. They knew that many of them were living there, and one would wonder how long it would be before one of his South Vietnamese neighbors would be forced to talk. An escape would require a good deal of luck, a daring plan, and the courage to finally execute it. Refugees were streaming aimlessly along the way….soldiers were guarding every street corner and occasionally used bayonets to prod along the stragglers.

A serious food shortage struck Saigon immediately after the Viet Cong Tet Offensive attack, affecting everyone living in the Vietnamese economy. The hardship had to be alleviated. A strict street curfew, and the inability of farmers to transport fresh produce into Saigon virtually closed the local markets. When they did reopen, food was available only in limited quantities, and prices skyrocketed. Vice President Nguyen Cao Ky made a plea for donations to the refugee relief fund. U.S. forces and installations in the Republic of Vietnam have been subjected to unprecedented enemy activity, and few areas of the Republic escaped the attack. Almost every site where American personnel, military and civilians were stationed was either attacked directly, or as part of larger compounds, brought under attack. All the glory of the Tet of 1968 was buried amid rubble and bloody bodies. All hell broke loose….

Chapter 6

This was WAR….Before we were able to settle down in our new quarters, I heard a commotion not far from our villa. Within blocks, there was the painful sound of shooting echoing in our ears. We ran to the upstairs balcony, and Doug grabbed the binoculars to see what was going on and how far away it was. He said he feared for all of our lives as the war had escalated again since the Tet Offensive, and he actually had second thoughts about us being in the midst of it. A few blocks behind our villa and in the direction of the winding Saigon River, we saw a small, thin man fall down a spiral staircase that entwined a concrete police observation tower. He was a Viet Cong, a "Charlie." Doug presumed he had swam the river that flowed like a snake behind our villa and had attempted to climb and infiltrate the police lookout tower, but lost his life in doing so when the local militia, or "Consots" as they were called, had gunned him down in cold blood….a gross welcome for the children and me; a ravaged, raw welcome to Saigon after the tiring flight. That was an initiation to the realities that I was to face, all the while being a civilian and non-combatant in Vietnam during the worst years of the war. "Juni Allen, NCO #E162034" was a title I would earn, and if in no other way, during the months to come.

Between Doug, Chi Hia and Lon, we were getting situated in this new land of strange customs, dress and speech. We had a lot to learn and soon found out that the best way of grasping local ways was through the maids; they were constantly attempting to get a message across to us in broken English or sign language….And before we knew it, we were actually communicating. One of the first words I learned was that I was a "ba," an older lady, and the kids were "babysons." When they were good, Chi Hia would praise them, saying "Number 1, number 1" with love and adoration, but when they were bad, which was pretty often, she would chase them up the spiral marble staircase, yelling "Number 10, number 10" as loud as her tiny Asian lungs would allow her to yell. She often exhausted herself caring for our children, and we wouldn't see her for hours on end, knowing full well she was hiding out in the maid's quarters that were off-limits to the kids and me, a fully respected "gentlemen's" agreement. They deserved some privacy; a place where they could go and pray, or scream, collect their thoughts, or whatever they found necessary to do away from the small Americans. Chi Hia needed this peace and quiet, a solace from the nerve-wracking chore of being an oriental nanny to three wild kids. I often wondered how she survived, yet she showed such a deep love for them that she could have easily been a natural parent or grandparent. She was constantly concerned for their safety and often held them in her arms across her lap when the rockets were coming from afar, and fear was much closer…. within us. She was wonderful, and we soon became very attached to her.

Doug helped the children and me get "comfortably settled" in the new home, a large, refurbished French villa constructed of grayish/pink clay and stone. It was complete with marble floors, porches and staircases, which Chi Hia and Lon mopped and polished till they glistened. The villa had a French bidet, and 3-foot-deep, square, tubs for bathing constructed by masters of glistening tile. We had our own water purification system, and when it rained, which was most of the time for the average rainfall per year was well over 100 inches, the raindrops were purified by flowing through tiny pebbles, smooth with wear, and then into storage tanks to later be pumped to the rooftop for the gravity flow to the flush the bathrooms. A generator sat out near the driveway. The power plant in Cholon, the Chinese sector of Saigon, was rocketed or plastic charged quite often, and the ceiling fans and the 40-year-old refrigerators would go off. The ceiling fans had to be kept running if the power was still on, as they kept the mosquitoes away….and this emergency, private power plant was welcomed when power outages were caused by invading Viet Cong, the never-ending enemy of Vietnam.

The refrigerators cost us $600 each, and that was used, and we had a pair….quite a distinction for any resident of Saigon. They were truly outdated but probably leftover from the previous French rule. They did cool our food, greatly, and that's all that was important. Milk was secured by friendly officers from the officer's mess hall and was "reconstituted" and bagged with a spigot on the lower front of the big bag. We set it in the refrigerator, and when someone wanted a glass of milk, they just opened the door, pushed the little button, and "presto"….milk! The kids thought this was pretty nifty, quite unlike the paper cartons they had been so used to back on the U.S. mainland. It sure beat powdered milk, and we soon learned to appreciate it, even though it was a far cry from the fresh milk of the dairy farms in Missouri and Kansas, where the cream floated with a fluffy lightness atop the glass, with the richness of yellow staring back at you like the morning sunshine. Actually, the reconstituted milk was good, and we had enough friends on the base that the kids were never without this essential basic, something I was very grateful for. The kids drank it like it was going out of style, or so it seemed….

The massive teakwood furnishings in our villa were intricately carved, lending depth and warmth to the castle-like structure we called home. Teakwood is a very beautiful wood, and its colors vary from a yellowish brown, to a rich brown. Teak comes from Latin America and Africa, as well as Vietnam, and because of the cost, it is mostly used for decorative applications. We had an ornately carved 8-foot-high china cabinet with glass doors and sides, two buffets and back bars of teak, as were tables, chairs and bed frames, all in the rich brown tone. It is similar to our oak in structural capabilities, and it is relatively easy to work with. It is used often in boat construction because it does not cause rust or corrosion in metal, and it resists moisture, so it is ideally suited to jungle temperatures, high humidity and constant dampness during the monsoon season. Should we decide to take up permanent residence in the Asian Far East, such sturdy furniture would outlast the children and their children. In the corner was a built-in Sansui 3000, complete with a reel-to-reel unit for taping messages, music, and the real voices and sounds of war. It held a place of distinction neatly tucked in under the marble staircase just beneath its curve, which provided protection in future months from falling dust and debris during rocket and mortar attacks.

The Big Indian loved Laura's Theme and constantly hummed "Somewhere My Love," and I was dumb enough to think he was thinking of me. How wrong I was. It reminded him of Kim….the little gal who held a special place in his heart those years he was in Saigon, and I was still in the States. I was told by many of his employees, "Mr. Doug had moved her out to make room for Mrs. Doug and his babysons." Well now, how do you like that! I accepted it; there wasn't anything I could do about it, and I had been raised to believe that "What you don't know won't hurt you." But I admit that I looked for this lady named "Kim;" I inquired about her wherever I went, and I questioned him about her whereabouts. I found out he had been very fond of her; she had a small child, a girl child, and some thought it was fathered by the Big Indian. I'll never know….I found scattered amongst his papers many photos of them, and what really hurt was the happiness shining in their eyes, the holding of hands under the banana tree, and his arm around her in others. They shared tenderness; I like to think of it as "sharing loneliness." I told myself he had to love me. He moved her out of this lovely villa for us, so I never brought up the subject of past love again. But I was hurt, and I wanted revenge. One of the men who filled me in on "Missy Kim" was Nigh, the Big Indian's driver and shotgun rider at all times….his "protection" as they called it. Nigh mentioned her often and used to openly tease Doug about how he used to sing "Crying Time," and how he could make Missy Kim cry. God, it hurt me….I had traveled halfway around the world and over 2 dozen hours of flying, and with three children to a war just to be tortured by stories of her. I became more bitter; I wanted to hurt him badly. I planned how to take revenge in a subtle manner; one that would show deviousness and slyness if only I could pull it off, and still manage to live near his Cherokee temper; an inheritance from his genes.

I missed air-conditioning, especially at night. The ceiling fans barely moved the air, yet I managed to rest. Jungle temperatures and monsoon rains were difficult for me to adjust to, but the sight of the little lizards that crawled up and down our walls, and over and across the ceiling made me forget the discomforts and inconveniences of being here, and on my own accord. They came in a rainbow of colors, mainly greens, blacks, browns and blues….and they were adorable with their swift antics. Their amusement kept our minds off of the street fighting, and we laughed at their childish games of hide and seek. The Big Indian always taught us to respect these tiny friends on the walls. They ate almost all the monstrous mosquitoes of the tropical climate, the mosquitoes that grew to giant-sized proportions, and could and would carry off airplanes!! That was one of his favorite stories of how this big mosquito swooped down and carried off a fighter plane that was parked on the runway for refueling. Yip, carried it off before they realized it wasn't a friend of the family. Another story that made the rounds was how this airman pumped 250 gallons of fuel into a mosquito before he realized it wasn't a fighter plane. They took these and other mosquito stories and twisted and turned them into dozens more. Big was not the only word for the Vietnam mosquitoes; they were monstrous. And they were aggravating, and they didn't just bite; they devoured 12-course meals!

Saigon had rats and rats and more rats; they were everywhere. Often, they were eaten by starving refugees who had swelled the city to unbelievable population figures. Saigon grew from one million to three million people overnight during the Tet Offensive of 1968. Dogs were unseen, as they, too, were roasted by hungry citizens fighting for their survival. Even raw garbage from massive street heaps made many pots of a kind of soup for millions of street people. The Filipinos working at the base often had "dog roasts," a delicacy to them… .a native dish. We soon taught Chi Hia how to cook some American dishes, yet her traditional dishes were our favorites. She had two kitchens, as do all French Villas: one off of our formal dining room, and the other more of a traditional oriental outdoor kitchen beyond the main villa, and closer to the full servant quarters off of the inner courtyard. The "outdoor" kitchen was not at all "outdoor," but enclosed on two sides by the walls full-tile roofs, yet open on both ends. The two open walls were folding doors that could be closed at night…. or opened during the daytime for fresh air. This is where the maids preferred cooking over a tiny low flame or charcoal, preparing succulent native dishes in a wok. The inner kitchen was more modern and complete with a double sink, a four-burner stove, a toaster and other items of comfort. "Her" kitchen, as she called the outer one, had shelves and cabinets on both of the walls, and she was more comfortable out there where her oil could smoke, and she could spatter without harming anything. I had the services of these three maids who cooked, kept house, and did all of the laundry. Chi Hia's lover, or "husband," worked at a bank, and soon started hanging around too, sleeping "over" with Chi

Hia when he thought we weren't looking, sneaking some happiness of his own to compensate for the war-torn days.

They had come to Saigon as refugees from Can Tho in the capital province of Phong Dinh, and found they could not travel the enemy-infested jungles; thus, they had moved lock, stock and barrel from the Mekong Delta area to the south of Saigon. They were good to the kids and another father image we could take! The kids had missed having men around the house and were delighted to have Chi Hia's husband as their friend. He brought them gifts, and I can recall one day especially when he came to the big gate, hands so full he couldn't reach up to ring the bell….but the kids spotted him from their perch on the balcony and ran down the stairway yelling "Chi Hia, Chi Hia, open the gate!" I ran out to see what all the commotion was and saw he was carrying an aquarium under one arm, and a plastic bag of what turned out to be tiny tropical fish in the other. He said, "This for babysons, the little monsters," which he had laughingly been taught in English! His feelings towards the children were a bit softer than those of his wife, who had to chase them all day. The kids were delighted and spent many hours feeding, caring and cleaning for their new pets.

Other fish followed….he was really good to them and showed love and concern for their total welfare and happiness. However, as days turned into weeks, we saw less and less of him. He was a mysterious person, usually he came at night and stayed with Chi Hia in her quarters, seldom letting himself be seen. By morning, there was no trace of him, and you may not see him again for several days. He was a neat person, with fine polish on his shoes, pants creased and clean, and always the banker's white shirt and tie. I used to wonder how many bodies he would have to step over on his way to work….we always saw the bloody aftermath of the night skirmishes, so I wondered if he ever encountered a corpse as he walked to his bank. I thought, "In America, you don't have to step over bodies to get to the bank." But this is Saigon, and you never know what will happen here. Not with Charlie in front of you, beside you and behind you; he was everywhere…. He let his Communist presence be known in so many horrible ways.

Our street was secure, with guard posts in towering open huts at each end of the block, rolls of concertina were stretched from curb to curb and surrounded the thatched roofs. They were perched on tall bamboo stilts, and usually manned by 2 or 3 soldiers with machine guns readily pointed at anyone entering or leaving the block. The Big Indian had felt this block was a fairly secure place, especially because of an Army-affiliated training consort, i.e. the local police camp, just across the street. And the Vietnamese Immigration office occupied the villa next door also, so we had reason to believe all security possible would be given to the other buildings and government offices in this block.

The training camp was ruled by a friendly South Vietnamese Major who soon learned that little American boys are pretty fair at roulette and chess. They played a mean game for their tender ages. Steve and Jeff soon became his partners, delivered to him by the aid of 5 or 6 army guards ringing the bell at our massive gates requesting the honor of the boys' presence for a game…. and off they would go. One of the more humorous sides of this war was to see a half-dozen uniformed guards and two little barefooted boys stroll down the street…. and picturing this Asian officer awaiting them with cokes and treats, sitting by the window of his office awaiting the start of the "game." The boys thought they were really big shots, and they loved the attention. It was just "one more war story" they could relate to their classmates in later years once we got out of here….that is, if they did at all. While some of the things they saw sickened them, they still learned and laughed every day, saving their tears for the blackness of the jungle nights, when one could be alone with one's fears and feelings, and one's God. Seeing all the starvation and nakedness made our children much more appreciative of America, as they had a wealth of knowledge to pack up and bring back to Missouri….when the war was over.

Troops roamed the area, and often Cindee and I got our laughs for the day by climbing to the front balcony of the villa and giggling, as the consorts at the camp across the street would strip to their underwear-type shorts for their daily bath in the outside water troughs, all the while unaware (at first) that the fair-headed, blue-eyed American women were enjoying their antics from across the street. It didn't take them long to spot us, and as word traveled fast, they started to enjoy their baths to the fullest, putting on little shows of dance and mimicking for us. They actually enjoyed knowing we were there, and though there was never any vulgarity, there was a certain boyish cuteness in their pranks. They would towel dry their behinds for us with a sideways motion that took the towel back and forth, grinning from ear to ear as they went through this little show. What they were really doing was towel drying their undershorts…. but they enjoyed doing it, so we enjoyed watching it! I know they didn't enjoy their bath to the fullest on the days we didn't appear on the balcony. No audience, no show!!

We watched these consorts train as they marched daily, held dress inspections and went through combat motions, pistol range, and physical exercises. We even observed them as they hand-washed their clothes and hung them on lines to dry. They had a crude army of men, but they were doing the best they could with what they had. If Cindee and Kim, or Cindee and I were on the balcony and paying no attention to them, they yelled. They liked showing off, and more than once, we observed them being reprimanded for yelling at us. I was convinced we were the highlight of their days…. and they gave us some fine performances for only a smile or a giggle in return. I can still see the wall topped with barbed wire surrounding our villa; it was our security fence, and with it, we did manage to get some sleep, but without it, there would have been none. Down the two sides and across the rear of the villa, our protection was 12-feet-high, 14-inch-thick wall of concrete, topped with 8 rows of barbed wire slanted at an angle, so as to tear out the heart of anyone attempting entry. Across the front lawn of the villa, our fortress was complete with heavy cast iron decorative fencing, complete with a 12-foot-high massive iron double-gate set into a 16-inch-square corner post anchors that only Goliath could have broken down after a hearty meal of wine and red beef.

Our little rag-a-muffin street kids, complete with swollen bellies and big eyes, often stood for hours and stared through the iron fencing….and often, they were rewarded with Tootsie Pop suckers or gum. Our kids were willing to share with the orphans this war had created, the less fortunate. Sometimes, if mom's mail had not caught up with us and our candy and gum supply was depleted, they just shared laughter. Neither understanding the other, it was a battle of wits, yet I overheard this type of conversation often: "You gum?" and Steve or Jeff or Cid would reply, "No, me no gum." So, they did have an open line of communication, and the orphans were advised by the Villa general store operators to "come back tomorrow." And they did. Sometimes balls, colored pictures and candy were handed through the fence… many of the kids left there smiling because of a small favor handed them by the little tow-head Americans. It doesn't take much to make a war child happy…. anything is better than what he has, and that's usually nothing. One 8-year-old boy often came with a street kid in tow, an American-Asian girl of 2 or 3 years old, the sad product of an Asian woman and an American lineage…A very unrespected mixture in Vietnam. The fair blond little girl was probably the offspring of a Vietnam prostitute and an American G.I., and she was shunned and spat upon.

Chapter 7

The Big Indian stayed busy on his job; a site supervisor at Tan Son Nhut airbase as a Telephone and Communications Engineer for Page Communications, Inc., working out of Washington, D.C. The system has been called, without exaggeration, the "AT&T of Southeast Asia." What a thrill when I was allowed to see inside the American General's conference room; examining the intellect and expertise of the plotter board situated between navy blue velvet drapes in a room dominated by a master's conference table and complete with matching velvet chairs. The décor was not that of war, but of aristocratic military power. It could have been the CZAR's battle headquarters; complete with a massive throne. Page Communication employed a total of well over 2,000 people on its staff during early 1968 in various capacities, and being Site Supervisor of such a massive system was indeed a big job. General William C. Westmorland was in charge of the IWCS System, the "Integrated Wideband Communications System of Vietnam" site supervisor, and it entailed construction and installation, Maintenance and Operations. Tan Son Nhut employed Americans, Filipinos, Koreans, Canadians, British, Thailanders, Germans, Australians,

French, Polish, Hungarians, Turkish and South African people, both men and women. My Big Indian played a big role in the communications of the Vietnamese war; I hadn't realized just how big his responsibilities were….

An insight into Tan Son Nhut Air Force Base and its communications system, I can give you some unwell-known facts and information about it:

General William C. Westmorland praised military and industry teamwork being put forth in the installation and operation of the whole microwave communications system: a set of new Microwave communications, embodying satellite, troposphere-scatter, and line-of-sight systems operating in Vietnam that have conquered terrain, distance, climate and time to provide the largest communications system ever to support a military operation. Radar systems provide air safety and navigational assistance to friendly aircraft, while also providing the means to rain destruction on the enemy with great accuracy. These systems have been installed and operated by the finest joint military industry microwave team ever assembled. These personnel have given their talents, and some, their lives, to the cause of freedom. Because of them, no combat operation in Vietnam has ever been hampered by the lack of communications and electronics support.

This system, we left behind….

Today's microwave system made a significant contribution to tomorrow's newest Vietnamese telecommunications and air traffic control system. Outstanding among the U.S. Army Strategic Communications Command, i.e. "Stratcom"….is the IWCS, the "Integrated Wideband Communications System" in Southeast Asia. It is the largest backbone of all-electric communications in both South Vietnam and Thailand. It is the largest, most sophisticated single communications system ever attempted by the U.S. Army. Its ultramodern equipment, using the latest types of solid-state components, provides the most refined sort of high-quality trunking for the continually increasing needs of the entire national effort in those lands….needs that are civilian and governmental, as well as military. Tan Son Nhut, with over 648,000 flight operations in 1967, and Danang, with over 714,000 operations, make John F. Kennedy Airport, with 481,000, and Los Angeles International, with 483,000, look rather quaint by comparison. Tan Son Nhut and Bien Hoa together total over 1.4 million, making the Saigon area the busiest air-traffic control complex in the world. This was Saigon's hub-bub of the military; a complex of air power and traffic, almost too large to comprehend….

The Big Indian was gone much of the time due to his total devotion to the system at Tan Son Nhut. He often worked late at night or all night if an emergency occurred, and it was necessary for him to be there. In

Saigon, emergencies were frequent, and Saigon was under curfew most of the time. We were not allowed out of the Villa after 6 pm, nor could we be on the street, so if his particular job or repair to equipment was not completed in time to make the 8-mile drive back to Vo Tohn Street to his family, then he was forced to spend the night on the base….Saigon was never safe for a non-combatant civilian woman or her three children, so we rarely ventured out, only with the Big Indian, and under the cover of Nigh, riding shotgun ahead of us. Nigh was molded of the universal design for bodyguards, and the AK-47 machine gun he carried scared off all takers. The Big Indian had a friend and co-worker at the base, Mr. Chang Lee, a Korean gentleman and scholar, a Personnel Representative in the Saigon office. He honored us by celebrating with 25 friends at the Koreana Club in Saigon, an authentic and pleasant dinner club. The Korean meal was served complete with Kimchi; the Korean staple represented by potatoes in the American diet. The meal was served Korean style at a low table with celebrants sitting on cushions on the floor, and that's where the two dozen or so American men that were present had some difficulty getting back on their feet after the three-hour meal….

The cushions were ornately embroidered with silken threads, and they were large enough to accommodate even the largest American man, and comfortable enough for a King. Our shoes had been left at the entrance of the Koreana Club while we sampled native dishes, including marinated and raw fish, a first for me. No main platter….but rather two dozen assorted bowls served to each guest, offering a tasty delicacy with each bite. A venture into another land, and an evening of honor and friendship by a gentleman I shall never forget. I had the distinction of being the only female at this gracious dinner….it was shortly before my birthday, and it was a double celebration: Welcome to Vietnam, and Happy Birthday rolled into one. I made numerous friends overseas, and certainly, Mr. Lee was high on my list of respected acquaintances, whose kindness and generosity will remain in my heart forever as cherished memories. Soon, I realized I needed something to do to pass the time away while he was gone. I was becoming bored with the war stories and its noises and tragedies; they were getting on my nerves, and I wanted to be a bigger part of what was going on around me.

I decided I wanted a job with a military-based construction company or engineering crew, something more than just sitting at home all day. I bombarded the Big Indian with my requests for information; I wanted to know where I could apply, who may be hiring American secretaries….and as an American citizen in a foreign country, what procedure I would go through to apply for employment to satisfy this burning desire to "do my part."

He drove me across town for some reason, and Nigh was not available to ride shotgun for us…. and as unsafe as Saigon was, we daringly and straightforwardly visited one of the construction firms after another, inquiring about secretarial positions. I filled out several applications at many American companies that were under contract to the United States Government. Their employees were unlike the tanned, robust, beer-drinking construction crews of the good ole U.S.A.….their faces were kind, but war- torn, and showed signs of the stress of war. Yet through the smiles, I saw happiness as they welcomed this real American woman, and I knew they were thinking as they interviewed me, "I have a wife just like this back home." or "She reminds me of my sis back on the farm." I was treated royally by all these men, many of whom Doug knew. He, too, enjoyed visiting with these old friends….some he had seen around Saigon for several years, so he rekindled old friendships. Many of these men would later be our houseguests or dinner guests, they grouped together for social life with each equally missing the homeland. There were many long, lingering dinners full of conversation about the U.S.A. What had been left behind, and what they hoped to go home to. Some brought tiny ladies as their guests, but I accepted this as "instant sexual satisfaction," knowing they would be returning to the wives they loved so dearly. Sex for cash is not a forbidden act, and as one president of a company told me, "It does satisfy the hungry appetite….but only temporarily."

On the third day of job hunting, we drove to the Vietnam Regional Exchange, USAAF PACEX

Headquarters in the Chinese sector of Saigon, known as Cholon. It closely resembled Chinatown in San Francisco….conical hats and sandled feet scurrying everywhere, quite different from downtown Saigon, more of an area of shanties. This American Military Exchange was known as the VRE Headquarters. I was tested, given a G.S. rating, and hired as Secretary of Administrative Services. I was to report the following day after a photo-taking session for my Identification card. The military card read "N.C.O. #E162034", complete with my fingerprints and photo. It was to suffice in case of capture by the enemy.

The VRE Headquarters was a very impressive building, an old classic theater in its time. It was now converted into dozens of offices on several floors and secured by machine gun-toting guards everywhere. The rolls of barbed wire at the entrance would scare anyone, except Charlie, that is, because he soon became a real nuisance. The Cholon section of Saigon housed the power plant, and Charlie the Viet Cong struck often, usually in the dark of the night. We were often under attack, and the sign on the wall less than 5 feet in front of my desk testified in flashing bright neon lights that there either was actually an attack, or we were being alerted to a possible attack….But I somehow managed to learn just to keep on typing as though nothing had happened. This was not too much different than learning to sleep through the rockets, knowing they were a couple of blocks away, only to turn over and return to dreamland. In war, you soon learn not to worry unless it's YOU, right then and now, life does go on, at least for some of us. We were the lucky ones who returned to tell about it….my first day at VRE was unforgettable. It was so different from any other position I had ever held on the mainland, where everyone looked alike! Here, we had many nationalities representing every corner of the world, and I made new friends as I met other employees. Amidst the machine guns and barbed wire, I started missing the rolling green hills of Missouri, and the familiar faces of co-workers and old friends I had left behind. God, I missed home, and that's saying it lightly….

I was frightened; this position was unlike any other job I would have had. We first dealt with the passport, then the medical/immunization records and a jillion questions during an interview, all the while asking why I was in the ravages of a war-torn city seeking employment. How I got there, why I was there, and how long I would be there? And of course, what did I expect to gain from this job? The first half of the day was taken up in this lengthy interview….first with a G.S. 11, with a Captain Workman, and last but most important, the Adjutant General. I convinced them Doug was doing his bit for the war as a civilian engineer, and I wanted to do mine….and I wanted to "get this war over with" by assisting at PACEX Headquarters, i.e., Vietnam Regional Exchange, Pacific Exchange headquarters…. USA/AF, where the name sounded impressive to me then and still does…. Officially, we were a branch of the United States Army and Air Force, so you know I was impressed with my N.C.O. card….one that I was to carry in case I was captured by the enemy, and stating I was to be treated with the same respect as that of a non-combatant officer. WOW! It was this card that said to me, "Juni, here you are! This is really it! And you are a part of it, so do your best!" I went home that night and read the card, every word on it, and it scared me half to death.

It simply said:

"Notice: The bearer of this card is a Civilian Non-Combatant serving with the Armed Forces of the United States, whose signature, photograph and fingerprints appear hereon. If the bearer of this card shall fall into the hands of the enemies of the United States, he shall at once show this card to the detaining authorities to assist in his identification. If the bearer is detained, he is entitled to be given the same treatment and afforded the same privileges as an individual in the grade, rate or rank of the military service of the United States indicated below, with any and all rights to which such personnel are entitled under all applicable treaties, agreements and the established practice of nations. According to the International Geneva Convention in 1949 and Geneva Agreement. Signed 7/21/1954"

These were big words, and I wanted to be worthy of them, so I tried hard to absorb everything and get into the swing of the procedures as soon as possible. I wanted to just be one of the crew. As secretary of Admin Services, I typed travel orders "up-country" for the purveyors, vendors and military exchange employees, and we plotted ships at sea so as to know what was on what ship, whether it be toilet tissue or Tide, and just how many days out to sea it was. It seemed the commissary and the P.X. were continually out of just what I wanted or needed, but it was reassuring to know the tissue was only 11 days out, or the deodorant was just 6 days offshore….It puts a little humor in long days and longer nights of tension and fright. The VRE was the warehouse and General Office Headquarters for this government military supply system, and the exchange provided the main commodities for the Allied forces throughout Vietnam, both "up-country" and south of Saigon in the Mekong Delta.

I assisted with the gathering of data for a manual to be used by employees of the military….sort of like the second-grade information telling you when and where to go to the bathroom. I thought it a waste of taxpayers' dollars, but I admit, I was well paid during the research of information and typing of hundreds of pages so it could go to press….so who was I to yell "waste of money" to? But then, that's our government, 14 copies of everything and keep typing and/or marching on!! I also worked with a lady named Ho Thi Cam Tu, who was our translator on the VRE Voice, the exchange's newspaper. I was fascinated to watch her type from English to Vietnamese for the reproduction of the "Voice" in her local language for the many Viets employed at headquarters. Cam Tu did a fine job at VRE. She had more and more responsibility with each promotion she got. Her English was very good, and she gave her job everything she had. She was much more fortunate than other Vietnamese girls who had fallen to the prostitute level of employment, or even lower, like the ones who were so hungry and depressed that they just gave up. And many did. You could tour the streets of Cholon and peer into one of the many shanties, settlements of crudely built dwellings that provided shelter of a sort…as that's all it provided.

They had dirt floors and no windows or doors…. just openings in the hut to go in or out of. Hammocks were slung from the ceilings; placed there so as to sleep above the hordes of rats and snakes that infected this refugee city. Any beds other than the rags slung in hammock form from walls and ceilings, were rattan mats on a freshly swept dirt floor. Children ran naked till they were 8 or 10, and it was not at all uncommon to see young men beyond puberty stage frolicking naked in the streets, but usually, they had on a pair of boxer shorts, their skinny legs sticking out beneath like bamboo stilts. Starvation was everywhere, and there was no money to improve the tin, cardboard and wood shacks. Often, 10 or 15 people would live in one small shanty, or the elders would live there, and the children would sleep outside in cardboard boxes.

It was a pitiful community, yet happiness abounded, and women squatted in their "working" positions and cooked for their families….the staple rice or noodles as the children played as in any other country. Singing could be heard as a "ba," an elderly lady, would sing a lullaby, perhaps rocking a child who was frightened or hungry off to sleep.

A handsome devil of a youth from India worked closely with me on the VRE Voice Newspaper, the monthly publication from VRE Headquarters. He assisted me in the composing room and print shop, and we had the occasion to work closely, sometimes too close for comfort. I didn't always trust myself! He was dark of skin, and his eyes were deep and black, and glistened like deep pools of oil….a mysterious blackness I found hard to penetrate. Yet he was soft and kind, and devilishly handsome. I was a bit too old to giggle, as did the other office girls, yet I wondered….and I'll always wonder, for I kept my cool and let his youthfulness be unscathed by an older woman. I loved his long, thick lashes that shaded his cheeks, and it curled downward at least a full inch as though it was protecting his fine bone structure. His name was as pretty as his face….Pago Pago, and he was represented at the VRE Headquarters by a sharp-looking secretary built like the Strategic Air Command itself, and skin of cocoa; a beautiful adornment of the office. I often wondered why she spent so much time in the Adjutant's office, but too soon, I found out what really was going on….

On Saturdays, each secretary had rotation duty, usually located in the Adjutant General's office. It wasn't an affair type of duty like I had presumed, at least not with me. In fact, it was scary. The building was more or less vacant on Saturdays, and you could hear the general beyond the reception desk talking of "big things" pertaining to the war, and you went home after your "once-a-month rotating Saturday duty," knowing more fully that it was indeed a real war. You had heard him say so; in his planning, his plotting and his maneuvers that he discussed quietly, yet firmly, like that of a great leader. The job consisted of getting his coffee and typing correspondence or orders, being on the field phone. Interesting, but not difficult at all. The playful games I felt sure that Pago Pago beauty had with the Adjutant General were real. He was 50ish, business-like….and yet a gentlemanly officer; appreciative of my Saturday duty. As my Saturday duty officer, C.J. Lambert, Major General, U.S. Army, was a kind and respectful boss. Where as R.J. Pugh, Colonel, USAF, Director of Administrative Services at VRE, was distant and seemed too burdened to make small talk. A big difference between the Military General boss, and the Civil Service boss at VRE.

I was happy to be here to share these months of war with the Big Indian after those long years of separation, the children and I were now experiencing something we would talk about for the rest of our lives. Ages 7, 9 and 11, and war stories to tape and mail home to grandma and grandpa Jeffers. What an experience for them, to live it, then live to tell it! They soon grew up too fast, to put it mildly….for it was new to them not to have a corner drug store to run to for a comic book or an ice cream cone. Here, they found out how to play baseball with a beer can and a stick and had a good time doing it. They soon learned to say "out" and "strike" in Vietnamese, and it didn't take long to participate with "Bup," the young houseboy next door, an employee of the Vietnamese doctor we leased our French Villa from. They became good friends, teaching each other as the days went by. Steve and Jeff soon learned to "learn" how they play in Saigon, or to not play at all. So they learned, and they revised, and they loved every minute of it, picking up new street friends daily…. friends beyond the massive gates or through the fence. Bup and Cindee had this thing going….she flirted with her baby blue eyes and found when she went to the balcony that Bup would soon appear in his yard next door, climbing up a tree like a monkey. They had their own special language to communicate, mostly smiles and eye contact…she and Kim made Bup feel very special with their giggling and ogling. I'm sure they both wanted to leap the concrete wall and barbed wire, but resorted to their flirtatious actions over the wall. At least for now….

After the enemy was repulsed from the early 1968 attack during the Tet holidays, and things started to return to some normalcy, we, too, adjusted to life with the three maids in our lovely home. The kids were tutored from the books the Buchanan County School District had allowed me to ship through the efforts and courtesy of the school board president, Mr. George Markley, and a few of their favorite teachers at Noyes School back home. These fine people all took a genuine interest in our move around the world, and the children reciprocated by letters and gifts of collector's dolls in glass cases, and smaller items being mailed back to old chums. The kids learned well, partially through Kim's willingness to both teach and learn, which soon rubbed off on our children. She was anxious to master English from the kids, and we were learning fractured Vietnamese slowly….a very difficult chore for all of us. Many an afternoon was passed on the balcony, or in the inner courtyard, repeating after each other and smiling under a mutual bond of friendship that only children can share and understand. Kim and Cindee were the same age, and a close relationship was there for all to see; a wonder of all wonders for these children to communicate, even though their individual language was yet to be fully understood. Before long, I could hear "mot, hai, ba, bon, nam, sau, bay, tam, chin and muoi." WONDERFUL! Counting from 1 to 10 in Vietnamese! Often, Doug was hinting he hoped it was safe for the kids to study on the balcony. Snipers were always in the neighborhood, and we had a constant fear for their lives….yet some semblance of normality had to be achieved to make each day bearable.

Chapter 8

His concern soon brought his crew from the base to build us a sandbag bunker in the inner courtyard at the rear of the villa; just outside our bedroom door. One humid Saturday, or Thu Bay, a flatbed loaded with sandbags and dozens of men ready to do what they could for their boss. They respected his knowledge of communications, as well as his talents for eyeing a pretty girl when he was out on the town with them, drinking Bom-e-Bom, a Vietnamese sour beer, or a San Miguel. He could hold his own with either, and they enjoyed his macho company, too. Their utmost respect for his family came first, so I know when he requested that they spend their day off building a bunker….there was not even the slightest hesitation. It was a dismal day, misty and hot as hell when the big flatbed rolled into the drive, followed by several jeeps and trucks pulling trailers of sand. They worked diligently filling the sandbags and putting them "just so" to make our private bomb shelter. They stopped for a beer now and then, and mostly now! It was too hot for man or beast, but they labored till the bunker was complete, doing a fine job. It was a good feeling watching them build it, knowing we now had a safe place to go during severe night attacks. And boy, did we go in there on many a night!

A friendly medic attached to the 14th Field Army Hospital, located a few distance blocks away, graciously supplied our bunker with the necessities and niceties of survival. Some of the necessities turned out to be 1940's issued WWII War rations, which somehow ended up in Vietnam in the late 1960s….And we never quite figured out what, or who, was responsible for sending the goodies for our G.I. to eat. It's for certain, though, that the civilians back in the States would have gagged and vomited if they would have opened one of the cans as we did. Green bread? I'll never forget it…. And black eggs? UGH!!!! But other items were much appreciated, such as medical kits, the whisky produced magically by the Officers' club, and the water hauled in from the base, purified and safe for drinking. Too, blankets were welcome to keep the bugs off of you as you sat in dark silence during an attack, afraid even to whisper because you could hear the Viet Cong on the rooftops, and the twang of their bullets racing by the bunker entrance. The children were perfect little angels….we dared them to be good, and by golly, they were. I think the terror of the Viet Cong night snipers outside their bedroom window and around the bunker had put the fear of God in them, and they realized they, too, were living in a full-scale war. It was a distinction they may not have realized at the time, being the only

American children that we were both aware of, and living, in Saigon, Vietnam, and in the middle of a full-scale war. Other construction American men perhaps had wives stashed somewhere in Thailand, Australia, Singapore, etc., but we never saw American children, as they were a rarity. Vietnam adults and children alike appeared from nowhere and stared through the Iron Gate bars to get a glimpse of these tow-headed American children, as fair hair is considered almost reverend to Buddhists; the golden locks were a symbol of good luck.

It was on the third day of work I knew how dearly I cared for all Australians. What creatures of fantasy… they live and love and enjoy life even in this war-torn city. I admired their poetic attitude to life, quoting great works of literature and taking pride in their knowledge of the arts, yet slugging down more beers than most Americans ever thought of drinking. And with gusto, but with manners befitting a British Lord. What gentlemen! What love they spread, I knew then I was in love with all the "down under," and I would fantasize about a secret lover….just for the hell of it. Perhaps thoughts and dreams with my secret love would make any future torturous nights a more pleasant affair, and I would give it a try, dreaming if at all possible of my very own Aussie, yet knowing full well I loved them all. Australian officers sauntered in and out of the VRE Headquarters, and I melted like a giddy schoolgirl. God, what they did to me….Chills ran up and down my spine when I heard them talk. When they turned on the charm, I wanted an instant divorce. OK, I'm only kidding! But my God; please forgive me for such selfish thoughts, I wondered why our feelings were bruised and hidden away, rather than caressed and warmed in total love and affection in our master bedroom. Yet, we shared the enjoyment and sexuality of normal beings, and I shouldn't be grasping us for an Aussie's tenderness.

Boots Peonies was one of my dearest Filipino friends and co-workers; she typed and charted whatever wartime office personnel did. A cute little young lady of chestnut skin, almond eyes and jet-black hair, a by-product of two lovely islanders who were back in Manila worrying about her safety. She spoke perfect English and was every inch a lady. She took me by the hand, introduced me to the area, and helped me with my one-thousand-and-one questions during that first week. She and Cam Tu were my side kicks, and I really depended on them. She had a handsome husband to whom she was devoted to, and I knew she never had an evil thought about another man, regardless of how fine he was. Boots loved her two tiny children also, and she did not hesitate to pull out their photos and let you dwell over them….A good wife and mother working overseas to get her share of that good money that was there to be made by anyone who was brave enough to live amidst the war and the Viet Cong. I cherished the lovely silk robe Boots gave to me, pure silk with mandarin collar and twisted silk knot buttons; it was true Asian/ Eastern and absolutely lovely. We had a lot of good laughs together, making the days of war a little more endurable and pleasant, and even though the alert sign was on, we still laughed. Boots had a great sense of humor, like the time we drew pictures during an attack just to keep from crying. We had "Charlie" with a pig nose, pointed ears and a devil's tail; hardly grotesque enough to do him any justice….And we did quite well with homemade Charlie Brown risqué posters, anything to keep our sanity during an attack. Sometimes, we drew Viet Cong and black pajamas on The Adjutant General, and then passed them around so everyone could share in the fun; at least it calmed some nerves while the bloody stuff was going on outside. I seldom cried at the office, but I did my share in bed at night, usually while staring out the bedroom window, listening and quivering from the sounds of weapons in the distance. Boots and Cam Tu kept me calm at work, laughing and talking about things unrelated to war; they were my closest allies for eight hours a day….and my best friends, all day.

And then there was Captain Workman, he was a cute little thing….we dubbed him "Little Boy Blue" due to his blond hair, childish features and small stature, with no offense intended. He was a great guy, just that he reminded you of your kid brother….he was young and should have been back in the States playing second base on the neighborhood team. I have fond memories of him and recall with joy how welcome he made me feel at VRE Headquarters, always smiling and throwing the tassel of flaxen hair back with a jerk of his head and a cute smile out of the corner of his mouth. The photos I have of him show his boyishness, and his fresh, scrubbed look shines in all the pictures. He never appeared demanding of our Administrative Services department employees, rather more congenial and understanding of us, and he was everyone's friend in the middle of the damned war. Sgt. Gray was from the motor pool….he was the exact opposite of Captain Workman or the Adjutant General. He was tall and big, the kind you wouldn't want to meet in a dark alley, yet tender and good to the kids. He dropped in often to visit and to inquire about the kids….sometimes just to say "hi," which proved his loneliness for his family back in the States. Most of the soldiers, marines and sailors at our villa were there for the same reason: Loneliness. It must have been a good feeling for them to be around the company of an American family, and I'll never forget the common saying from all of our guests: "Wow, a real American family. Complete with wife and kids!" Sgt. Gray's olive drab khakis and his limp-billed soft khaki hat were his trademarks, no class, just a common sign of a big man in a small war.

Lunch became the highlight of the day because of a Vietnamese translator and friend I mentioned before, Ho Thi Cam Tu, a lovely young Vietnamese who worked at the next desk and behind Ms. Boots Peonies. Cam Tu was so gracious in her native Ao-dia, the flowing slit dress of the Vietnamese woman with long pants peeking out from underneath. The dress and pants were ankle length, beautiful garments of silks and satins, sometimes of batiste cotton, with a high neck and narrow long sleeves, showing their oriental beauty in all its glory. They are tiny, dainty people, very short in stature compared to Americans. Her personality was big and one of "You are an American, please be my friend, and I will love you forever." And she did…. We ate lunch daily at the company headquarters café sharing a menu of American hamburgers or fried rice. It was there that I learned to love a lot of foods that I still prepare and enjoy, but I can savor the long ago taste of my first fried rice. And I'll never forget how she laughed at my awkward attempt with chopsticks, her native utensil; I had rice from one end of the company lunchroom to the other, and all commissary personnel were cracking up with laughter. Cam Tu giggled uncontrollably, and we fell in love that day…. sisters till death. She is an oriental beauty, and a lovely lady; we tied a bond that could never be severed. This bond was shared by the bearer of a Non-combatants Officer, ID #E162034, US Army. It was a good feeling to be an active participant in this war to assist South Vietnam in maintaining their independence….

A constant fight, and after the fall of France in 1940, the Japanese occupied French Indo-China till 1945, when Japan granted Vietnam its independence. And now again, fighting against their communist aggression here in early 1968, I was part of that fight for freedom. I was proud, and I vowed to do my utmost, both at headquarters and in my villa, towards making life a little more enjoyable for the fighting forces whose paths crossed ours. I vowed to make them all welcome and to be a good listener for their homesickness and problems; to love each and every one of them who were giving of themselves, whether by their voluntary enlistment, or by draft. Our French villa would be a stopping-off hotel between new assignments and a return haven after 30-day jungle bivouacs, and the joy my children brought would be shared with every G.I. entering my home. Our food and beds were theirs, and this was my decision and my promise.

Life was becoming more of a routine for the kids; they had taught Chi Hia how to make bun Ma (toast) for morning De-Ong, and she had taught them how to ask for it in Vietnamese. They had command of the language, or so they thought, by learning "water," and soon found by stating "nook" that little Chi Hia would take off shuffling to the kitchen to wait on them. They loved it, but I still wonder who enjoyed the relationship most… .I think she did because she was secure, appreciated, and needed and loved in the safety of a secure block and under the roof with Americans. We were one big happy family, and life went on, the children studied and observed, picked up Vietnamese habits and traditions, customs and language very rapidly and were soon to be known as "Chi Hia's sidekicks," her babysons. When they were ornery, Chi Hia yelled "ma-bun" (good for nothing), and the kids would reply with "sin Lowie" (I'm sorry). Common household words were: "Cam on" (Thank you), "Cam quachi" (You're welcome), "Doi-tit" (I like), "chop-chop" (eat), "café" (coffee), and the list just keeps on going.

Back at the office, and as a new hire at Administrative Services, I soon realized how plentiful the machine guns were when the "red alert" sign on the wall flashed red. The G.I.'s in our office jumped as they grabbed for their M-16s and aimed at the entrance near my desk, as it was part of their survival training as soldiers. We managed to continue typing or proof-reading, or whatever our jobs were, though fear gripped at our hearts, and our mouths were dry of saliva, like cotton had been the main course for lunch. Our hearts pounded wildly in our chests when we heard the rockets and incoming mortars outside of the safety of the headquarters building… A few weeks prior to our landing in Saigon, the Tet attack on the city by enemy troops focused mainly on the American embassy, not too far from our villa. The entire population of over three million was equally frightened. God didn't single out the young or old, men or women, and civilians or members of the military when it came to being frightened. Everyone was scared. I glanced at the young man riding shotgun at my desk and realized he was reading the Bible….a rare sight indeed. I'm certain they all read it at one time or another, but so openly and without shame, whereas others could have made a mockery of his doings. I saw another reading his Geneva Convention Booklet, so I knew we all shared the same fears.

Another G.I. assigned to Boots' desk was freckled and maybe 19 years old. I glanced down to see the steel-plated boots that were "punji proof," a bamboo-type weapon made into the ground that the G.I.'s would fall on and it would puncture their feet, and I saw the bayonet reaching out from his gun. I realized he was ready for hand-to-hand combat with an entire Viet Cong regiment! These kids had guts….I just hoped he didn't spill his on my desk. I picked up a book and read about the booby trap course, the escape and evasion chapter and thought of the thousands of protesters back home. Were the kids on the university campuses right or wrong? Who could answer that? Did we really belong here? Just the afternoon before, we were jeered and yelled at with a loud "Yankee, go Home!" It was a very unappreciative attitude for ones who had traveled halfway around the world to assist with South Vietnam's quest for freedom. Shit….Why was this kid here at my desk with a gun pointed at the door? Why was I here? Did the Big Indian really belong here? Questions that would never be answered spun through my head again and again. I was scared as I watched the alert sign on the wall. It did not go off. I thought of the three million people, and I wondered if a correct count was made of the ones sleeping in cardboard boxes and burned-out cars along the streets….in crowded schoolyards and parking lots. Three million seemed to be the right figure, or at least a good estimate. People were everywhere: children without parents, parents crying as they searched for their children, families broken and hungry and without a roof or security from the invaders. These people were raiding the local garbage piles in the streets, piles 10 to 20 feet high, sharing with the rats whatever they could forage to boil for their evening meal. A few outer leaves of cabbage could flavor water into a thin soup, or one American's garbage could make a tasty stew for starving children. Starvation and nakedness were everywhere. So sad, these refugees, mountain and hamlet people, had trickled into Saigon seeking refuge from the dark eyes of the jungle.

The war had again escalated; the evidence was plain as we passed dead bodies in the streets, a daily sight to and from work. The gutter-sleeping victims shared the streets with roaring tanks, troops in trucks, supply trucks loaded with everything from artillery to medical supplies, droves of people on the move, elephants and water buffalo, dark-eyed people of the land, all under suspicion and dodging the cyclos and taxi and pedi-cabs of this Asian nation….A freak sight for an American accustomed to Cadillacs, Chevy's, Jeeps, football games and golden wheat shafts, someone that was accustomed to the sparkling of the Midwestern late-day sun on the cleanliness of a city without blood. I found this to be quite a sight and hard to comprehend, yet it was a city of past and forgotten beauty left over from the days of French rule; Indochina and France were showing everywhere in the architecture and language, beauty amidst the beast of war. Then I heard yelling and sporadic rat-tat-tat in the Headquarters neighborhood… .I presumed they had killed the Charlie that had presented a threat to our area and to our Exchange Headquarters. The alert sign went off, and G.I.'s left their manned posts and returned to their desks. I had typed throughout the alert, and as I counted the pages, I found I had a total of 14, an automatic reaction to keep the fingers busy, even though the mind wandered and worried over a probable attack. After a couple of deep breaths, we had survived one more alert….With the alert sign "clear," my G.I. friend and his punji-proof boots returned to his assigned desk and went back to his normal routine. This had been one of our luckier days, no infiltration of our particular building, although it had been rumored Charlie was in the neighborhood. This information came from documents of the captured Viet Cong, so we were always prepared. I gave a long, silent prayer of thanks.

The weekend of my 36th birthday was celebrated with a surprise pig roast. It was my Indian's gift to me, and, I guess, the finest gift ever. His Filipino employees were very adept at pig roasting, and they had arrived very early that Saturday morning to dig the pit so the succulent meat would be tender by late afternoon. They were pulling into the villa driving flatbed trucks and were followed closely behind by a jeep towing a canvas-covered trailer as Doug was taking me to work very early one Saturday morning. I said, "What are they doing here, Doug?" As we drove out of the heavy iron gate that protected our villa, these trucks were waiting in line to turn in, and Doug calmly stated, "They are going to do some work for me today." I accepted that, thinking they would reinforce the bunker, perhaps work on the generators or water system, never giving it a second thought that they had anything remotely connected to my birthday. All I knew was that it was Saturday, and I hated to go to work; it was my once-a-month-duty day, and it fell on my birthday. The Adjutant General told me at noon that I could go home, and I excitedly called Doug to pick me up. Although, it was prearranged with the General that I could take off at noon, and he never let their secret slip. He only said we were not too busy, and why didn't I go home? I felt guilty leaving his field phone unmanned, but he assured me it was okay. It was fine with me, and I meandered out towards the thatched hut of the guard post and waited for the Big Indian to come after me. While I waited, I pondered the evening ahead. What would we do to celebrate? How could this birthday be special in the middle of a war? Did Chi Hia even know it was my birthday? Would she have something special prepared for dinner? Would any friends be dropping by for a fun evening? Had the Big Indian even realized it was my birthday? The guard asked why I was taking off at noon, and so I replied, "It's my birthday today!"

He leaned on his rifle and gave me a hug and a big kiss, as somehow it seemed okay....Hell, neither of us may even be here tomorrow. Little did I know of the activity going on at our villa, and as we drove up to the gate, I could see our villa was one big lawn party. People of many colors and many nations were there yelling "Surprise, surprise, surprise!" and surprised I was! What a thrill! What a celebration! My heart pounded, and I cried with joy because the Big Indian and our friends were here to celebrate with me.

Soon, I spotted two very large pigs roasting over a pit in my honor; this had to be the best birthday anybody ever had. The crusty skin of the pig is cherished as the finest of delicacies, and everyone, especially the Filipinos, requested the skin first and meat later. They dipped the crisp skin in a cooked sauce like poi that resembled cooked oatmeal....a concoction simmered in a huge black pot. It even looked like oatmeal, very sweet and thick like oatmeal, and it was delicious. The swine heads, complete with apples in their mouths, were placed on a tray and paraded around to the rhythm of a drummer, then put in their place of honor on the picnic table in the shaded front yard so we could take pictures. We had a great time, and some placed the tray on their heads for that special photo with the birthday girl....some danced around with it and chanted and sang while I clapped and laughed. It was a wonderful party amidst the incoming barrage of shells that broke up the party later that night. Even the papaya and banana trees that were sheltering their tiny spider monkeys had a good time at the party, as they swayed with the breeze and seemed to give extra shade earlier that day, just for my birthday. There were dozens of handsome men at the party, and some lovely Vietnamese girls, all looking like Kim's photo. I was looking for her at every corner, wondering what this woman was really like; this woman had stolen his heart, all the while I had waited so many years in the States. I inquired about each and every one, but never knowing if she was there or not. But I have reason to suspect one particularly pretty girl could have been her because the Big Indian appeared to spend a lot of time with her, and I wondered, "Does she really have a little girl fathered by my husband?" as I had been told….

Most everyone had a date for the celebration; even the American Chaplain brought his little Vietnamese beauty. They, too, partook in the festivities, and sang and danced with the crowd, having as much fun as anyone. The drinks flowed, gaiety prevailed, and it had all been a wonderful and complete surprise. The children told me later they had known about the party for a long time, and Chi Hia had been forewarned, yet they had managed to keep it a big secret! There was a large, round cake, frosted prettily in pink and white, and written across the top was "To Juni, from the boys at Tan Son Nhut," to complete the wonderful day. I was anxious to cut into the cake….because from the time I was a very small girl, I had always loved the confectioner's fluffy-white icing that adorned store-bought cakes. We hadn't had cake for a long time, and this was a very exciting moment, taking the knife in hand and cutting the first piece. The cameras were turning; this moment was to be "recorded for posterity," as Doug put it. This moment was mine! Something red oozed out from between the layers, and I knew it would be a sweet fruit filling. Anticipation was such that everyone said, "Juni, you eat the first piece," and I didn't give them any argument.

My mouth was watering, and I could hardly wait when that first piece rose to my lips with a smile about four blocks wide, when, lo and behold, I almost gagged; It had no sugar in it! It was tasteless and did nothing to arouse the longing taste buds in my mouth. I wondered if it was a joke….Shaving cream? I kept my composure, not sure if a prank had indeed been played on me, yet wise enough to realize I couldn't hurt anyone's feelings. Stranger things than dull cake had happened here, so I ate another bite, but quickly set it down. I proceeded to cut and share the rest of it, as I had done the correct thing, and it was not a joke. I know that the Vietnamese do not sweeten their celebration cakes with sugar, so I laughed to myself and thought, "So, it's not sweet? Who cares? Whatever gave me the idea it was even easy to get a lovely, decorated cake in the middle of a war?" Some ate it, but most Americans did not. I was thankful and appreciative, and let it be known. I was glad I had not asked aloud, "Is this a joke?" Because, as it turned out, it certainly wasn't. It was a thing of beauty, and I still treasure the photographs that attest to its decorations. But the biggest disappointment was that it surely didn't taste like the finger-lickin' good bakery cakes from back home!

The G.I.'s had come to the house to be comfortable, to be a part of a family, to be out of the jungle or from the base and into a house filled with American children and their laughter. This was something to remind them of what life was like back in the States, and they took advantage of it as though it were a hotel. Many G.I.'s spent the night as we had several spare rooms. It was "Allen Hotel" night when we had a pot of beans and pork and mixed up a batch of spoon bread from a mix sent from the States. They ate like farm hands and then settled down for games of cribbage and checkers with the kids. We often entertained all nationalities, all branches of the Armed Forces, and the civilian employees from both my husband's company….and the VRE Headquarters. It was a good life amidst all the blood and hell; it was an experience. And tonight was no different, only more people. The many lovely gifts from the far corners of Asia, the singing in many different languages, and the native dances were a welcome respite from what was outside the confines of our block: WAR….

I was becoming accustomed to dismal days and long nights; monsoons and sweltering heat were of no important significance. Only the far-off sounds of war bothered me. Acceptance of the conditions within the city gave you a feeling of security; we had a job to do, and we were there to do it. I felt a sense of pride to be a part of it. It was the darkness of the night that held the greatest fears….I was a prisoner to the noises that shattered my sleep and my faith in God at times. It was difficult to pray during a rocket attack when fears overwhelmed all lip movements and brain functions. I found I was reaching deeper within my gut to find the words of comfort the kids so desperately needed. Sometimes, it was as though the words lay hidden deep under my toenails, like lizards under a desert rock; not wanting to be a part of the outside world easily. Words never came easily….not during the night. One night, I tiptoed to Cid's room and woke her, and the two of us went into the boy's room to check on them. The Big Indian was on the base for a cut-over project, and I knew the kids were scared when daddy could not get home at night. I suggested perhaps we should be thinking about returning to the United States for their safety, as daddy was having to spend more and more time on base. They assured me they were doing OK, and did not want to go home, yet….

Brave little liars, they never could explain the sobbing noises coming from their rooms that had all too often awakened me during the night. They were too damned proud, lest their fighting buddies, the G.I.'s, may call them "chickens" in this hellish game of war.

Could God forgive me for bringing them to South Vietnam? I barely found the words to explain the war game that was so different from any other game they had ever played….unlike a game of checkers or chess. This game hurts badly, and occasionally, tears have to be shed. Pain and tears are allowed in the game. I held them tight to me, a huddle of love and bravery combined. We were becoming accustomed to war and its terrors. We talked of death, funerals, bodies, blood and starvation that night. We spoke frankly and openly about the things that scared us and the problems we had encountered as Americans in Vietnam. We talked about what we missed the most, and everybody agreed it was their Grandma and Grandpa. They were beginning to miss school, and the achievements school brings. Here, there were no report cards, no "99's" at the top of their papers, or "77's" for that matter. There were no close friends to go to the movies with, no neighborhood Saturday afternoon games at the corner lot. And yet here, there were curfews that kept us from attending many movies on base. We cried. We prayed together, and aloud. It felt good to thank God for all the things we had in America that were always taken for granted. The four of us slept together that night, secure in knowing we could reach out and touch one another….

Chapter 9

The dawn brought heat, more miserable heat and more incoming rockets. The farmers had a difficult journey getting into town, with Napalm and Agent Orange being sprayed alongside the roads, killing foliage and children alike. It was dangerous to travel any road outside of Saigon, but they had to get their crops to market. Farming is primitive, and the rice fields abound in the countryside. The Vietnamese raise a few cattle, but cattle are considered sacred to some of the religious sects, so many just roam freely and are never slaughtered to feed the thousands of starving citizens. They will raid garbage piles before they slaughter their cattle. Garbage piles average one to each block in the residential districts….no pick-up routes like in the USA. You just take it out and dump it. Someone will appear as though out of nowhere and take what you have just dumped, especially if the maids that were depositing garbage worked for the Americans. The Americans usually had choice garbage as we instructed our maids to take off the outer leaves of the lettuce and cabbages, take off the tops and outer stalks of celery and bok choy, and not bother to boil the chicken carcass or bones after we had our meal….thus it was a staple to starving people and far better tasting than the rats they often ate. Or the dogs; you never saw a dog roaming the streets of Cholon or Saigon, as they were precious food for the hungry families and Tet refugees and demanding a good price.

If you had a pet, beware; it would be kidnapped for food. I have observed from our balcony as natives would rummage through the nearby garbage pile about a block or so away, digging and prodding for something the Americans may have tossed away, something that could be salvaged to boil flavor into their meager evening meal of rice for their skinny children and respected elders. We were fortunate to get all the T-bones and pork chops from the officers of Tan Son Nhut that we could use, so we always had bones to be boiled with plenty of meat left on them.... Or they could be chewed on after they seasoned their rice, a real delicacy to a hungry family. So when Chi Hia made her daily trek to the garbage pile, she would gather quite a following behind her, like the Pied Piper leading the way to salvation. Our garbage never had time to rot in the pile. They would be fighting over it and yelling, "It's mine," and "No, it's mine." in their Vietnamese language. I have seen pushing and shoving over a few leaves of cabbage and bones that made me cry. Starvation and swollen bellies are not pretty sights. Farmers climb from their overloaded carts for a rare day of trading and price haggling at the open market, shopping and browsing with their families, "the big day in the city." Water buffalo pulled the cart laden with cut bamboo, the hand-carved pipes, and all the mother-of-pearl trinket boxes produced by wife and kids. They had dodged mines and sniper fire as they trekked the muddy roads from village to town. Rice crops have failed, and people have starved by the thousands. Thousands more barely survived with their sweet potato soup….one piece of potato boiled into thin soup to feed many members of the family. The sweet potato crop is usually good in the tropical climate with over 95 inches of rainfall each year….so this watery soup was edible but not too nourishing, considering it was a staple replacing their rice. It was edible, but that's about all. Our maids were 99% monophagous of their rice diet, the Big Indian brought it home in 100-pound sacks. They dumped it out on the freshly scrubbed and highly polished tile floors and sat for hours in their squatting position to sort each and every grain, searching for any foreign particle, bug, rock, or imperfection that would ruin theirs (or ours) daily staple. The 100-pound bag fed not only the three maids, Chi Hia's husband and daughter, Kim, but occasionally, I would see a small brown paper sack handed through the iron spikes of the massive gate of our villa….I strongly suspected some little person was getting a handout, compliments of the Big Indian via our maids. Little did it matter. We never went hungry, so we couldn't complain if some other family had a little happiness with our black rice marketed right out under our noses.

We longed for Coke, Pepsi and 7up. Being deprived of our favorite drinks was like being deprived of a swim on a murky summer day back in the Midwest as the temperatures soared over the 100-degree mark. Bourbon and nook became the drink after a hard day at the base or at headquarters. Chi Hia always managed to have it ready when you arrived, a cool drink of V.O. and nook or a stinger over rocks. You could depend on it, just like you could depend on your slippers. What a gal….and all for $65.00 a month wage. Live-in maids, mothers and friends! A bargain in any war. Gambling has always been a major pastime for our armed forces serving in any war; and this war was no different. There was not much else for the guys to do, except pass the time away by drinking Bom-e-Bom beer and chasing short-skirted prostitutes on Tu Do Street, which soon became known as the "Street of Love"….And later, the "Expressway of Love" as the girls got faster, and the guys got hornier. G.I.'s often spent a large portion of their pay envelopes buying "Saigon Tea" for the bar girls, a watered-down "tea" of weak bourbon and water. Sometimes, just colored water, usually costing $4.00 or $5.00, of which the house kept half, and the prostitute got half. I was told by one of the girls that they could knock down $2,000 or $3,000 a month easily off of the free-spending G.I.'s out for companionship. So, it was either drink or gamble, and the clubs were everywhere; complete with slot machines to deprive them of the few coins the girls missed.

My kids were guests of the G.I.'s often, usually going with their friend and favorite houseguest, Benny Fraley, to play the one-arm bandit machines. Benny was employed at MAC-V Headquarters….The top source of information, but he drank too much after working hours, and if the truth was known; probably during working hours. After the kids spotted him throwing up a few times, they soon dubbed him "Benny Barf." He was never Benny Fraley after that; he was just simply known as Benny Barf. He was a lovable guy, and he worshiped the kids….he delighted in taking them to the military club and giving them a handful of money. Endless hours of pulling the handle on the slot machine, waiting and watching for the lemons, oranges and berries that made the winning combination that allowed the coins to flow like liquid silver down the spout and onto the floor. Benny never drank when he took the kids to the club….he cherished his friendship with them and valued the house they shared and the time they spent together. He always brought them home on time, and he was always sober.

Quite often, they won!!! The kids would come home with $5.00 less, or $5.00 more than they had left the villa with, all smiles and proud of their accomplishments, not realizing that luck had no role in their newest war game. They soon made a deal with Benny Barf and told him, "Take me along, and I'll split my winnings with you." Because of their extraordinary "luck," they were bankrolled and soon became "heroes" of sorts.

They had their own war stories to sit around and tell, of how much they won, of what day at what club and with whom. Celebrities of sorts? They were sought after as gaming partners, both with the G.I.'s and with the Major of the Consots across the street. Oh….the glory of the Major sending what looked like a full regiment of uniformed M.P.s for those kids, demanding they accompany the men back to play roulette with the Major. We were always told, "The Major desires your company in a game of roulette." Very proper, very formal….you didn't dare refuse the uniformed men at the gate. The kids thought they were big shots in a war; although heroes only to themselves, proud and elated at their new status. It had never been quite like this back at Noyes Elementary.

Chess and checkers became a regular pastime around the 12-foot teak table as the evenings became more dangerous and we dared not venture out. At 5 pm the daily curfew was in effect, so everyone scurried in, closed the shutters, and passed the time the best we could within our own walls. Many times, I heard a guest make the statement, "Well, I am down $3.00, Jeff," or "I lost $4.00 to Steve", and it's safe to say our children were the best-heeled kids in Asia!! I wondered what they spent it on; no corner drugstore or movie houses for them to run to, perhaps they rat-holed it away for a rainy day? No, because it rained almost every day….I'll never know how the Rockefeller twins parted with their fast fortune, one of the secrets of the war, buried like some of Charlie's victims, and forever God's secret. Some things just were not discussed with mom, and their own finances and gambling were two of those prized secrets. Win or lose, they never disclosed their full set of books to me. Many a good poker or crap games ended with the sun coming up. Our house should have been dubbed the "Allen Casino" rather than the "Allen Hotel," but we welcomed the guys anytime, day or night. We loved each and every one of them and considered them part of the family. It sure beats digging foxholes or pulling blood-sucking swamp leeches from their skin. And "Allen's" meant hospitality, hot showers and an occasional Missouri newspaper. It was always interesting to read about our war in a hometown paper because the mainlanders never got the whole story. Only we, here in South Vietnam, knew this police action WAR; because we ate WAR, slept WAR, talked WAR and fought WAR on a day-to-day basis. And desperately wanting to be allowed to fight to win; the attitude and saying of the day was "vogue la galere, or "keep on whatever may happen."

Shopping in Saigon was fascinating. The main shopping areas were the boulevards or streets of Tu Do, Le Loi, Nguyen Hue, Le Thanh ton, and Dong Khanh in Cholon, and the huge city market known as the Saigon Central Market were the gathering place. The Central Market was a most interesting house of barter and exchange, stocked with everything from jade jewelry to water buffalo harnesses, and from hand-carved

Ivory candlesticks to an over-ripe durian. Fishing nets and swords were near the delicate silks, and across from the Chinese celery, a "one-stop market." Many alleyways….and a maze of crowded stalls made this a rich margin center for visitors, but the war had turned it into a snake pit of inflated prices for local peasants and farmers merely desirous of trading for the bare necessities of life. Refrigeration was at such a premium that only the very wealthy had it. Natives with no refrigeration found it necessary to shop daily for their perishables. I have seen chickens hanging aloft at the open market covered with flies, and bearing a price equivalent to $4.00 American money.

Few could afford such exorbitant prices, and few made such a purchase. We never bought meat at the open market….I gagged when I saw all of the flies clinging to the foul-like maggots, "YUK," I said out loud to anyone who would listen. I thought I would throw up. We were fortunate to be Americans; having the privilege of marketing at the P.X. and Commissary provided for all troops and civilians employed under government contract, whereas local citizens had no choice but to shop in the central market, or from street vendors. But I can't honestly swear I never ate a Central Market chicken, mainly because Chi Hia often disappeared on one of our Honda scooters, so who knows what she bought besides bok choy and ginger root? Yes, I may well have eaten "Saigon chicken" and never even knew it….The native crafts and silks were lovely, and we spent many a lunch hour buying "pretties" to ship home. Tortoiseshell and ivory goods were reasonable, and one intricately hand-carved Ivory fan is one of my most prized possessions. The pottery is pretty, and blinds and room dividers were a good bargain, though they posed shipping problems with their bulk. Conical hats and totes were bargains, as were lacquered jewelry boxes of a black, shiny finish and adorned with bright colors, another native work of art. I received a set with matching smaller boxes and a hairbrush for a birthday gift, and I loved them like I loved my children. Well, almost!

Having shoes made to order was an experience the children will likely never forget. We walked into the boot shop and had to duck beneath the dozens of skins hanging from the rafters, brushing them aside to get to the rear of the shop to find the proprietor. We picked our style of shoe from an old American Sears catalog and chose the skin of our choice from the selection hanging to the floor. The female attendant took a paper and pencil and said, "Stand on paper, please." She outlined our feet and then politely announced that we should return in one week for our shoes and boots…. Steve chose python for his boots and wallet, which is wildly beautiful. Jeff chose leathery elephant hide for his boots and wallet, and Cid and I decided we'd have both! And purses to match! And one for my sister, one for my mother, and one for a girlfriend back home! But I found out later I could have bought the business for what we spent. They did a remarkable job fitting the shoes and boots though; it's hard to believe they started with an outline penciled on plain white paper, just like a butcher tears off to wrap your meat purchase in. They were very careful to tear off just the exact amount that would cover your foot, as not an inch was wasted in this land of war, this land of short materials. They had also carefully measured around the instep of the foot, so the shoes had a remarkable fit and comfort, complete with fine insoles, silk lining and leather soles. Where they got all the materials, I don't know, but they had a booming American business in this tiny back-alley shop. We cherished the crafted footwear, tremendously….

Elephant hide is so tough it should be worn for years and years and years; it could well be passed on from generation to generation and never show wear and tear. It had been a fun experience having our shoes made "while we waited," so to speak….something we'll never forget. We found tailors and shirt makers along Tu Do Street sandwiched in between the famous Tu Do bars and prostitutes. And according to many of the visiting G.I.'s, the shirt makers and prostitutes both did a fine job, workmanship unequaled! Both had fixed rates: cheap for locals and expensive for Americans. Jewelers found it very profitable when the Americans and third country Nationalists and G.I.'s hit their shops on payday to purchase precious stones…. those of the likes of jade, coral, tiger eye, opals and pure gold for their wives and girlfriends back home. Opals were cheap in Australia, and armed forces on R&R leave brought back dozens to have mounted in Vietnamese gold. We purchased pins, bracelets, necklaces and pure gold with no alloy added as in American gold, thus a pureness that is also soft and bendable. Their gold is truly beautiful, to say nothing of its extremely high value due to purity. No visitor to Saigon could depart without buying one of their native dresses, the Ao Dia….It is the first thing that strikes the foreign visitors' eye when they set foot in this strange land: raven-haired beauties in this unique, sexy native dress looking almost reverend, yet vixen-like as their tiny dark eyes dance and try to speak another language to these fair headed visitors. The "Ao Dia" has a close-fitting bodice; a long flowing slit-sided tunic worn with the pantaloon, which today are a bit tighter in the leg than in years gone by, almost losing their allure and grace that is the Vietnamese charm. But with all the Americans around to entice, the loose-legged pantaloons left with the breeze and the tightness shored up the ankle, as well as the buttocks to allure some G.I. into the night.

Chinese was spoken in most shops, as well as French and English. French is the language of the Vietnamese aristocracy and of the more luxurious shops, hotels and dinner clubs. It was not uncommon to hear the languages mixed in one conversation, so I was at a total and complete loss when ordering dinner at the Caravel Hotel. Steamships stopped in Saigon, and ships called on Tokyo, Calcutta, Rangoon, Djakarta, Bangkok,

Hong Kong, Manila, and Singapore, so there was usually an influx of world travelers. This slowed down during the war, though, but the port was still a busy place to be. Ships with up to 200,000-ton cargo are apt to pass between banks lined with mangroves or areas covered with luxurious vegetation, water palm trees and rice fields. Artillery, machine gun ammo, medical supplies, tide, toilet tissue, Jeeps and tanks bulged the holds of these giant-sized freighters. The bulk of war supplies were shipped via the China Sea to Saigon on foreign ships leased to America. Saigon and Cholon covered an estimated area of 51 square kilometers and housed well over three million residents and refugees. All the while, sampans and river junks, filled with rice, fish, sand or wood guided by men using poles or ores.

In this beautiful city, we visited the Botanical Gardens, blooming wildly with equatorial plants and the most beautiful orchids ever. The game runs free in this garden, bounding from one corner to another, fully enjoying Mother Nature's works of beauty, amidst all of the barrages of incoming shelling which cratered these lovely gardens a few weeks later. One day, the G.I.'s took the kids to the National Museum, located at the entrance of the Botanical Gardens, and they talked about it for days. So, I made it a point to visit and view for myself the hundreds of objects and documents relating to the history and evolution of Vietnam….Other documented antiques adorned this, the best-organized museum among the five throughout the country and related to other Asian countries. This includes Cambodia, Thailand, Laos, Indonesia, Malaya, Japan, China, and Tibet; all exhibited in this attractive museum which was first inaugurated in 1929. We ate lunch in the garden as rockets fell across town, and I thought, "The elite and the dead….they're for sure strange lunch partners." Taking Tu Do Street to the Bach Dang Quay on the Saigon River was a wonderful place to just loaf, drink Bom-e-Bom and watch the ships coming into the harbor. Its park-like grounds and childlike park chairs made a rendezvous spot for young and old alike, enjoying the breeze and a beautiful view. We enjoyed driving to the end of Tu Do Street to the Quay and browsing around, sometimes purchasing tasty snacks from vendors, on down to the Pointe Des Beleaguers, which was better known as Bull Slingers Point, and then on down towards the National Bank of Vietnam. You could always find a bench under the shade and view the ships at the port in Khanh Hoi, their lights reflecting in the waters and taking your mind off of war. I thought to myself, "What a lovely city this would be if it weren't for the damned war, so sad…." Ships traveled some 40-miles upriver to reach the port, and the girls frequented the port area around the Quay, short skirts blowing in the breezes and hopes of making out with a sex-starved seaman. Prostitution flourished, just another phase of the war.

One sunny Sunday afternoon, I took the children to see the zoo, and to me, it was quite unlike the zoos we had visited stateside. The kids went on and on about how weird it was to purchase bamboo shoots for the elephants rather than customary bags of peanuts. Ah, peanuts….I remembered how I had spent a small fortune on peanuts at the Swope Park Zoo in Kansas City, until I discovered the boys were returning to the picnic basket with each new sack, hiding them under the red gingham napkins and a little left of the pickled beets. They had peanuts stashed for the whole neighborhood after a trip to Swope Park. Poor little friends who had to stay behind were rewarded with a bag of nuts. I hadn't planned it that way, and didn't even get my suspicions aroused until I realized I had purchased over two dozen sacks. And yet here in Vietnam, and all the time, I thought K.C. had hungry elephants! They enjoyed the baboons and monkeys, and they loved spending the afternoon gawking at giant snakes and birds. A lot of huge Asian snakes were on display in the zoo, alive and kicking. And so was I, alive and kicking; kicking right on by as fast as I could go! I detest snakes, especially the kind that can gulp you down for breakfast faster than you can say "Wheaties!" I kept my distance and drug the kids right on by….That's why they didn't enjoy going with me. The monkeys lured me closer and closer, and I fell in love with the little ones who craved some attention. They loved showing off for us. We had a tree full of them at the villa; their chattering lasted way into the night, and I often wondered if they would ever shut up so we could go to sleep. Soon, we learned to accept the noise, no different than the sound of the crickets and bullfrogs lulling around the farm ponds back home.

On another day, we ate lunch at the Chinese Embassy on Pasteur, which was rather close to VRE headquarters. One of the Chinese secretaries hosted a tea, complete with tiny cakes and crabmeat amidst the décor of silk screens and silken pillows around a low table. I liked the shark soup, but to this day, I know to this very day that she is wondering why we didn't care for the eel pate….My stomach can only absorb so much in new tastes, and its boundaries have been reached. I am willing to try most foods, but the thought of the slippery fish turned my stomach. She was a lovely hostess, and it was one of the highlights of my time overseas, she was so formal at the tea, yet so playful during office hours. She showed her socialite manners at this luncheon; a lovely daughter of an honorable nobleman, doing her duty for the war as best she could….

Chapter 10

Back at home that night, we were scared…. Rockets were landing all around us and forcing us to sleep with one eye open and both ears cocked and tuned in for the incoming sounds that were to send us scurrying to the sandbagged bunker in the inner courtyard. The noise was devastating, and we were gripped by fear as it tore at our hearts and shattered our nerves. We wondered if we would come out of this particular night alive. We prayed…. Life in the war-weary city goes on, of course. It's a part of life for everyone in Vietnam, something to live with and accept as best you can. We spent many hours in our master bathroom before finally having the sandbag shelter at the time. War shows in deep crevices across everyone's brow, making the young look old before their time. However, life went on as usual, and the few shops that were still open were filled with customers, and businessmen conducted business as usual between attacks. Traffic is as hectic as ever during daytime hours, dodging bullets and sniper fire and elephants and water buffalo….the streets of Saigon were always dangerous for one reason or another. Most of the Vietnamese people can't leave the city-proper, unlike the Americans who normally depart after a twelve-month tour, so the locals do the best they can and make it through another day. Another day of roasting rats, stealing food, picking the pockets of American civilian employees on their lunch hours, the poor robbing the poorest, and the sluts conducting business as usual in the rubbish-filled gutters of once flower-lined streets.

An officer at the base had invited the Big Indian and I, along with 6 or 7 other couples in for an evening of cocktails, cards and games, and we watched as he pulled the drapes across the massive windows of his base office that would cut down on the flying glass. He went on to explain that the storeroom next door would be the safest place in case of an attack and gave explicit directions and instructions on what to do in case of an attack. The same instructions were given at a cocktail party at the Embassy, along with an apology for the party room, an inner room away from entrances and windows, and with guards posted closer together than guests, or so it seemed….The diplomats had 100% protection, as did most of the people at the base. But it was more of a "Do It Yourself" at our villa, and that's where Nigh came in handy, as he always rode shotgun for us wherever we ventured in this war-strafed city, and he was always around when we entertained or had friends over. He was the number one Honcho with the gun, and protected the Big Indian's wife and children as though they were his own. Incoming rockets targeted their area, and there was no discretion as to women and children, or soldiers at their guard posts. "Kill one and all" was Charlie's motto….No compassion in this war, not when you deal with the ugly Communists. But the game continued, and all the Americans learned to live with the fear of incoming mortar and Hell. You couldn't just hole up and wait. You had to live, socially and mentally….or just fold up and die. It takes special courage to fight a war, whether from a G.I.'s point of view, or a housewife's point of view, especially if you are in the middle of it.

Casual precautions were commonplace, especially since Communist forces outside South Vietnam's capitol began to bombard the city with daily rocket attacks during the Offensive of 1968. "The year of the rockets." No, it was "the year of Hell," as far as I was concerned. And "The year the Big Indian forgot to come home." It was "The year I would like to forget." Native women send their children to sleep with different relatives each night so that they would not all die together in an attack. Best not to all be killed…. Some would hopefully survive to carry on the name. But for what? Old beggars and refugees who normally sleep in the street now move indoors; it is hotter, but much safer, and they, too, still have the desire to live. One old man rests his body near two small children huddled close together, perhaps children of refugees long ago found dead. He manipulated the remnants of a long-ago worn-out blanket over the children in an act combining protection, love and tenderness in one motion. I even doubt if any of the three war-weary figures lived through the night….the Viet Cong hit that block pretty heavily just before dawn. A young American construction employee, barely four days in the country, catches the first plane out and says, "To hell with you guys, I don't need that $100,000.00 a year that damned bad!" Well-to-do Vietnamese send their families to safer cities on the coast, like Vung Tau. Street vendors, café patrons, workers, merchants, soldiers and secretaries alike; everyone discussed the rockets as though the attacks were the weather. Very matter-of-factly, 1968 was known throughout the city as "the year of the rockets," and they were daily. You could mark your calendar or set your watch by the noises. Charlie consistently plugged away with his war effort, prodded and pushed by superiors who knew nothing else, except "Kill and conquer for the glory of our leader." The police action was bloody and ugly. A young Vietnamese girl at the VRE headquarters was begging the boss to get her some sandbags, explaining they have disappeared from the black market, regardless of how many piasters you have to offer in payment for these highly prized items, which can mean life or death during the long black nights. Many girls exchanged sexual favors for sandbags that could save their entire family. Sex for sandbags? It's not a bad deal; it's a pleasure in exchange for life. Think about it….

An old lady moves her bed from the window to a more sheltered corner. Whole families leave their bedrooms to sleep beneath stairwells, all the while plaster falls and prayers are silently spoken with all the reverence one can muster during a war. We did likewise. But the reaction, somehow, is more depressing nowadays than ever. It was worse than it was during the Viet Cong attacks on the city in January and February, and worse than it was during the street fighting that has taken place sporadically since then. The casualties creep upward, and rumors fly quicker than ever, rumors of our losing the war. "Hogwash," my daddy wrote to me, "Americans don't lose wars." But he was not there with the misguided leadership in the field, nor the directives issued in error, or the unauthorized memos and orders that sent our already intoxicated or drug-crazed boys straight into ambush….And often with orders not to kill, but to "observe." You can't win a war fought the way this war was being fought. It's impossible. Young Lieutenants overpowered by tears were clinging to their bunks, rather than leading their group. A commissioned kid-like officer was scared to death. But we felt these fears too, and no one was ashamed to cry in this war. The tears ran like rivers, and these psychological rivers were cause enough for gallons of beer and whiskey chasers, or an entire night of stingers on the rocks. A good sleep-induced night; a necessity in Saigon….The rockets have already claimed thousands of Vietnamese, and there were thousands more that have been wounded. The psychological impact is deep, while the bandages run short. It was a reality that Saigon's citizens were becoming accustomed to the "normal" sounds of war:

The rattle of machine guns, the rumble of the big guns outside the city and the roar of warplanes overhead, the constant whirl of treetop level chopper blades, and the screams of death within the city sent chills up your spine and a lump in your throat.

But the rockets are a new and frightening experience. They exploded with a nerve-cutting crack: always too close. The ominous whistle of incoming rockets is terrifying to people who have no place to run. Saigon is scared, and the summer's heat makes living in this war-torn jungle pure HELL. Aircraft carriers with their wind-whipped decks were doing a massive job at refueling the thunderous jets. Cockpit doors slid shut, and barely cleared the decks when they soared into the skies. At 6,000 feet, they dropped their deadly cargo of bombs on encampments, roads, river shores and hills below. Our fighters strafed the 2 eyed snakes below….and some of our luckier pilots made it back to base or carriers, while the others hit the eject button and were catapulted through mid-air. Many were killed when their chutes failed to open, and worse, many were captured by the Viet Cong after floating to a life of misery. Death was better, by far. I obtained maps of Agent Orange annotated with the base area locations in 1968, and the darkened areas represent approximate locations where the U.S. Air Force "ranch hands" spray missions were conducted. The spray tracts represent fixed-wing herbicide missions using Agent Orange. The U.S. Army and Joint Services Environmental Support

Group also sent me the group Herbicide Status Report and the Veterans Administration Agent Orange briefs. Talk about creepy....

The saddened faces of children were everywhere, their frightened dark eyes budding out of their sockets and hollow cheeks showing a lack of nutrition in their diets. They suffered greatly, and my heart ached for them. Their skin was the color of white-washed clothes, rather than the tanned browns of their healthier American playmates which were aglow with health due to jungle sunshine sent from God's heavens. Why He didn't shine on all of the children, I'll never know.... many certainly needed to be blessed by his hand on their shoulders and his food in their swollen bellies. Death lurked nearby for them, and they knew it. Though they attempted to show some happiness and participation in street games, their weakened legs and swollen bellies kept them from being normal. Gutters, curbs and doorways housed their weak bodies, and their little eyes often pleaded, "Let me die." Probably, they had already witnessed death many times: soldiers in the streets, brothers and sisters killed before they fled their hamlet in the jungle homes the Viet Cong burned, and their pets killed....So what was left for them in this; their lovely country of green vegetation, an Asian tradition and oriental pride? Life was empty, and their only future was hopes of a hand-out from a passing American or a third-country nationalist. They were known to carry American Hershey bars and chewing gum. The lucky ones may be taken in by one of the many orphanages in the area, such as the Santa Maria orphanage. I had heard of this wonderful place from a Frenchman at VRE headquarters, telling of the hundreds of children who called Santa Maria "home." Others at my office told me how the Frenchman donated most of his salary and ran the place with the help of a few natives, and how he had been trying hard to set up a dispensary for the children….many just babies. They said he was begging for medical supplies, clothing, whatever, and so I decided, "This is my project." I wrote Mother and begged her assistance, and she took the matter to her Ladies Aid Society at the church…a move in the right direction! And that's saying it lightly!

We adopted the Santa Maria and visited it often. My stomach turned over a couple of times when I saw the children searching garbage and gutters for a dirty banana peeling, and disgust filled my gut as I saw them toss it away, all in hopes of an edible bite, but now lost to the winds… I have seen children fall from tall trees behind the orphanage attempting to reach their tiny arms to the last fruit; the one the older kids forgot to pick, hopes of a meal banished when their little bodies fell to earth, crumpled and crying. Hunger and war go together; sickness and sadness, black and blue, hate and abuse….and I thought, "Jesus, why am I here?" The lucky children taken to the Santa Maria Orphanage found a haven from the street war. A small clinic was set up to treat minor wounds and illnesses, cuts and scratches, colds and fevers, and a lot of love was passed around between hundreds of children who shared the walls as one family. I often wondered why God had to let the little children suffer. I was never answered, though I prayed the same question over and over and over. The efforts put forth for the orphanage by the ladies of Mom's church were commendable; they stitched boxer shorts with nimble fingers, some of the ladies so aged they had already dropped out of the Thursday morning quilting club, unable to make the arthritic joints move the way they wanted them to. Yet somehow, these same fingers and joints sewed dozens and dozens and dozens of pairs of shorts for these tiny waifs of the Vietnamese war….their first clothing other than rags for a very long time. These kids got under your skin, tugged at your heartstrings, and begged for affection and love. They had no mama or daddy, and their shanties were destroyed, brothers and sisters scattered throughout the city; they had nothing except what we could offer. Our Frenchman was doing his best to give medical care with his limited knowledge and lack of supplies. The Ebenezer Methodist Church ladies came through for us; they packed their sewed boxer shorts of assorted sizes and loud colors amid the precious medical supplies they had begged, bought and borrowed. They were gracious in their giving in a true Mid-western spirit, and what they gave these tiny children was more than just material. They gave love and life and hope; the greatest of all gifts….

The boxes for the orphanage were APO'd to us at a much faster speed than surface mail. It's true, APO mail during the war moves fast, compared to the U.S. Post Office where it may take a week to move a letter in the States from Missouri to Kansas. The boxes contained everything from leftover Bible School supplies to stethoscopes. Packed in the crevices and tucked in the corners were crayons, stick-on's, picture stories, gum, aspirin, thermometers, Mentholatum, bandages and tapes in an array of widths and thicknesses, salves to soothe burns and ants and mosquito bites, cotton swabs, toothbrushes, soap, candy and suckers, disinfectant, alcohol, first aid cream, small dolls and jacks, paddle balls and baseballs….But the stethoscope was the most prized possession the Frenchman cherished more than anything. The games and goodies were welcomed by waifs with dirty smiles that will remain in my heart forever, and happiness is a kid with a starving swollen belly sucking on an American Tootsie Pop, purple and red suckers drooling out of his mouth as though their last prayer had been answered. It doesn't take much to make a dying kid happy, and God, how my parents and these people of the Ebenezer Methodist Church had tried. They kept the boxes coming day after day. "Airlift Santa Maria." sometimes, it was all I could do to load the 5 or 6 large boxes onto a truck for the trip to the orphanage….We had adopted the Santa Maria and gave gifts of love and life as best we could, thanks to the efforts of lovely farm people in Missouri and Kansas.

I would find out later how church members, led by my mother, would call for donations, spending many hours each day on the phone. How they contacted doctors and local hospitals for used equipment and medical supplies….Oh how they took this project by its ears and mushroomed it into the operation it had become.

We were grateful and delighted to deliver the supplies, seeing the happy faces and absorbing the cheers as we drove into the yard of the orphanage. Dust swirled as the healthier children ran to greet us, tearing at our skirts and pant legs, and tugging at your heart at the same time. Hungry for love, they climbed on us and held to our legs as we walked. These; our happiest moments of the war; looking into the small-dark eyes that awaited us at Santa Maria, "my orphanage." One small child stood back and only observed us….never partaking of the glee and joy during our visits. I had watched her before as she shrunk deep into the corner of the wall, hiding her head before she turned her back on us. She was a pathetic little thing, hair stringy and matted with lice. Sores covered her tiny brown body. Yet she appeared to be halfway healthy….thin, yet normal in size for a Vietnamese child of her apparent age. I asked about her and found out that she was only four. A magic age when little girls should be visiting the zoo with their mommies, having their curly locks trimmed at the neighborhood beauty salons, partaking of a chocolate double-dip ice-cream cone after the Saturday cartoon movies. But not this little girl. No pink ruffled dresses with satin bows streaming down behind, and no hair ribbons in her jet-black hair. Only sadness and fear surrounded her world….and she was staying within it. She wanted no part of these strange Americans who were visiting her new home at the orphanage; she distrusted everyone, and it showed in her eyes.

I found out her name was Maria, and she was half Vietnamese and half French, born of a native girl from a small village out of Saigon and a French mercenary soldier. She had witnessed one of the most horrible atrocities of the war, watching her mother being raped and beaten, and her grandfather disemboweled in front of the family as they were forced to look on. This child was scared forever. I wanted to take her into my arms and hold her forever, to give her new strength and faith in human beings. I went home that night and found I couldn't forget her….so I talked to the Big Indian about her, asking if we could adopt her and give her what she would never find in this; her land of horror and bad memories. We discussed it at great length. The following day, I approached the Frenchman to inquire where and how to start the paperwork. Doug had agreed that it would be wonderful to take this small child and give her a home with brothers and a sister. Cindee was elated at the idea of a new baby sister and anxious to get the process started. Little did we know it would involve thousands of dollars and mountains of paperwork. When the Vietnamese officials see an

American coming….they really "stick it to them," so the saying goes. Many Vietnamese politicians became millionaires during the war; if an American wanted something, he had to pay dearly for it, and the officials took advantage of every Yankee dollar possible. They wanted those "green" dollars, and they got them. Stacks of them…. absurd exorbitant prices for everything from rent, refrigerators, signatures, notary seals to adoption paperwork. You name it: you paid for it….

I was told it would be $4,000 to start the paperwork on Maria, and so I paid for it. Then, I was told to fill out this form and that form and have them notarized. I had to have letters from home attesting to our lifestyle and status, proof of employment and copies of tax papers; I then had to produce a ticket for her flight, although she was not yet "ours," nor did we have a departure date to return to the states. I had to produce medical records by the ton, immunization records for the entire family, more money and more papers. This went on for two months, and then I was finally advised Maria was not for adoption just like that. Quickly and to the point; a simple explanation. A big-fat-short-bastard-of-an-official had stopped the wheels of Maria's future before they really ever started to spin. We were only told that Maria was of some relation to him, perhaps a niece, and he forbids the adoption; how cruel of him to take away any future she may have….The possibility of going to America to grow up in freedom and have a family to care for her and see that she was clean, fed, loved and educated. I hated this man. I found out later he put the skids on the adoption, but planned to offer her through the black-market channels at a later date, keeping all the money for himself, rather than the officials getting the tidy sum they had requested and received from us. Most of our money was given back to us, but they kept a "small retainer fee" of $1,500.00 for all of the paperwork they had produced. Thanks....

Marie continued to live at the orphanage, and I went back to see her several times after that. We would sit for hours and play dolls and sing songs, she in her little singing voice that squeaked like a mouse and me in my English, which was all new to her. Cindee and I loved to take her walking, and we spent a lot of Saturday afternoons with Maria. Her new "father" Doug would take us to Santa Maria and drop us off for 3 or 4 hours, all the while he went to Tan Son Nhut to check on radar towers, phone and cable systems, or some other phase of his operations at the base. Maria took us into her confidence....and she finally smiled as Cindee offered her a banana with one hand, and offered her other hand outstretched in a plea for friendship. Maria accepted and came running, finally. I often wonder if she is even alive, and if not, I wonder if perhaps she isn't better off. May God bless her and all the other tiny children, wherever they are....I cherish my memories and pray she cherishes the doll we left with her, that is, if the communists haven't taken that away from her, too. She named her doll "Cindee," so somewhere there is a

"Cindee" still in Vietnam, and hopefully, that Cindee is being remembered and cherished, just as we remember our little Maria.

Vietnam….Damned War! Military officials often flatter those whom they wish to influence the VRE; the Embassy and construction secretaries loved it and accepted the frills of war, as did the bar girls of Tu Do Street. It was an inebriated good fellowship not totally unknown to both "Charlie," and to MAC-V Headquarters, and to a system that worked two ways on the street of information exchange. Tales were told while dining at the Caruso on Vo di Nguy and at the Koutouki on Phan Thanh Gian, or at the lush Caravelle Hotel, The Royal Saigon or the Embassy Hotel. Secrets emerged as military and civilians whispered among rooftop lounges, though often interrupted by incoming rockets, or plastic charges being set off in nearby shops or theaters. Secrets slipped out as nationalities entwined in the art of lovemaking in villas and back alleys, sleazy huts and French Hotels: blacks and whites, G.I.'s and officers alike screwing dainty, cute Vietnamese whores. The whites preferring the Pago Pago Island beauties, or the Singapore dollies, who, posing as secretaries, had invaded Saigon in polished linens and pure silks with plunging necklines. What a hellish place we found ourselves living in….

But the gals who made the abundant money, mainly due to low overhead, weren't the mamasons too old or too ugly to command a desirable wage on the Street of Flowers. Those ugly gals "flat-backed" their wares by yelling and advertising their bodies from the back of trucks, often in the back of the U.S. Army trucks that had somehow found their way to the black market. The night owl cronies….drunks and hard-ups bought this wrinkled flesh merchandise with a total lack of selection or pride concerning themselves, only with self-gratification, and hopefully, some satisfaction in mind. I wonder how many G.I.'s affiliated with the MAC-V Headquarters, and others having confidential information pertaining to the maneuvers of the war, had allowed top-priority secrets to slip out in those "after-hours-meals-on-wheels" as they were called? Or, how many conniving motor pool sergeants picked up tens of thousands of dollars in green as the provider of the wheels for romance? Jesus….What an ugly war. One G.I. told me the bar closed and tossed him out, but only after a night of heavy drinking and buying the bar girls Saigon Teas in exchange for a boob rub or an ass pat, when he realized he had paid good green for every tea girl there at one time or another in the past year. So, he left alone and broke, having sampled each young lady in the past. There were none left to conquer.

Stumbling through the endless maze of alleys, he encountered the fat mamason in her 40s, making her living as best she knew how in the darkness of the night. You guessed it! She was a conniving, old and worn-out whore descending on the Americanos, who were too tanked up to realize how they dispersed their dollars at this time of night. Many a child and husband had rice and tea the next day because of old Ba's actions and efforts the night before. So, thewar made a good living for the ladies of the night, whether on satin sheets in the French Caravelle, at the Ambassador's lawn party, or in the rusty old bed of a truck. My friend said it was a rather memorable experience. Grossly so, she, being in her late 40's, admits her cockroach and rat-infested, bidet-less bed-on-wheels, and he being virile, young and over capable of functioning at copulation. He mumbled something about wondering if a child had been conceived in the truck. The damned fool was serious….I laughed.

Starvation was everywhere, and the street children saddened me the most. Bones showed, and sores covered their bodies. I thought to myself: "Hell, this is not a war, but a horrendous mistake when children and tens of thousands of brave Americans are being slaughtered for nothing." Many of these boys died angry, frustrated and afraid many times over, but kept going because he was sent there to fight to keep his country free. Yet, I thought this war had nothing to do with Americas' freedom, yet they gave of their lives, making the supreme sacrifice for the things we take so lightly….Our freedom of the press, speech and freedom to worship as we see fit. I was troubled that our world is a divided people, I thought about a third World War and wondered if it would be here in Asia? I wondered if I would get out alive? These thoughts crossed my mind: "What will happen to Steve, Jeff and Cid if anything happens to the Big Indian and me?" War was getting to me. It seemed I could not collect my thoughts and fears, and then try to distinguish between them. The only thing I could be sure of was that Doug was here to help people. He had served his years in the Navy in his younger days, and now, as a communications engineer, he was giving of himself again. I was proud to be a part of this war and working with the Army and Air Force personnel at headquarters. The VRE was giving me a feeling of satisfaction that I felt no one else on Petrus Street in Cholon could equal. I swelled up with pride. I was the only American secretary on Petrus Street in Saigon, and by God, that was a good feeling.

The sleepless nights were long, no, longer….and tempers were short. It became more difficult to rest on the teak-framed bed sodden with only a rattan woven mat, which further aggravated my already aching muscles. Fast-flooding streets and alleys soon made any outside activity almost impossible, all the while Monsoon rains thundered down on shanties and villas alike. As I listened to the sounds of the night, and while trying to define the thunder from the heavy artillery, I wondered what it was like further out into the jungle…. outside of Saigon where the sounds of this real war were also interrupted by the storm. Were "our boys" dry? Hell no. I took pride in the fact that I had answered that one myself, and that I didn't have to call on our Maker in the black of that miserable night. Hell, He was busy anyway. God is always busy in a war, so many tears and prayers on a battlefield. It makes you wonder if He manages to get around to everyone when they talk and cry out to Him. Does He hold their hands as they die? Does He comfort them when their legs are blown away from a land mine? Does He hear their prayers, and does He cradle each and every man and take them on to heaven? About that time, the Big Indian threw an arm across my sweaty body; I threw it back. Charlie had plastic charged our power plant again, and the ceiling fans no longer whirled a breeze above us. I got up…. sleep was not to come for a long time. At the window, I threw open a weathered shutter to see the tracer bullets streaking through the sky. Damned war. Sweat trickled down my brow. I wish I knew how to start the generator; we needed the ceiling fans. I let the Big Indian sleep; he needed his rest. Maybe the power would come back on. My thoughts were across the inner courtyard of the villa and skipping over the red-tiled roof, jumping the river and beyond to communist-infiltrated jungle and on over the China Sea to America. I missed my kinfolk, my "mountain" people, as I remembered them. Maybe not "mountains," but hills at least, and smiling faces who didn't shoot at you each and every day or night. Well, at least most of them.

My family was a close family. My direction was changed. The war was momentarily forgotten as I searched beyond the red tracer lines in the sky. My soul was being transported through the air like an erupted tephra from a volcano, and I was truly carried home. My mind was in the USA, but my body was wet with perspiration as I listened to the choppers at tree top level and gazed at the lines of tracer bullets in the night sky. I was homesick, and the damned tracer bullets scared me….I couldn't sleep. I longed to see fields of green corn, or Noyes Boulevard full of leisure Sunday drivers. I missed the USA. The power is back on, and the night is still sickening with heat. The blades of the ceiling fan glisten in the little light squeezing through the rainforest and from beyond the shutters. The Big Indian woke once to ask if I heard snipers, and I assured him I had not. I was just hot and homesick and couldn't sleep. Really, he could care less. He mumbled something about Geronimo and took up snoring where he had left off. His concern for me was doubtful at times. Another thought flashed through my mind, and I smiled and gave thanks to my living children. "Wait, living children? With real breath?" That's really something to give thanks to in Saigon….But tonight, I was lonely, and I wished the Big Indian would wake up. I somehow began to feel frightened standing at this shuttered opening in the wall and gazing across the open courtyard, wondering just what the darkness holds out there in this war-torn city. This city was ravaged by nightly shelling and bombardments of rocket attacks, and the snipers were roaming the city while being performed nightly as soon as sunset.

Then I heard it. I came back from my Missouri days of long ago and listened closely. Yes, I heard footsteps, yet ever so softly. But damn it, where were they coming from? In my room? In the hall outside our bedroom, or at the base of the marble staircase that would lead to the children and the guestrooms? Was he headed to the second floor? Was he on the rooftop? Was he tiptoeing across the courtyard? My heart came up into my throat, and I shook like a shanty alongside some freight yard as Old Number 10 rolled by….Jesus, I was scared, and I thought I felt him breathe down my neck. I thought, "Missouri is a long way away from this war," and it truly was. I was edging silently toward the bed to alert the Big Indian when I heard "him" or "it" step on something, perhaps dislodging a rock, and that's when I wet my pants. I decided he was in the courtyard, as the wall between our villa and the villa next door would have been the only thing to crumble and send a pebble or rock skidding. Either that, or the rooftop. Oh God, I remembered the windows were open in the kid's rooms. I started yelling, "Doug, Doug, Help….wake up.…Doug….we have a snipe here somewhere."

We ran to the stairs, almost knocking each other down as we fought to reach the kids in their bedrooms. Somewhere in all the commotion, Chi Hia and Lon had managed to pass us; crazy women could run the mile in 10 seconds if necessary. They sprinted above and beyond the call of duty, crying loudly, "Babyson, Babyson, get up." Doug was searching the second- floor rooms….all of them. I was racing Lon to Cindee's room, satisfied I recognized Chi Hia as the one that had entered the boy's bedroom. Lon and I lunged for the shutter at the same time, and somehow, in the scramble, we managed to close it and lock it securely. She grabbed Cid, and we met two mighty sleepy-eyed sons in the hallway, one being cradled in Chi Hia's arms across her shoulder, the other being drug behind her like a sack of potatoes. Everyone scurried down as the Big Indian announced the sniper was on the roof and for all of us to "beat it, go hide downstairs in the bathroom." So we did as he told us, we huddled on the tile floor for what seemed to be hours….unable to reach the safety of the bunker outside. Finally, he gave the word that we could come out now; sniper fire had rung in our ears, and we heard yelling from outside the bathroom window. We were aware now that Mr. Sniper had been chased either by M.P.'s, or the local Consots….and if he wasn't dead by now, he soon would be! They rarely got away in the city. Doug went outside and returned to advise us everything was "O.K." The body was being carried off, and he advised us to go back to sleep. He had expected us to obey him, as though the order was from a top Sergeant. He truly thought the kids would just go back to sleep and obey, but war doesn't work that way; they were still scared. I remember staying up with them, whispering in the dark, comforting them, with all three in the same bed for security reasons. I thought, "Oh well, whatever makes them happy," and after a half an hour of convincing them the house was secured for the night, and daddy was going to stay awake just to be sure….they finally drifted off, probably to Missouri; the only good thoughts you could muster up in this damned war.

And me? Knowing full well the Big Indian was not guarding us anymore but snoring his heart out. I later crawled in beside him and prayed to my own private God, the one I turned to so often. This was my "Child God," the God I knew would look out for my kids whenever I called on him to look over us. He sure got a workout that year; it was almost like if he had been a card-carrying member of the teamsters local, he would have been rich on overtime pay! I needed him close by, and by golly, he was always on duty in my times of need; somehow, he snuggled up to me. We finally made it through another night; my God, my husband and me. Many nights were like this one….scary and full of wondering what and where the next skirmish would be when the sun went down. But monsoon season was the worst. No sun. With the rains drenching the palms and villas and spattering the streets and tiles, it was even more difficult to hear footsteps, rainy nights were feared the most, and people tended to stay in rather than chance any stalking by Charlie….

Chapter 11

Back stateside, the young wives worried about their appearances and if their "replacement lovers" would condone a short evening, instead of the planned "all-nighter" because the sitter had to be home by midnight. Young men worried about fitness and football, college graduation and the draft. They anticipated doing their thing with a slant eye if called to serve. If drafted, some worried about money for survival in Canada; the place where they had fled to avoid the draft in the "no-win war." They must have had premature knowledge that it would always be a "no-win-war," and I find no hate in my heart for the ones who chose to live rather than give up, as America did in South Vietnam. All of these are serious worries that captured the hearts of every American, as this war should never have happened.

Modes of life were changed, and experts from every field were mutilated in battle, or strung from trees and vines, tortured and left to die. Some were disemboweled, some with throats cut, and others carrying the bullets of Charlie but not yet dead. It was nothing for a patrol to come across a half dozen of our G.I.s strung upside down, suspended from a tree limb, in their final moments of life. They died alone, with no mother at their bedside and no priest to give them last rights. Damned war. Too many men died for nothing in this war. Artillery blasted away legs and arms, not unlike the way a small child tears petals from a dandelion as he sings, "He loves me, he loves me not." One by one, they fell….these young petals of boys who had been turned into men overnight, yet never knowing the full bloom of life. These were some courageous men, but their leaders were not totally committed like in past wars; I remember. I recall the risking of lives when war used to be a simple concept, not pleasant, just bloody simple in the 40s and 50s when daring, heroic men fought to the end, and hopefully alive. This Vietnam War never guaranteed America's victory, although the threat of communist take-over was one of high stakes. One nation coveting another makes an arsenal of impractical and irrational tactics, aggressors and victims searching for the guts to believe in a drafted cause; one they perhaps cannot wholly support. Something was lacking in this war; the permission to win.

These kids, these teenage warriors away from their mother's breast, were not allowed by their superiors to pursue the jungle full throttle; they should never have been there. We never fought to win. I remember the stories only too well of the numerous times "We took a hill," only later to hear them say "Let the Congs have it," only to later return and take it again. Each time, we were losing men. I used to want to throw up when I heard a kid telling me how many buddies he had lost "on a second taking of a hill." Hell, why didn't we secure it and keep it the first time? A war unsyncopated, and of bad form that had a lot of people worried over its outcome. Mothers were worried about their sons. Middle-aged men worried about the families back home, and that's if their wives weren't shacking-up with the family lawyer, and if the 15-year-old daughter had lost her virginity. Wives worried even more over this war….They worried about all the alcohol and drugs in Vietnam, the sex offered for sale to their soldier husbands, they worried over the fear of V.D. and of suffering and torture their husbands would be forced to endure if captured and/or injured. College students and hippies were rebelling and protesting because they believed in their cause; their cause being the bare fact that America's intervention and policing of Vietnam was wrong. It would take many years to prove this to the world….and they were right. President Lyndon Johnson said in the early 1960s: "This really is war." I thought at the time, "You bet'cha this is really war, a war of destruction," but yet it's only classified as a damned "Police Action." Why? Its purpose, as far as the North Vietnamese were concerned, was to extend the Asiatic dominion of communism further south. It was a war to later be told in notes and photos by journalists, photographers and cameramen; they brought the war into the living rooms back in the mainland like no other war before. The Vietnam War was known as the "TV war."

The press was headquartered at the Continental Palace and the Caravel Hotels in downtown Saigon…. and some evenings when curfew was pushed back, we would enjoy a chat with some of them over dinner and a few drinks. Some weekends, we had breakfast in the hotel Garden or enjoyed French coffee on the terrace of the aged Hotels. We met Navy Seals on R&R from the delta South Vietnam, where their 6-man crews worked river reconnaissance patrols, or dived for salvage or ambushed driving night raids. We even met some of the SEAL hunks while shooting pool. The pool was an occasional past-time….movie houses were off limits, as the Viet Cong were blowing them up with plastic charges. It was the first war lost. How many Americans are aware over 80 journalists and cameramen were killed in the Vietnam War? By launch grenades or mortar? Or at the hands of the merciless Cong? And there were many great third-country nationalists, many French or Australian or New Zealanders, and many more Americans. They told of this war for future generations, and they were there…they felt this war. And I felt this war. I lived it.

President Lyndon Johnson said, "We will not surrender, and we will not retreat." That was a Lie. M-16s and A-K 47s continued to maim, and the flak jackets became heavier and hotter, but so necessary. President Johnson said, "We will bring the boys home by Christmas of 1965." Another lie told by our politicians, all the while puffing on cigars in D.C.…

But by 1968, there were a half a million troops in the war. The biggest build-up of armed forces was in 1965. Pictures on the front lines told the story firsthand, pictures don't have to be edited and pieced together at a later date from notes….People were being killed by shock waves as they hid in caves, holes and tunnels. B-52s, the big 8-engine bombers used by our forces, carried 30-ton bombs each. They flew in an inverted "V" formation and dumped their target load all at once, killing directly on top of the ground, or indirectly below by the shock. The President had said, "The Viet Cong agents are among the people, and among the armed forces." It was hard to find trust in the yellow skin, never knowing who was who, or who actually worshiped the flag of the commies. The North Vietnamese and South Vietnamese comrades looked alike, causing mistrust and confusion. In 1968, the Allies were winning the war….or so the media convinced the public. Actually, I think the media believed we were conquering, but Tet 1968 proved wrong; we were losing badly. Napalm burnt kids presented the ugly side of war. There were 6000 rounds a minute pouring down on soldiers and peasants alike. The South Vietnamese forces were fighting hell; it was their war. Strafing continued to strip leaves from trees, knocking children down in hamlets and villages like toy soldiers felling old people like trees….death was everywhere. Four by four guns going all day and all night; 16 barrels giving shrapnel like Santa gives gifts to everyone regardless of age, color or nationality.

People could be heard yelling "dee dee mau," meaning "go quickly," or "ga dit," meaning "chicken shit," or a child crying for her elder, moaning as the blood gurgled from her thin lips; "Ba" as her voice was trailing off in death. A lonely death. Gunships kept you company day and night. And mosquitoes and leeches out in the miserable jungle. Damned war.

In 1968, the grounds of the Embassy were stormed by Viet Cong; tanks and troops with rifles pointed at whoever stood in their way. Nixon had come to power, and also vowed he would end the war. Being the TV war it was, a war almost fought in the American living rooms; it has been said the USA saw too much of this war, causing unbearable grief. To fight in a war is one thing, you are there, and you have a purpose. That purpose is two-fold; to win, and to stay alive. But when it was brought into the American living rooms, it was too much blood and grief for the average citizen back home. The slaughter was shown on TV to the parents of our soldiers in their Eastern New England cottages, and to the ranchers on the Western plains, to the Gulf beaches, board meetings and bars, and brothels and reception rooms. Everyone saw it….It was actually more than the average American on the mainland could handle. No other war had been so close to home yet so far away. The American public had lost confidence in both military and political leaders by now; they felt they had been lied to and cheated out of a win. Their boys were not coming home with honor, and it was going to prove to be a lost war that was hard to accept with dignity. Losers have a way of letting their heads hang low….Americans didn't need this. Congressmen began to search for answers. They investigated and asked questions of people in power, people who had made decisions in this so-called "TV" war. Many had quit making all the decisions and had lost all that power.

When the mere mention of the words "draft" and the "Hell no, I won't go" bunch took the streets in protest, I shared their views on Vietnam. The United Nations policy action was more than a "war"; it was a horrendous mistake, as 10's of thousands of Americans were slaughtered for nothing. Our existence as a nation was not threatened; the war was so many miles away that no one really cared whether we won or not, no one really understood what this action in Southeast Asia was all about. Protesters were marching in Washington, D.C., and millions of young Americans were angry over the invasion of their privacy entailed by the mere thought of the Military's draft. Yet, at that precise moment, another young American was wading in mud up to his neck in a steaming jungle….was his freedom lost? What frustration was he fighting for? No doubt he was frustrated and angry, many times afraid and bitter, but he kept going because he was fighting to keep his country free, or so he was told. But he was not allowed to fight to win a war so misunderstood that it would go down in history as a total mistake. Meanwhile, protesters were burning flags and draft cards, hurling insults at the greatest nation on earth, while the boy in the jungle gave his life. The ultimate-supreme sacrifice for the things many of us take too lightly….freedom of speech, of the press, freedom to worship as we see fit. The Soviet Union, being ahead of the U.S. in military power, made the tiny, suppressed nation of South Vietnam very vulnerable, so we answered their cry for arms and assistance.

The Soviets were steadily mass-producing and shipping war materials to the North Vietnamese, while the commonality of the Vietnamese people showed the war scars etched upon the faces of former youthful beauties. Their suffering showed in their own personal battle scars in the form of deep wrinkles with frightened eyes daring to dart about, half scared to look around for fear of seeing death. Dreadful what war does to pretty people? I watched two young boys dismember a dog one day….and then sharing its parts with other neighbor children; I could but presume all were orphans, hungry and destitute. This act took place on a side street in the city near our villa, and rather close to the 14th Army Field Hospital. They were jabbering and fighting over the choice loins, perhaps the easiest to pierce with a stick so as to roast over an open fire; the only way refugee children knew how to cook. All cooking was done over open fires in the refugee camps, and the luckiest ones had a tripod and a hanging bucket-type kettle. Sometimes, it was a gutter fire of twigs and trash, sided by discarded corrugated metal for purposes of a type of a windshield. Gutter fires and metal sufficed as "home" for many children. Inside the tin walls was warmth from rainy nights. Then step outside the tin to relieve yourself. A pathetic, instant home….

Other children, fully armed, slithered through rice paddies, as some soldiers were as young as 12-years old; war was all they knew. The people's faces showed little signs of hope. All had the improbable dream of peace or escape. The streets of Saigon were lined with shacks, dirt streets with ruts and holes; one never knew whether to dodge the masses of bicycles or the ruts in the street, or the rats….Rats were everywhere as you meandered through the city, especially the alley streets where women worked repairing streets, as the men had gone to war. They tended to their children as they worked. The war had disrupted normal education, and schoolyards and buildings had been taken over by refugees seeking protection and shelter in the city following the influx of refugees during the Tet of '68. Children often wandered about aimlessly, avoiding the tanks and supply trucks lumbering down the streets. They passed the time kicking cans or stealing food, a matter of survival in many cases. It was a dismal neighborhood, yet it looked the same as it had for years and years. This was the way they lived, having never known any luxuries. An old woman once told me her biggest dream was to have a refrigerator….her dream was like an American wishing for a yacht, and they lived the same way in Asia, whether in Kuala Lumpur,

Bangkok, Singapore or Jakarta….I saw depression, filth and hunger wherever I went, yet the deep green countryside had once been so beautiful before the defoliation and craters.

But the Orient holds more fascination than one could ever absorb; it's like no other place you've ever seen. The South China Sea is beautiful, and the forest and wildflowers were lovely, yet one had to go just outside of Saigon to see the destruction and devastation of all vegetation from napalm, Agent Orange and the bombing of war. What a lovely country to go up in flames, so much of its beauty had been lost over the years, as fighting was all that many Vietnamese had ever known. A constant war had made Vietnam truly another world. The war went on, but we found occasion to frequent the shops, hotels, markets, cafes and bazaars. Art flourished, and little shops showed authentic works…. attractive pieces were picked up for a small price to be cherished in years to come; cherished as mementos of a world lost to communism. Much of their art reflected the Buddhist religion, and many miniature statues were brought home by G.I.'s and engineers cheap in the markets. We were fortunate to find a small shop close to the P.X. that catered to the money of American secretaries working for Army/Air Force headquarters, PACEX, and they gladly took whatever we offered. I take great pride in the articles I shipped home; I'll always tenderly remember them because they represent so much suffering and pain, memories of a war we never won….I was so proud to have been a part of that war, yet so ashamed to have been a part of a war that America gave up on. When troops finally pulled out in early 1975 and gave leftovers of South Vietnam to the communists, I cried. What had we gone for if we weren't supposed to win? Why had our men died? This war had cost tens of thousands of lives in America, and for what reason? Could it ever be justified in the pages of history?

The country had been proud, as were its people, and yet somehow, life managed to go on day after day as the little shops opened their gates for business. It was amazing to me how fast they closed, though. One trip down a neighboring street showed shopkeepers dusting wares and hawking to each and every passing American to "buy here." But the same street a few weeks later, or perhaps the following day, showed signs of midnight destruction, and what was left of it would be totally boarded-up against thieves. And I always thought to myself, "Well, those little children won't get any rice tomorrow….Daddy's out of business." What a hell of a way to support a family in the middle of a war. Stealing was rampant; children grabbed and ran, yelling as though daring anyone to catch them. They would grab fruit and go hide beneath rubble to munch out, perhaps their only meal of the day. Saigon broke my heart, yet it earned my heart and my respect for the people's gumption to continue living amongst the incoming daily shelling. Americans should have to live just 24 hours the way they lived. They would quit complaining about the new TV they want, or the new car they are about to finance….and they would get down on their knees and thank God for milk in the refrigerator and an apple in the crisper. To think American kids can trot to the drugstore for a chocolate bar on Monday, go to basketball practice on Tuesday, Boy Scouts on Wednesday, go to the shopping center on Thursday for that model kit they had been wanting, and Friday brings a teen dance to abound with fun, laughter and pretty girls. Saturday meant bowling lessons and a trip to McDonald's for that Big Mac and fries, and Sunday meant a movie at a local theater….My God, what a good life. Yet they don't realize it and can't be expected to realize it until they live in Saigon for 24 hours.

Many stories are told of eating rats, but my favorite was the little boy I saw standing outside the gates of Tan Son Nhut hawking dead rats. He made his living killing, catching or trapping the rodents for less unfortunate people who were willing to buy or trade for the only food available. He was a cute kid. His long, dark hair was unkempt, and his body reeked of his wares, but he made money the best way he could. I observed a lady one morning making her daily purchase of three rodents, and as they made their exchange of barter, I got a glimpse of her part of the deal: she slipped him two black market canned Cokes….a rather high price to pay for rats, hardly worth the black-market price, yet the rats would make soup for her hungry children. God, that was an awful way to live in an awful war. It wasn't really a war, but it certainly had all the symptoms: Starvation, living in the streets, refugees into the inner city, bombed-out huts, businesses closing, curfew, guards, tanks, artillery rolling down the center of the main streets, people fighting with water buffalo and elephants jockeying position in the line of traffic, bloody children, wounded civilians, bandaged soldiers, choppers, strafing, tracer bullets in the sky, sniper fire, and black market stands set up on every corner and dangerous back alleys. This certainly was a war, and it virtually closed the city once dusk fell. It was a God-awful war….

We were as vulnerable as the peasants sleeping in the tents of the schoolyard, or the children matted down for the night in a burnt-out automobile in Cholon, or the young mother and her baby huddled in the cardboard box in the street gutter. No one was safe. I remember reading of the Viet Cong who swept across the police compound in Saigon proper and killed the wife and 6 children of the live-in-Colonel. The General "My Lon" was the Godfather to some of those children, and he blew a man's brains out in the center of Saigon to prove his revenge for young deaths. A sick war, and there was torture….stories of the quick-little jabs with a punji stick, whittled to razor sharpness so that the jabbing would be severely painful, and often fatal. These were the "instant" tortures of the hidden ones that lay far beyond in the jungle, where a G.I. might step on a vine tied to a limb or tree, which had been fashioned to quickly form a loop around his foot, causing him to fall off balance and onto the punji sticks stuck in the ground. Many of these were shoots of bamboo up to 1" and 1½" in thickness….and with this razor point on the end. Can you imagine one of these piercing your neck? Or your groin? So, they lay there and bleed to death, slowly.

The guys that visited our villa often told of finding one of their buddies strung up by their feet, hanging from a tree, and often disemboweled. Sometimes, 2 or 3 Americans would be found hanging from a tree with a rope around their necks, but minus their hands. It leads you to believe their hands were cut off before they were hung, otherwise, why would Charlie have bothered to torture them? Certainly, not after they had been hung from the limb? And there were cases of rifle butts being inserted into the anal opening of a young G.I., just anything to cause pain. Our boys suffered, but for what? A victory? No….It's a celebration, complete with a ticker tape parade. And what really hurt was to hear of the guys found in the jungles bleeding, but still holding on to life within them, yet covered with leeches and snake-bitten, all the while they awaited a medic. Often times, the injured could not be reached for hours, especially if it was in the middle of taking a hill; the battle had to go on until there was a winner, so these kids, your sons and brothers, fathers and husbands, often bled and suffered for hours before the medic could reach them. Many were given no medical assistance…. but they were captured and imprisoned instead. Sometimes, the prisoners were made to sit caged for hours, days and weeks in a small animal cage, hardly big enough for a dog.

They were only fed bread and water, and sometimes one ration of rice daily that was either soured, or bug-infested. They told of leeches and flies, and mosquitoes biting them as they caged and baked in the jungle sun, having no protection from the environment at all. These cages sat out in prison or camp yards in the sweltering sun day and night. No relief from the elements, or its creatures. I say, "its creatures," because the mosquitoes did belong to the element rain, and they grew to enormous sizes when the monsoons started. They bred where they could find swamps and rice paddies….and that was 95% of South Vietnam. So, in other words, there were mosquitoes everywhere. They carried many diseases and sent thousands of young men home with malaria, plague, yellow fever and Asiatic cholera. The men forced to curl in these cages had no exercise, and often, no water to drink. They were not allowed the courtesy of bathroom privileges, and they lay in their own filth and excretion. They would gag and vomit from the stench they had been imprisoned with. Many of them prayed they could die….They would have definitely been better off.

Although, some were imprisoned in tiny dark rooms without sunlight or facilities; just 4 walls, a dirt floor and a door. The door was solid, so there was no communication or light. The only living things were the roaches crawling across their faces as they slept. The only meals were, again, soured rice and water, or they caught a roach. Meals depended on the mood of the guards….certainly, not conditions as set forth by the Geneva Convention regarding the treatment of P.O.W.s. Many were kicked in the groin and had their eyes gouged, and we often heard the story of dripping water on a man's forehead, which supposedly would drive him totally out of his mind. Also, water poured up their nostrils as they were forced to lie and choke to death. Or, of punishment in the form of snakes being put in cells with them; if they didn't bite and their venom wouldn't kill you, you were certain to die of fright. These were our enemies, the North Viet Cong. Vicious communists, soiling their hands for future generations, yet proud of their wicked atrocities. They tortured civilians, and many times, they took servants, maids, houseboys or politicians and gave them the same treatment.

Chapter 12

One night, many Vietnamese arrived at our gate, fully armed and with stern faces. They jabbered with Chi Hia when she went to answer the bell, and then she came running as she yelled, "Mr. Doug, Mr. Doug, they try to get me." The children and I watched from behind the iron bars of the living room window, knowing fully well he preferred we stay out of view; an American wife and children should not be advertised after dark. They tried their best to take her from us. They were trying hard to convince the Big Indian that her papers were not in order….for if they had arrested her, we would surely never have seen her alive again. She was on her knees, crying, begging, and pleading for her life. She came in and gathered her papers and clutched them to her breast….running back to somehow convince the South Vietnamese soldiers, or the North's Viet Cong soldiers, as we'll never know which ones they actually were, that she had everything in order. "In order" in Saigon meant much money; you pay this Chieftain, that Hamlet official, then this policeman and that politician, you never get through paying a sort of blackmail. I don't know exactly what pressure Mr. Doug used to convince them that they should leave her alone….but after much wailing and cursing, I saw them coming across the lawn towards the villa, her head on his shoulder and his arm around her for protection. Probably, he threatened to castrate the bastards, I don't know for sure.

But I do know he could be one tough man, and he would give our maids the same love and protection from this damned war that he would give his own children. He had actually saved her life, maybe paid cash for it? We heard many stories of other American maids being "carried off" in the middle of the night, even though their employers swore their papers were in proper order, and had been checked, rechecked and then checked again. Whenever the authorities, whoever they were, pulled a "villa raid," and all the locals were petrified, they knew if they were yanked out of their villa security in the middle of the night, they would never be seen again. To this day, I thank God for his persistence, loudness, and forcefulness with the intruders. I thought, "What if it had been one of those nights he stayed on the base? Oh god, we would have lost her." And too, they would probably have managed to get inside the gates and perhaps murdered us….we'll never know. I often stared out into the night beyond the courtyard, praying, sending my thanks to God for saving us that night. Tears creased my cheeks as I shivered nervously in the heat of the night. Chills racked my body: war nerves.

Raising children in the environment of war proved to be successful, as far as health was concerned. They were never healthier or happier. Vietnam presented a tragic gap between the ideal and the real. Share or take? Gunfire or music? Mud or flowers? Heal or kill? A good deal of confusion goes on in your mind in a city of conflict. Confusion that stirs thoughts and disrupts normal sleep. If you let yourself go off the deep end, you were a goner. Thoughts would range from amazement to condemnation, to skepticism to fear…. Total confusion. But so was our being there. Today, war is a rather pleasant recollection of the past, an important part of my life where most of us have opinions on the war and feel compelled, as self-respecting citizens, to openly discuss the intervention in Southeast Asia. In discussing issues of importance, we find we may know very little about one another, so another's purpose and point of view are always welcomed. The Indians were God-like beings and possessed their universal and complete knowledge, whereas without taking thought, I flashed opinions as to the most righteous reasoning to justify Americans' presence in Vietnam, or of the most dangerous plans its future held. We spent many hours absorbed in our own abilities, forming and expressing our personal and private convictions without really a moment's forethought….we were the live-in's of this war. I was oppressed by the war, yet excited. We did a lot of serious talking during the rocket attacks in '68, not a hell of a lot more to do other than to talk, and to pray, and I'm not sure which one comes first. I know what it means to be scared though, and to fear for the lives of my children.

One weekend, we entertained the crew of an off-shore patrol boat, swabbies of the greatest breed, as they're called. They had a tough and lonely job, skirting the beaches off the southern shores of South Vietnam and keeping their eyes peeled across the blue of the horizon for the enemy. These were America's youth, searching for Charlie in a remote, damp and endless position in the China Sea. They had earned a few days R&R and chose Saigon. They relayed stories of skullduggery; their devious behavior when it came to tracking Charlie across open waters of their ships equipped with a private strike force….and of radio equipment that had a significant range for reporting their sightings back to the mainland. We knew they had their land legs when we went to a local hotel for dinner, and a night of dancing in town. Curfew was lifted till 1:00 a.m., so there was no hesitation on their part when it came to chasing the bar girls who were trained in flirting, as they soon picked up the floozies and perched them at our table. But I watched and enjoyed their antics. The pinching, the buying of Saigon Teas and the closeness of the mini-skirted bodies pressed close to the swabbies on the dimly lit 14' X 14' dance floor. The girls were definitely planning an attack; that was their strategy. After a long evening of no one understanding what the other was saying….yet laughter prevailed as the guys bid us goodnight and asked that we leave our maid alerted to their late homecoming. We assured them either the Big Indian or Chi Hia would listen for the bell, providing early morning access to our villa and to their guest rooms. They were super kids, out for a good time that ended in the Penicillin line at the field hospital later. It was not too high of a price to pay for an evening, I guess, and they certainly weren't alone in the line for shots. I was told on a later visit they had been joined about 30 deep in line by a local base chaplain….I guess love comes in all flavors, and attacks all who hang in its way, specifically during the war and especially in Saigon!

Chaplains were not exempt from love in this war. One was a guest at our home many times, a red-headed Irishman who was a teller of tales, and the good humorist of the base chaplains. He always drank more than his share of the Saigon Stingers with us, and never tried to heal or minister when with a social group. He was "one of the guys," and I know how deeply the guys felt for him. He was a father, a Chaplain with a capital 'C' and a buddy…. He administered last rights when necessary, and he was a peach, to say the least, but not unblemished of bruises and dust. He was often brought to play the buddy role, and they embraced, danced, and had as good a time as any grunt on R&R. He was a real person and loved by all. He wound up many nights with tall war stories, taller than I could accept sometimes, yet I knew he spoke the truth, as others volunteered to vouch that they had been in the field with him saying, "Yeah, I remember that night." He was one of God's best representatives of love, compassion and fellowship in the war. I know because I, too, gained inner warmth and faith from being his friend, and the men in his outfit spoke so fondly of him. I was told he was always there when he was needed….and in my opinion; it was men like this who made this war bearable. His name was fitting of his person, "Corey," short for Corrigan, and the boys soon found out they could even beat him at chess, and once, they had him down $20! He returned often to get even, but even with God's hand on his shoulder, and his private angels looking over his shoulder, he lost, a lousy opponent, but a good sport. The boys looked forward to his visits and jumped at the chance to corner him for a game. They pegged him as their "Number one Sucker!" and I doubt if Corey will forget either. The boys claimed their total losses for the year were around $40 each; it's not a bad take for pre-puberty kids in the world of glitter and gambling.

Chi Hia and other domestics had privacy in their quarters off the inner courtyard, as we let them live their lives the Asian way, so long as they met our demands and needs in return for their monthly monies. They worshiped when they felt like going to church…. and if a curfew was in force, they were welcome at any time of the day or night to go to their rooms and burn candles; we had a good arrangement with them, and they loved living where they felt safe, knowing the Big Indian had a position of considerable power, and 800 men at his fingertips for sentry duty if the scale of the action called for guards at the house. They knew we would always have food and drink and that they would be getting "hand-me-downs" to wear, and prized Western clothing that would bring a fine price on the streets, even if it didn't fit them. The potential for benefits was unequaled to anywhere in Saigon, and they appreciated what they had, just as we appreciated their loyalty. It seemed like a tight-knit family, yet none of us were related to another. But one day, their privacy was invaded, and it took Chi Hia many days to face me again. I was led to believe the kids were napping in the mid-afternoon….and upon hearing sniper fire in the near neighborhood, I had gone to close the shutters of their bedrooms.

Lo and behold, Steve and Jeff were not in bed and I immediately became alarmed. I ran downstairs and straight out our bedroom door, across the inner courtyard to Chi Hia's quarters, where I caught her in bed with her husband/boyfriend/banker/lover, really showing him what love was all about! "Oh my God," I heard myself say as I looked to the floor in shame and embarrassment. "I'm sorry, Chi Hia, but have you seen the boys? All she could say was "ga dit, ga dit," and what sounded like "dee dee mau" when I forgot the boys were missing and she fell from her perch astride her man. We both laughed till we were sick; she with the sheet drawn close to her body and totally exposing her lover….and him cursing at the top of his lungs as he flung his hands into position to cover his private parts. He was knowing shamefully well that the Asians are a smaller people in stature and build than their guest Americans, and he was hiding what little he had. Oh God, it was funny, Chi Hia and I were both laughing at him trying to cover up, when he finally ran out of the room in shame. He hid in the laundry room for what seemed like hours. And the boys? They had been on the balcony with an infrared lens that a Sergeant from the motor pool at VRE Headquarters had given them…. They could have been killed or kidnapped from the balcony because, within 5 minutes of locating them, I heard a shot close by and lots of talking and jabbering. I then saw three consorts from the camp across the street dragging a body into their compound and closing the gate behind them. They don't know how close they were to death. It was a certainty that if Charlie Cong had spotted them on the front balcony, they wouldn't be around to get the lecture I was giving them now!

I think it was when the balcony was "off limits" that they really discovered the fun you could have with a bidet, and they soon spent more time in the bathroom than was necessary. Chi Hia or Lon had to mop up the messes they made, and often brought the little monsters down the curving staircase with a twist of their ear. After all, you just don't hold your thumb on the flow of bidet water to spray your buddy across the room. "Pow… I got you!" and "Bang, you're dead!" Shit, what dumb war games they played, yet they managed to entertain themselves quite nicely for Americans in a war zone, practically chained to the house. Sometimes, I conceded that chains may actually be the answer to their corruption, but I never resorted to such restraints. Cid was a different story because she had Kim, and they spent many hours teaching each other their respective languages and soon were able to discuss 'boys," so they could finally understand each other. They wasted many hours giggling and gendering at the soldiers on the streets and in the yard of the compound across the street. Typical young teens….they thought boys, they dreamed boys, and now they were talking boys, in two languages! She had finally met a friend.

An evening at the Officers Club soon made you forget the war. Most everyone was spit and polished and socially proper, yet there were the occasional tears as Dear John letters from home came out in the open, or the loss of a buddy or friend was often the topic of conversation. But there were the good times too, like the night the guys dressed in women's clothing and put on the "Saigon Follies." A cute young Lieutenant had the lead and was getting raves from the audience when one of his boobs slipped, and he looked like a severe case of acne….you know, one here and one there! He had his "confidence" up prior to the falling of Mt. Rushmore, but with the avalanche of phony flesh, his act fell apart and he left the stage! Then there was "Foxy Red," a masculine 200-pound woman of lead and guts covered with hair. I never knew some women had such hairy backs till Foxy Red came on in her bikini, strutting in such a way that her calves literally bulged with muscle. And biceps? She had them!!! She looked like a linebacker from the Steelers!!! She did the skit with a Sailor….a beach scene, and she stole the show when she floored him in a very unfeminine manner. They were crazy, but for a couple of hours, we laughed and forgot about the war, all the while the Huey's and F-102's were taking off and landing at the base just a mere quarter mile across the long stretch of concrete. These chicks brought a lot of laughter to the boys that night. Dinner was good; it was like dining at one of the finer restaurants back home, a place where you could don a pretty cocktail dress and pretend you were not in Saigon, or you were welcome in the uniform of the day….a cozy lounge and fun bartenders to help you forget that Charlie was out there somewhere lurking behind the scenes.

The USO shows were great; Martha Raye is the greatest of all entertainers next to The Master, Mr. Bob Hope. Martha was warm and real, and she gained more respect in her lifetime than probably any other woman. She sure as hell did her part in the war, a fantastic woman of great talents. I saw her about cry when the crippled and maimed were wheeled up front for her show….even the finest of entertainers can't always hide emotions. She saw it at the opening, but she gained composure and went down and kissed each of them.

She was a touching, tender Lady, a lady with a capital "L." The entertainment branch of the armed forces is of the finest, the musicians are of the most talented, and the shows are of the most appreciated by the guys and gals who so desperately needed to laugh. This was Martha's job, and she did it well. There would have been no U.S.O. shows without Hope and Martha…. We visited with Martha and invited her to the villa for dinner, but being the real trooper she is, she explained dinner on base with "the guys" could make hundreds happy, so she graciously declined. The following day, a military messenger delivered a large brown envelope containing a glossy 8 x 10 of Martha. She had written on it:

"To my friend Juni, Thanks for the dinner invitation, maybe we'll do it next time. Love, Martha Raye."

Grunts and G.I.'s had total indoctrination, being taught to kill from day one. So, in this war, thousands of civilians and peasants were killed. This is a war? The only answer can be "Yes." Our sons and husbands, and brothers and uncles had this drilled within them, so what went wrong? There was a lack of compassion for Asians involved in this war, and it was constantly difficult to tell the enemy Charlie from the South Vietnamese alongside you. We took a hill, we lost a hill so we would have something to do the next day, or next week. Shit, WWII wasn't fought like this, this war had a pattern: take, lose, then retake again; just keep the men busy. This damned war was never fought to be won; someone in Washington had to know this before the actual surrender. It was politics; dirty politics! Some had to die to appease those who would not let them win. Damn, it makes me sick to think about it and all of the friends I lost here. I recall a Cambodian summed it up properly when he spoke of an inevitable tense situation, saying, "Death is a lady…."

Chapter 13

The rains had slackened, and it appeared it could be a nice day, a cheerful thought for everyone after days and days of musty, humid monsoon weather. Even the sounds of war seemed more distant today, and the sun peeked from behind the clouds. Boots suggested we hail a cyclo or taxi and go to Fuji where the cuisine was reportedly the greatest in Saigon. She assured me I would like it, so I accepted her gracious invitation, though fear gripped me when I thought of using chopsticks. Chopsticks and I went together like fine China and a defensive quarterback, and I chuckled as I recalled an event that happened at our dinner table a few short evenings ago. I was showing off for the kids proving my recent adeptness with the sticks of wood, and I thought I had done rather well….only to find out when I excused myself from the table that I had dropped the rice on the floor, and I slipped on it and fell flat on my face. The rice had accumulated under my chair like gooks assembling for an attack; it was everywhere! It was embarrassing, to say the least! At least I was ridiculed with laughter and teasing, and cheers of "Ha, mom is just learning!" set to sing-song tunes. Needless to say, it was "back to the fork" for me.

But I mustered the courage to eat native food, and we proceeded to the Fuji, accompanied by two friends from headquarters. These guys would not hear of Boots and me taking a taxi to Fuji alone. They said they would go along with us, and we were grateful for their consideration and company for the simple fact they shouldered machine guns. The Fuji was almost hidden behind palm trees and down a side street, a beautiful place with exotic foods. The Orientals have a knack for making things look so appetizing, and they put love and expertise into every dish they serve. The meal was excellent, especially the asparagus soup as an entrée. I was both appreciative and relieved when the waiter brought an odd-shaped spoon with my soup, a spoon with a deep ladle and a sharp crook in the handle, unlike American spoons. It closely resembled a "dipper," as we used back in Kansas on my sister's farm when we dished up the ham and butter beans. I found it to be a handy gadget, and I was hoping they would leave it for my vegetables and rice. But alas, the main course was indeed presented with the customary chopsticks. How I managed, I'll never know. Boots had a good laugh with me, and commented that it took me noticeably more time to consume my meal than it did the others….

We talked about her two lovely children, and she showed me photos of her son and daughter. We talked of her loving husband in the Philippine Islands, and for a moment, I forgot we were in the midst of a war. The warm conversation and the friendship we shared were beautiful for both of us. It was evidence of an inner beauty being felt, even during the aggression in the Far East; one just had to make happiness and look for it and grasp it when one could. We were living from day to day and taking each minute for what it held….as death was all around us, but we were bound and determined to find our own happiness as best we could. The guys had been good company and brought us more up-to-date on the war, telling things they shouldn't have been telling, yet of little importance to us and our families there in Saigon. We always managed to be informed better than the other girls at VRE, mainly because we had children to consider; their safety was on our minds constantly. On a few occasions, Cam Tu and Boots could talk me into lunching with a neighborhood sidewalk vendor, which is always a new experience. These people presented convenience. "Fast food" Asian style, and they were found on every corner selling their wares and carving out a meager living for their families.

Sometimes, the vendor would be a young boy, weighted with the hardware of a complete kitchen, suspended on his weak shoulders. We presumed his mother had sent him to the streets in order to earn enough to feed the elderly, and the younger members of his family. Sometimes, a bearded old man sold his noodles to fellow customers. Cam Tu told me that he was supporting his grandchildren; children who were products of war and prostitution, and who had been denied a father. The vendor's kitchens were complete with a stove, pots for noodles, soup kettles and a rice pot slung from a long pole across their shoulders. A walking kitchen. The aroma was a great advertisement for their foods, but I had a premonition of food poisoning and turned down such lunch invitations as often as I dared. The vendor one day was rather interesting…. although of minute stature, he screamed advertisement of his foods with explosive lungs. Rags covered his body, yet an attractive and well-groomed goatee gave him a certain air of dignity, commanding respect as a businessman amid his kitchen clutter. Dining with him was an experience to write home about, but it was neither a favorite, nor a frequent lunch spot. Our favorite was at our headquarters company lunchroom, where the native Vietnamese could prepare a mean skillet of fried rice, or an American hamburger, both equally tasty. The fried rice….sprinkled generously with boc choy, onions, bean sprouts, pork, chicken, black dried mushrooms and water chestnuts, was my favorite. Flooded with nuoc mom, it equaled a medium-rare 16-ounce T-bone at the "Hoof and Horn Restaurant;" the Midwest's corn-fed happiness at its best!

Lunchtime was always a welcome fun time; it was a chance to meet and visit with other VRE employees and assigned military from many different countries. Captain Workman, dubbed "Little Boy Blue" to fit his look of innocence, dined with us often, as did Sgt. Gray of the motor pool. I had every reason in the world to "play" like the other secretaries, but I was in a group of my own, probably the only Civil Service Headquarters secretary with my GSU rating, a husband in Saigon, and no lover! Visiting Reps and purveyors tried to break down my fence and enter, but I stuck with my "No's," firm and hard, at least for the time being, fully aware my eyes were only for my Big Indian….The days were long for the kids; they played, studied, and read what they could find, yet they found it difficult to accept the fact they could not go out of the yard. They spent many days just peering through the massive gates at the villa entrance, watching the local children and friends playing their games of kick the can or baseball, without a baseball. They used a rusty beer can, and a stick, and it worked fine! Make do; they did, with whatever they could find. Vietnamese children would wander up to the gate to see the fair-headed kids….if they had not been there before. Blondes were a rarity in Saigon, and only because a good part of the population were Buddhists, and a fair-haired person tends to bring good luck if you can get close enough to touch them. Many times, I saw laughter between the childish figures, unable to communicate except for smiles and international signs of friendship. Occasionally, Chi Hia or Lon would take the kids outside the wall and let them run and play in the street. Soon….they became acquainted with neighborhood children and would yell their names from the balcony in the later days. They finally had friends by the dozens, and names were more easily pronounced on both sides of the fence. These friends were less fortunate than most of the world's children; skinny scavengers of the warfighting just to survive. Our kids shared their goodies and cold drinks and toys with these street people, and as smiles crossed their faces, a small bit of happiness emerged from this awful war.

Next door, the 15-year-old houseboy "Bup" gave a lot of himself to make their long days a bit happier, as Steve and Jeff would go to the balcony to observe him over the 12-foot concrete wall between the doctor's house and ours, and if they could spot Bup somewhere amongst the lush vegetation, it was then a verbal exchange of laughter and gibberish only "buddies" can understand. Two languages, all mixed up like cake batter, but soon smoothed out to a final understanding. They were good friends and spent many an hour together….yet always this tall wall separated them. One day, Bup found a big lizard, a foot-long sized one: beautiful in its natural colors of blending greens and blues. He playfully tossed it over the wall to the boys and motioned for them to toss it back, and with a yell from Steve sounding "Play ball," they tossed it back to Bup. This game of "Ha, ha, who's got the lizard now?" went on and on until the reptile was showing definite signs of bloody wear and tear. Its guts were hanging out, but the kids kept playing on with a "who cares" attitude. It was something to do, laughter entailed; who could be happier?

Then, the curdling screams of Chi Hia pierced the air, and I ran to observe her in her finest role: that of a Maid mother. She was shaking hard, and she grabbed the two boys and ushered them into the courtyard, her voice that of great distress and concern. She kept yelling "Number 10, number 10," which indicated something was awfully bad; no, the worst! She was telling us through broken English and sign language that the lizard was very poisonous, and she took us back to the mangled lizard lying in the driveway and pretended to eat it. Then she gripped at her stomach and curled up and keeled over as though in unbearable pain. She made signs of pain, moaning, and then, as quickly as it started….it ended. She lay prone in the driveway and was dead. Well, she's not really dead, but she sure got her point across to the kids and me. She had saved their lives and taught them they should never again play with poisoned animals. I think it was this incident that made me realize she was indeed a wonderful mother for them, doing a hell of a lot more for their safety than I, and simply by being a Vietnamese and mothering them in her country. Her love was concrete and forever, although just a few short months ago, we had been strangers. She could be explosive, yet easy; a ruler of sorts when I was gone to the office. They loved her dearly, this humble tiny woman with wisdom creviced within each wrinkle on her muddy brown face….a face of an old woman, not even age 40 yet.

Our Missouri home had always been a haven for stray kittens that some other mother had refused. Any stray, injured, or just plain "cute" animals in the old Midwestern neighborhood, so it seemed reasonable that I should say yes to Cindee's request for a pet here in Saigon. I discussed it with the Big Indian, and he forked over bahts and dong to Lon when she offered to cycle Cindee to the local pet shop on a rather quiet day. I had fully expected a tiny kitten or a puppy, maybe some exotic bird or a funny monkey, but found total dissatisfaction with their final purchases. One white rabbit named Peter Rabbit: (what else?) Six white mice....or were they rats? And a duck she named Clarence! The mice were the first to go. I told Cindee there was no way all of us could live in the same house, and she was told to discuss their "disposal" with Chi Hia and do whatever this wise old lady thought best. The next thing I knew, she announced she had turned them loose in the yard and explained, "This way, I can still see them once in a while." Well....you guessed it: I didn't want to see them occasionally, so never was much too soon for me. I hated the thought of them hiding behind a blade of grass when I took a sunbath or walked through the yard barefooted, or even worse, perhaps crawling to the balcony where I wrote my letters. Damn her anyway, now I had more to worry about than just losing sleep over Charlie, and wondering if he was climbing to our rooftop at night. Too, I worried about the sniper bullets he may whiz past our bedroom windows….SHIT, I longed for home; the peace and serenity that awaited me in Missouri, without war and mice.

Her menagerie of pets allowed her and the boys a new way to pass the time. They followed the duck, and he followed them, quacking like a "Clarence" all the way. They soon became very good at imitating Clarence: so good that I ran a kid out of the house one Sunday afternoon, thinking that dumb animal was playing in the bathroom. One Saturday, I found Steve and Jeff giving Clarence a bath, and the tub was a deep tile tub, and Clarence thought it was a farm pond; he loved every minute of it. Chi Hia had snitched on them. She came running down the staircase yelling and screaming, "Babysons number 10, number 10," and I recognized that old familiar phrase. It meant trouble. She took me by the hand, and upstairs we went where I really thought someone was in bad trouble, and I expected the worst….but I had to laugh when I saw that silly Clarence having a field day in the bathtub, and he was actually getting the royal spa treatment! He was a frequent visitor to the interior of the house, and an occasional visitor to the kitchen; I thought about making feather-down bed pillows, but I decided to pamper their whims, and I even learned to understand them. Having kids in a war zone was difficult, to say the least, so let them have some happiness. Just keep the damned duck off the dining room table, please. Damned duck! Have you ever seen duck tracks….after they had been through the nuc-mom sauce? Clarence felt he owned the table and fluttered up whenever we had just filled our dinner plates, a feathered nuisance; but a lovable friend….He got to stay.

Chapter 14

Happiness is a warm puppy, or an Australian officer with mysteriously penetrating green eyes, which makes you wonder if he really belongs on this planet, and in this war. He belonged on Wall Street in a Botany 500, yet here he was in my villa, ever so dapper, blouson uniform and spit and polished boots topped by a cocky beret, a most welcome guest. But something about him troubled me, and I could tell he was receiving my vibes right between his ribs, caging his heart so it wouldn't burst out of its ivory cage. God, we had to have each other from the first moment we saw each other. I thought, "Heaven, help me to be good. God. I know two wrongs don't make a right." I said to myself, "The Big Indian has done enough on the wrong side of the fence for both of us, so please don't let me be weak. I can't succumb to this….to my new Greek God in human form, not here among the marble and tile in my lacquered temple of a home. Not here among my people, my family, my fellow employees and my house servants. This can't be the place to throw us together in desires of fire, God. There must be another solution." God and I continued our discussion: "Curfew? Not allowed out on the streets? A husband in the other room swearing his love for me when I know he's lying….

Hell, he moved a Vietnamese broad and her kid out to make room for the three children and me when we arrived from the States, didn't he? Would I have him here under our tiled roof? Did I dare?" I knew I would. My mind was reeling at the thought of Hank holding my body close to his, and I felt the weakness in my knees as I passed by him in the crowd of party goers…. with my cocktails in hand.

Loners, lovers and lookers, yet all devoted and promised to someone back on the mainland, but lonely in this damnation called war; "Live today," was their motto, "for tomorrow may never come. You won't get to come this way again." I said, "God, don't let me become one of them, sucked into love and passion by this damned war and forgotten tomorrow." I quietly said, "Go away, Hank, leave….No, don't go, I want you." My thoughts confused me. I was fascinated, overwhelmed and anxious for this handsome blond Aussie to conquer me. Satisfaction at this point was inevitable; there was no turning back. Then I laughed, I remembered that I had experienced this same feeling before when I lost my virginity, the feeling of total lust and the "who gives a damn" attitude. But now, here in a strange land, I am shivering again from anticipation and want for this Aussie. The pains stabbing at my groin are severe pains of lust. A shudder passed through his body, and he raised his arm from my waist and with his finger, he drew a path from one shoulder to another and whispered in his lovely down-under accent, "I'm going to have you, birdie." I thought, "Can this voyage be possible?" I smiled reassuringly, letting him know it would work out….somehow, somewhere. I made his drink as I glanced around the room to see about my Big Indian, unafraid of being observed as I was; a charming hostess, obligingly catering to my guests. Hank's remark had left me numb and aching, yet I managed to mingle and make it through a formal dinner, feeling very secure from distant skirmishes and war noises. Gaiety prevailed, the music and dancing continued as the champagne flowed, replacing pre-dinner cocktails and dinner wines. Guests relaxed, and laughter rang out from small groups as the latest Charlie and Cong stories made their usual rounds….

Pushing towards my own perfection as a Ms. Perle Meste, the "Hostess-with-the-mostess," I chatted openly and freely with the visiting Adj. General, Sergeants and the Privates of the motor pool, and the officers from MAC-V Headquarters. I visited with the 3rd country nationalists from the air base, but the Aussie officers were my favorites. They were the favorites of everyone; charming the ladies and being daring and down-to-earth little-boy ornery, and always the life of the party. Soldiers of fortune or men of the night, they were accepted and loved by all. A crap game had started….noises of "Little Joe from Kokomo" and "Hello Seven" drifted out from the inner courtyard, and then a blasting "Fighter from Decatur" pierced the air at the same precise moment the bell rung alerting us of late guests arriving at the Iron Gate. Thinking all invited guests had indeed arrived in time for the dinner party, we never suspected news of the party had spread. The Big Indian and an elderly maid crossed the marble entryway and down the drive to greet the late arrivals, only to find a group of local consots, the South Vietnamese military police, and with drawn guns. They were requesting a search of the premises and indicated they were interested in the high walls and roof area at the rear of the inner courtyard….It seems Charlie was in our neighborhood, and his presence put a damper on the whole party. They searched all the rooms, the closets, and every square foot of roof and courtyard to no avail. Shots in the distance led us to believe he, the Viet Cong, i.e. Charlie, had made it down Vo Tanh Street towards the thatched guard hut tower at the end of our block. The consots had a cold drink, thanked us and went on their way, shouldering their rifles and smiling as though they actually knew they had sobered us up and put an end to the evening's festivities. It had been such a good party, but with such an abrupt ending. Fear alone had sobered up most of the guests, and the crap game followed the way of any fad; it just disappeared….and left you wondering how it started and ended so fast. Damn war. Damn Charlie.

Losers and winners alike, they hit the black coffee before staggered departures down the drive and onto the streets. It was well past curfew, and many of the guests had not planned to spend the night and chanced to get beyond the guards at the end of the block. Some made it, but most were told to return to "wherever you just came from in this secured block."

They were told to take cover indoors. Neighborhood action beyond curfew time made for a "no travel tonight, sorry" type of situation. With the tired guests bedded down, the villa gaiety soon again bounded from wall to wall for the die-hards, but one by one, they, too, passed out or retired in guest rooms for the night. It was premeditated with all the detailed care of a murder, the intent being for this Aussie and his new bird to have the greatest gift that any one-being can give another….the gift of oneself. I recall it was a master plan conceived by drunks. Step #1 is the same as step #Final: to out-drink the Big Indian; be the survivor of sorts; and be alone with my Aussie Hank. But where? How? Did I dare? Guests overflowed from the bedrooms both upstairs and down. Guards secured both ends of the block, so there was no other location where we could safely make love. And it had been many years since either of us had back-seated it in a car, or wallowed in the grass! The suspense was building, and man-made feelings were enlarging faster….nothing was superficial about the desires now burning our bodies. We uncorked another bottle, always aiming at an imaginary Charlie stealing across the shadows of the ceiling. With each new cork shot upwards, an empty was tossed aside with cheers and laughter of "Who gives a shit about any tomorrow?" We decided we would all be dead tomorrow, so we would live for tomorrow, but live it out tonight. "Another Charlie...Get 'em!" and another fresh bottle of the bubbly was popped open, when all of a sudden, a "POW" pulled the shadowy Cong bastard down.

Should have cut an ear off for proof of each kill, as G.I.'s on bivouacs do….but with no rewards for our kill. Keeping their ears lost importance, and our scheme for sex predominated the night.

Everyone passed out except Benny Barf and the Big Indian. Benny was so far gone, his last drink slowly tipping and spilling across the tiles. His nightly heavy drinking was either a habit for survival, or a survivor of habits. Either way, who gave a damn? Now, the only important feat to accomplish was to drag him upstairs to a bedroom and roll him in beside someone. Anyone. I secretly hoped we dumped him in with Nom, the vexingly sweet half-South Vietnamese and half-suspected secret agent bitch friend of Danny Fraley, the older brother of our beloved Benny Barf. Didn't know which bedroom she was in, but I sure hoped we could manage was a good American piece for Benny Barf…. she had always eyeballed him anyway, so I thought we may as well oblige her with who wanted the other. We just dumped him in the nearest room and never did know who the nut caressed all night; that remains one of the untold secrets of the Vietnam War! If I ever run into old buddy Benny Barf again, I'll sure put the question to him and hope for a straight answer! Hell, he doesn't know himself. He couldn't. He was a goner!

The struggle with Benny narrowed the party down to three: My Big Indian, my Aussie and me. Now, what do I do with my drunkin' husband before I pass out from the bubbly stuff? Damned Indian. The old saying that Indians don't drink very well is bull shit. Hell's bells, he popped corks at Charlie's, even Hank and I couldn't see. While the Big Indian played "Kill the Gook", Hank and I played footsie under the table. I squirmed and twisted as I laughed with my Big Indian, knowing he was fully aware of plans to "outlast" him in his numb brain. He could always read my brain, and he picked it like a monkey picking lice. But, by now, he was beyond helping himself, and I last saw him stumbling blindly through the French doors to pee on the tiles of the courtyard. I hoped he would miss the water system….pebbles only filter some things, but not pee. He was gross at times, and peeing in the courtyard angered me, but he was drunk and had turned west when he should have headed east to the restroom door. He could have cared less at this point in time as he passed out. Hank and I managed to roll him back inside, where we assured him that he belonged in his bed. With each and every snore rumbling like an echo through the rooms, Hank and I drew closer to the finalization of our plan and anticipated what we had only dreamed of as a realization now. His magnetic appeal filled me with intense passion and feistiness. I was a gutsy young woman, allowing him to win my heart. I was obsessed by my desire for him. But what cheek got turned, or what chicken decided to peep instead of crow; I'll never know. I guess it was mutual, and we called it off as a tender, tear-stained face was gently kissed goodnight. But God, I wanted him, and bad….

God had intervened to answer my prayers, and I was still a faithful wife under the Big Indian's roof. I was hurt, but proud. Hank had aroused his drunken buddy, and with a mutual feeling of "We're hurting, but we're doing the right thing by saying goodnight" type talk, he and his buddy climbed in their Jeep, then Chi Hia and I locked the massive gate behind them. I was saddened, and empty, and lonely….They didn't get very far, a half block. The security guards sent them back. Charlie Cong was still in the area, and our neighborhood was unsafe for travel. They were told to return and spend the night within the block's security. So, as I wiped my drunken tears, and assured my burning desires that they would be satisfied at some future date, the gate bell rang. Someone was at the gate. I snuck back out to the iron horse and swung it wide with the aid of Che Hai, who was always there with her protective key, one of only two coveted keys to the big gate. I had no need for a key as I didn't drive, nor did I ever venture out without the Big Indian or his shotgun buddy Nigh at my side. Enter Aussie….now pray the Big Indian had not rallied with the hasty departure noises and the sudden voices of their second arrival. Oh God, let him still be sleeping. He was.

Hank and I were alone again. Another kiss, another cork. Ceiling on target; countdown: 3, 2, 1, Fire! Hell, we were winning the war by ourselves! The night was suddenly anew, and our show was replaying, catching up to where it had left off earlier. The night was hotter, and I don't mean the fire between us. Charlie had plastic charged the power plant again, so our ceiling fans came to a halt. We shadow danced by candlelight. Murky, humid weather. Jesus, it was hot. The Big Indian knew how to switch on the generators for our emergency power, but I wasn't about to rouse him for his electrical talents. He was right where I wanted him; asleep and unconscious. Charlie was still in our area…. and the rumbling and rattling of automatic weapons pierced the silence of the night. Or was it morning? M-16's could be heard close enough to cut the darkness of our room. I was scared, but too intoxicated with my high to realize I had children, and I should be caring for them. Then Chi Hia flashed through my mind, and I knew she would come yelling if danger warranted an adult's presence with the children, or if we should go to the bunker. I knew it was time for Sergeant Major Hank Williams to fade into oblivion. I had to let go. I had been obsessed with my desire for him. There was no shame, no remorse… Everything differs in times of a war-torn country. With the first glow of morning's daylight, my Aussie made his way down the winding marble staircase, where he was met by our number one maid, Chi Hia. She was up at the crack of dawn, probably up all night, knowing it was her responsibility to let any guests out the gate. I secretly think she knew that she had to be on duty to assist him in making his escape from guilt, and from the Big Indian.

Chapter 15

It was late summer of '68 now, and the Big Indian continually prodded me to depart Vietnam and take the children to safer territory, i.e., back to the USA. He suggested many alternatives to the mainland; among them were Australia, Thailand, Hong Kong, Singapore or Manila, but none of these locations appealed to me without him, and I told him I was staying in Saigon with him and refused to leave. I remember telling him many times I had a feeling that if I were to leave him behind in Saigon, then I would never see him again. I remember the tearful Sunday afternoon he and I sat on the marble porch; just the Big Indian and I….He was putting in overtime as far as I was concerned because it was the same story, over and over, and over again: "It's not safe here anymore, Juni. I really think you should take the kids and get out while you can." He assured me he would fly to whatever destination we chose so he could spend time with us, a neighboring country like Laos or Cambodia was out, but Bangkok or Kuala Lumpur would not have been so bad. I asked how I would survive in a new country, not being aware of their customs, their rate of exchange of monies, how to dress, the types of transportation, or even their language. He assured me we would be alright because of what he called "my determination" and told us he would fly in every weekend….

Things were going well between us, and our love was still constant. We had friends we had made during R & R weekend in Brisbane and Sydney, and so I wanted to go back to Australia, but too much distance for weekend flights. We also discussed returning to Missouri, and he told me it would be best if I returned home to the States. I cried so hard, God, I was crushed. I remember looking tenderly into his eyes and saying, "Doug, if I leave, I'll never see you again." And I knew it. Call it women's intuition or whatever you want…. but I felt it. He decided this was the thing to do, but I was still fighting with all I had. I would not move out and make room for Kim again, just in case this is what he had in the back of his mind. It probably wasn't, but I wouldn't give him that chance. I was holding onto what I had. I recalled those lonely years back in the States while he worked overseas for several years of it….and I hated it. We were together as a family, and that's the way I wanted it: "The five of us together, or not at all." We loved each other. None of the locations we discussed appealed to me without him, and I was adamant in my refusal to leave. Period.

If I had been wiser, then I would have left late summer following that Sunday on the marble porch when he was so persistent. The days wore by, shelling and blood, incoming noise and fright. The war was hot and heavy, and we found ourselves spending more nights than usual in the bunker due to constant attacks. The G.I.'s that visited and bedded down in the "Allen Hotel" were now hostile, as tension and tempers flared as the fighting increased. No one could really relax, as decoded messages were coming from MAC-V headquarters whenever an attack was imminent….and we were fortunate to have inside information to give us advanced warning of area trouble. We always got an anonymous phone call when a skirmish was expected in our neighborhood, so as to "take cover" or impose an all-day curfew on the kids, or when we should go to the bunker. Friends were lifesavers to the kids, and not a G.I. in Saigon didn't love them and worried about them. The circumstances were that our dear friend, Benny Barf, was in a position of information gathering, and while he was not harming our actions of war in any way, he was advising us when to give special consideration to the kids and keep them in. He was so damned concerned; he would literally let us in on advance warnings especially if captured documents indicated there may be an attack within a few blocks of our villa. He was "sent from God" as far as we were concerned; we had a bond of love and safety between us, an all-out effort to keep the kids safe from harm… Benny was impressive with his dark curly hair and square shoulders; just one of the millions making up the armed forces fighting to suppress communism halfway around the world.

Benny came from the hills of Virginia, backcountry people. He was one obscure young man of Dunbar, Star Route, Virginia, who gave of himself endlessly, and he had his share of girlfriends in Saigon. The dainty but hard bar girls of Tu Do Street, with their mini-skirts above their backside cheeks, they accompanied Benny whenever they got the chance; he was loose with both his morals and his money, and they loved both. They bluntly flaunted themselves when we were out on the town….and they whispered, "Buy me Saigon tea, Honey?" I suspect they made good wages off of just Benny, as he loved them all. Tu Do Street for blocks and blocks was loaded with women, a good choice of "Tea Houses" and "Bars" for the G.I.'s to choose from, and they were always full. Benny "Barf" and his acquired name were our most welcome guests. And our most frequent. As I had said before, he had been found in his own vomit one morning, half dead from overindulgence in sex and booze, his two favorite pastimes. The kids ran and told me Benny had barfed all over the floor, fell in it, and slept there. Benny's brother was a civilian under a government contract capacity like that of Doug's, and Danny was the opposite of Benny in looks, temperament and manners. Benny was a polished officer on duty….an officer of MAC-V Headquarters. Danny, and on the other hand, lived with a little Vietnamese girl called Nom; a skinny, disturbed and mad little girl. I liked Nom, she was good to the kids, but she was distant. She would hibernate for days with her sewing machine in her room on the second floor of our villa. You wouldn't see her for two or three days, and then she would suddenly appear and be wearing a new outfit. She loved to be alone and read a lot of books waiting for Danny to return and make love to her. They stayed out of sight most of the time, unlike Benny….who was more a part of the family and constantly downstairs visiting, playing with the kids, taping new reel-to-reels with the Big Indian, or engrossed in a serious game of checkers or chess with the kids. Benny was always there, and we enjoyed him around the table at mealtime; you could always depend on Benny to be cheerful and cute, full of war stories and smiling. He was fun to have around!!

Nom was a moody little girl, perhaps 19 years old, she stayed mad about 99% of the time as Danny wasn't always there when she wanted him to be. He, too, frequented the bars, and she was often alone overnight. She would lose her temper and run down the staircase, hop on her little Honda and disappear into the streets. We wondered if she ever found him, and what she said or did to him. She was insanely jealous of Danny and didn't like sharing him with the Tu Do girls, but he was good to her. He bought her very expensive gifts, and tried to appease her as best he could. I never knew anything about Nom's past or future….she never talked of a family or discussed where she went. She would say "go shopping" as she buzzed out the driveway, but would actually be gone sometimes a couple of days.

Then Danny would rough her up a bit…and she would stay home for a few weeks, then coming and going at her own will on her little market trips. Sometimes, she would bring Cindee a gift, as Cid tried hard to be her friend, but we found it hard to get close to her. Just about the time you felt you were in touch with Nom, she took off again…and came back with her temper showing. She and Danny fought, and I mean a lot, both verbally and physically, abusive to each other constantly. I always wondered when they found time to make love, because their lives were filled with war on both the streets, and in their bedroom. Danny ran around a lot, and when he finally showed up, that's when Nom came down the circular staircase crying and yelling "Home" while pointing her finger out the door.

She would crank up her cycle and yell, "You son a bitch" as she turned the corner. They were never truly happy; I think. Passionate occasionally, but only when their souls eased back to norm, usually at each other's throats. They were alike, yet they had nothing in common except they both liked our kids. But it was Benny who totally won the kids' hearts; they worshiped him so much, and he spent a lot of time with them. He would come bouncing in with that boyish smile across his face, and the tensions of the day would ease a bit. Benny was the one who would alert us if there was to be an attack that night….and he was always right. He would rush home from MAC-V Headquarters and tell us confidentially to keep the children inside and to be on alert tonight. They had captured a Cong carrying a certain document, and an attack was expected at a certain time before daybreak. He was a big help in securing our villa, being on guard, and taking no chances in letting the kids go outside to play in the yard or on the balcony. The balcony was our "lookout post." Many an hour passed away just watching the distant, and sometimes not too distant war taking place.

Benny was like an uncle to the kids; one day he had camouflaged material made up into small army uniforms for the boys but had to apologize to Cid that his maid had run out of material before she got to hers. So, the boys posed for photos, the "little soldiers," hardly any smaller than some of the Asian "boy soldiers" actually fighting the war. I remember Cid was hurt because she didn't get camos, but she finally accepted it. Benny proudly announced one evening that he had secured a captured Viet Cong enemy flag, and he presented it to us as a souvenir. We were thrilled in a distasteful way and managed to get back to the mainland with it. It was taken during a battle on "Hamburger Hill," and some G.I. said, "Give this to the little American kids….you know, the Allen's kids." All the while, captured plans, maps, and military documents were vital to security, and of utmost importance in preparing to repel any enemy attack on the city. General Creighton Abrams took over as American Commander from General Westmoreland, and Doug was telling me foreign intervention would come to an end in late 1968. Amidst a jumble of reports,

I kept hearing the words "evacuation." I constantly needed to be reassured….being here was sensible, yet foolish. At times, I felt a little bit rich for being with the Big Indian. And yet other times, I felt a whole lot poorer. I was mixed-up and scared….

Benny had access to much of this information and passed it on to us for safety reasons, and his tips kept us alive more than once; we treasured and heeded his warnings. He never jeopardized the security of headquarters in any way; he just gave us a simple warning of what to expect and when, that way we would stay inside and keep the children inside, being alert as we tried to rest during the frightfully black nights. One night, a rocket hit our area, and plaster was falling as we made our way downstairs. With the help of G.I.'s living with us, and our devoted maids, we safely brought the kids to our inner courtyard bunker….The rocket had entered through the thick concrete from the Doctor's villa next door, and debris had scattered like red and yellow maple leaves on a fall day. Chunks of colored ornate plaster that had once adorned their garden rooftop now shot out in every direction. Concrete, scraps of metal and broken flowerpots, vases and statues were flung from their rooftop garden, and the debris tore into Cindee's bedroom wall leaving 17 holes. The worst night ever, and it was this night that the final decision as to whether or not move, and when we would return stateside, and leaving Doug there to finish out a contract with his company before proceeding on to Heidelberg, Germany, sitting on the River Rhine; his next assignment to build a Command Center.

So, by the fall of 1968, I agreed with the Big Indian that we had been in Vietnam long enough, and that the children and I should return to the mainland for our own safety. But, before I left, I made him promise that he would arrive in the States in time for Christmas. He assured me he would be following me in just a few short weeks, just as soon as he had checked out some radar towers up-country, shipped and relocated his crew of several hundred, and had disbursed all equipment to new job sites around the Far East. Yes, he would be in Missouri for the holidays, so I begrudgingly started packing and shipping APO boxes to my parents; preparing for the massive move back to the good old USA….It would be 24 straight hours of flying time, and I didn't want to go. This was not an easy decision; returning to the States and leaving the Big Indian there; I was heartbroken. Separation again. I'll never forget the day. The mood was one of sadness, and tension hung in the air like Louisiana moss from a tree weighing me down. Skirmishes had been heated during the night; fear gripped the hearts of everyone. Alerts were constant, and 5 p.m. curfews were still imposed on all Americans. The word from MAC-V was not good, as the war appeared to have really picked up momentum. There were no more "lulls" in the war, no more "quiet" days….just constant sounds of bombers, choppers, rockets and missiles, and enduring every 24 hours was becoming increasingly more difficult.

Co-workers were finding it hard to smile, and the cheery hellos were changed to "glad to see you this morning," as though they really hadn't expected you at VRE Headquarters at all. Being close to death day in and out is normally a requirement of war; but in my case, it was voluntary, and it was getting dangerous. Rumors had it that Charlie and his Viet Cong buddies had dug in real deep under the Phu Do racetrack, an elaborate tunnel system stacked full of ammo and gear, waiting for the right moment to hit Saigon with all they had. Was there to be another Tet offensive in the near future? Could the city stand another? Fear reigned, and the streets were deserted except for troops. Breathing became difficult at night as you listened for footsteps….someone on the tiles of your roof. Then came the tingling sound of "ping" ringing in your ears, wondering just how close that bullet was to the screen on your window. So I ran upstairs and carefully closed the shutters on the children's windows, and then creeped back down to the master bedroom and silently awaited the thundering of incoming rockets, praying they were at least a block away. Knowing somehow, secretly within, that they were as close that night as they had ever been. The heat was stifling, but closed shutters meant more security. No air to breathe, only a miserable night ahead of us….The fans are off. Charlie got the power plant again in Cholon. "Ping." There it went again. I cried, "God, will we get out alive?" Damned fans. Damned sticky air. Damned mosquitoes.

It was this constant tension and worry that formed the decision the Big Indian had to make; us returning to the United States for our safety. It was not my decision. In fact, I fought the decision with uncontrollable tears, though I knew within that this had to be for the kid's sake. The war had become WAR with capitals, WAR in the worst possible way. Bodies lay in the streets riddled with shrapnel, and the nights became a circus of lights in the sky. Sleep came harder as the noises outside tensed one's nerves to the breaking point. It was unsafe to venture out even to the base, or to my VRE Headquarters in Cholon. No more leisure evenings on the floating restaurant ship docked at the end of Tu Do, partaking of Eastern Cuisine and watching foreign ships unload the tools of war, and the staples of survival….Many an evening had been passed on the floating restaurant, and it was a pleasant past-time to cycle across town with the children, and to walk the swinging bridge that led across the water's edge and up to the Saigon River. An old, converted ship that obliged one and all to partake a cold beer, and a meal of luscious oriental food. We spent many evenings there observing the ships of many nations unloading their cargo of tanks, medical supplies, food for the commissaries, troops, Jeeps, flatbed trucks, ammo, chopper parts, but no more; it was war….Tide and toilet tissue, the occasional lipstick or hair spray. The ships were from all nations: Scandinavia, Germany, Libia, Monrovia, Britain, the United States, Egypt, etc., all under contract to the United States of American Armed Forces to freighter supplies for our "Police Action" in Vietnam. The balmy breezes blew gently across the deck as you dipped your spring rolls in nuoc mom and sipped your beer, but now these days were gone. Charlie was all over the city and docks, swimming the river at night, infiltrating Saigon from every crack and crevice….like cockroaches, multiplying with every sunrise. There was no end to him, the sneaky little bastard. He had his way with everyone there.

On one particular occasion when the war had let up, Doug and the boys headed to the Floating Restaurant where we were to meet him. The Big Indian realized he was almost out of gas in his Honda, and so he was sloshing gas by rocking from side to side as he motored down Tu Do Street. The rocking motion was getting to both boys, one riding in front of him, and one behind him. They were soon yelling, "Be careful, dad;" but when he sloshed just a bit too much, they went over, skidding down the street. The 14th Field Army Hospital was within sight, and it seemed the thing to do….solicit attention from Medics to care for the kids' bleeding elbows and hands. No one was badly injured, only shaken up, and we realized minor medical cleansing was in order. There we were in the Emergency room, unlike any other emergency room I had ever seen, hardly like the ones I had taken the kids to back in the States. There were glistening white, pretty nurses dressed in white, tile floors and children playing in the reception area. This was war…. this was a field hospital, and it was set up with rows of cots: row after row, and by each was a stand to hold the apparatus for intravenous feeding that may save a life. Alert and ready always, they never knew when a truck or ambulance full of wounded soldiers would be brought in from the jungle just outside the city. The room was empty when we entered, and the young Medic was actually elated at the sight of an American family; a term we had heard many, many times in Vietnam as G.I.'s would exclaim: "And with kids and a wife, and blondes at that! Wow! Am I seeing things? Is it a mirage?" We were respected and stared at, often hugged and kissed as we reminded the kisser that he, too, had children and a wife back in the safety of Montana, or Arkansas, or New York…. who knew, but we were his family at that moment; a moment he spent reminiscing as a tear slid down his face. Memories of "back home" kept many guys going from day to day, we were only an instant reminder. In one fleeting instant, they had both a smile and a tear, and neither really belonged in this war. Soon, they were gone, waving in the distance, their day happier just for having seen us. If in no other way did the children and I give of ourselves towards the war effort, those smiles and tears were our bit….

The young Medic respected us, planting a sweet kiss on the brow of each child, he then turned to me and said, "Lordy….a real American blond. I had forgotten what they looked like!" He hugged me and kissed my cheek as he reminded me that he, too, had a wife back in the safety zone of Montana, and we became his family for just that fleeting moment. He quickly got over his awe at the sight of us and proceeded to care for the bleeding children, his hands going over and over the scratches they had received from the pavement. With his wash basin of disinfectant suds and a stack of sterile towels, he proceeded to scrub the gravel from around the elbows and knees. He playfully….but gently, hoisted them to the gurney and was cleansing their scratches when an alert light came on. An ambulance entered the area with a siren blazing, and what I saw took about 15 years off my life, but I also grew up 25 years at that very moment. The truth of war hit me in full force. Six young, uniformed men not a day over 19 years of age appeared. They were bearded, bedraggled, dirty, covered with scum of the swamps and leeches of the jungle, as well as their own blood. Some were holding up bloody stumps of hands, others had fingers missing, but all had hands and arms held out in front of them, and with blood running down their bodies.

They spotted the young Americans being cared for on the tables and immediately smiled through their pain. The kids and Doug and I clamored to get out of their way, knowing fully well the young fighters needed emergency attention before they died in front of us. We knew we had to get the hell out of there. The war had come to us whether we wanted it or not. I felt sick to my stomach, and terror showed in the kids' eyes as they scampered down from the tables. The one Medic on duty was yelling, "Medic….

Medic." as he needed an assistant, now and pronto! These boy soldiers, Americans from back home, said things like "Finish the kids first," and "No man, that's O.K., take care of them first." Those words still ring in my ears today. Talk about a lump in my throat; I knew I was going to throw up, yet I fought it. Seeing all the guts and determination in those fighting young men, courageous even in pain, tender with compassion for the young, I wanted to cry, but I was too sick….These had to be the bravest Americans I had ever seen, painfully insisting we get cared for first. We finished cleansing our own wounds off in a corner of the emergency room, and the wounded young soldiers were immediately taken care of. By then, there were 7 Medics that had swarmed upon the room, and a plan of action was in force. Hell, it was their war, not ours. God, I felt selfish for a moment, yet happy at their courage. That was a moment of war most mothers and wives never saw. It was like a scene right out of a movie to see, a movie about a war that took place somewhere else, but not here. No, there was no way a war was happening here. Or was it?

That evening is embedded in my mind, and I have said it over and over again: "Every mother and wife should see war the way I saw war." The war made me sick in my stomach more than once, but it made me appreciative of the United States of America and our freedom, and I often feel our Democratic society does not work as well as it should. I am so thankful to be a loving American lady….I sometimes lay awake at night wishing I could call every single mother and father of sons in Vietnam, fighting somewhere in a hamlet, a village, or a rice paddy or behind a hill, or lost in the darkness of the jungle." I wanted to tell them, "I am here. I have seen your son, and he is O.K., well, for today." I wanted to tell her, "He is tough, and you should be so very proud of him." I wanted to Mother all of them, and I fell in love with each and every man I met over there. I felt I had a thousand brothers, sons or whatever. I wanted to care for them and spend 10 minutes with each one of them just visiting and reminding them that they, too, had blondes, brunettes and redheads back home…. to hang in there and not to give up faith. I prayed for them every night, "Either we will build peace sensibly, or we will rebel against sense."

The Vietnam "Police Action" was no solution to communism, it spawned worse problems than those intended to solve. There were no accomplishments to pride ourselves in, as nothing was really solved by the years and lives spent by our occupation in that country. Looking back, our being there was just a "shot in the dark," a shot that still rings in the ears of our veterans. Just dirty memories of a war we never won. When the wheels of liberation movements pick up speed, Communism tailgates closely by. The Soviet Union has not hesitated to act with harsh force in Czechoslovakia, Hungary, Vietnam, and Afghanistan, and more recently….Poland, Iraq, Nicaragua, South America and Chechnya. It sickens you to see freedom so randomly drained; it was as though it were a Midwestern sink clogged with the peach peelings left from the seasons canning, the pits to be dozed under in mass graves of God's Earth, and never to grow and nurture again in the form of life on this planet. What are we doing to ourselves? To our future as a race of humans? I am glad I live NOW…. as I fear for the future of our children, as the rich soil of ranches and farms is being bought up by Arabians, Iranians, Japanese, Chinese and other oil barons from Eastern countries. I want my children's children to have a wild country to be young in. It makes me want to throw up to think there may be a day when my grandchildren "rent" American soil from an oil sheik; the same soil our men fought for to gain freedom and protect what was rightfully theirs from labors of love and blisters and tilling the old thyme soil. And this is supposed to be America? It's changed. It is still today's soil, and the soil of yesteryear, but will it be tomorrow's farms? Bitterness….that's what I feel. It was this same bitterness I felt about the Vietnamese war. By being there, we were not fashioning a durable institution that could ever maintain world peace; thus, the justification for analyzing and categorizing us along with the Soviet Union. It never will be the same here, never.

Whether Americans like that closeness or not, we had no sanction for being there. Our motives were not to win, but apparently to prolong! Sadness lingered in the hearts of the G.I.'s serving alongside the Vietnamese, whose feelings were "I care less if you Yanks are here or not." In fact, many, some say most, yelled obscenities like "Go home, Yank, go home." The American grunts questioned, "Why aren't we allowed to win?" Not being a pro, or an intellect, and a novice at putting my feelings and memories on paper to share, I am the first to admit my feelings are not those of everyone who served in South Vietnam. Yes, I felt, I saw, I touched, I listened and understood, watched and cried….I saw war. That in itsel is a big statement from a wife and mother who had never been much further than family vacation travels north to Canada, west to California and south to Mexico. I viewed a jungle of secrets, sadness and heartache, blood, booby traps and Viet Cong. The youth of the armed forces sickened your maternal instincts with patriotism, wanting to cradle, soothe and mend them. Like the lost cats the kids brought home, they all needed a home full of love and tenderness, cats and G.I.s alike….Their childish eyes danced at the sight of the blonde-tousled kids, laughing and standing on their heads, though the hardness of the tiled floors must have dented their brains. It was "home" to many of the visiting servicemen; a welcome was always awaiting them at our villa, and somehow, they knew. No invitations were necessary, mealtime was hotel style, and they always chewed the "meat closest to the bone, "greasy fingers and all….They were grateful for home cooking.

Invariably, they requested cornbread, and a game of chess or checkers afterward with one of the kids. Games followed mealtime. Ours was a house of love; it was Mother's Day, every day; it was the corner drugstore and the YMCA, and it was the pub on the corner. It was home to a lot of Vietnamese, G.I.'s, sailors, Marines and 3rd county nationalists, home to a lot of kids, some not too young, but still kids at heart. We loved them all; Cindee, Steve, Jeff, and I looked forward to evenings, to the guests and friends who soon became like members of our family. The sense of protection from having them around was like….praying at an altar; an inner sereneness only God can understand. I knew the kids would be taken care of during each attack or skirmish, whether it was rooftop snipers, or down-to-earth incoming mortars and rockets hitting Saigon and jarring the plaster loose from the walls and loosening the marble tiles and ceramics that adorned the villa. We had a private army in our villa, ready to fight and protect the little Americans so far from home. God Bless each and every one of those military men and civilian engineers, our friends….Australian,

Korean, Vietnamese, Filipino, mercenaries, soldiers and all of the other third-country nationalists who had their private reasons for being there. God knew it best to send them to 331A Vo Tanh, and it was a mercy mission of protection and love. I'll never forget their faces. I don't do well with names at all, but faces are etched into my memories forever.

On my way to VRE Headquarters one day, we counted the bodies lying on the roadway. Doug was driving, and I was counting. I got to 14, and I cried. It was not at all unusual to see the secretaries coming into VRE Headquarters in the mornings with mascara running down their faces. Some had lost a loved one during the night, and others had become sickened at the sight of bodies on the way to work just as I had. No one ever asked any questions; as in war, there is a mutual understanding….everyone has the same fears and tears are just accepted. The little boys with plastic charges strapped, or taped to their backs, or their midsections hidden by a shirt and being sent into public places with one intention: "Destroy" saddened me and broke my heart. They were probably told, "Carry this into the theater or market, and a nice man will be waiting for you, and he'll pay you money for this package on your back. Don't lose it now, and don't tell anyone about it." Then the child innocently strolled into the business, and "Ker-plow-iee!" and he was blown to bits along with patrons of the business. This happened in a theater near our villa, and the explosion could be heard for miles, and it totally destroyed the theater and everyone in it; an act of war by Charlie again….The innocent child was scattered over to Vo Than Street, across the intersection, and parts of him even hanging from nearby rooftops. God, this is war? Starving children begging for a handout the minute our maids left the villa, knowing we had food and drink inside and hoping they would prey on her mercy. Skinny little kids, naked and shameless from the war tugged at your heartstrings, and our kids often passed goodies through the massive iron gate to starving tykes in the street. Before long, it became too risky to pass food through the fence….they were yelling, "Go home, you damned Yankee," apparently not aware that at that tender age, our presence was not winning their war. They were envious of our health and well-being, all the while they nursed and patted their swollen bellies and soothed their cuts and scratches. They were hurting from within, and badly. Damn war….

Chapter 16

Chi Hia, Lon and Kim loved to be invited in for an evening of television, a rare treat for them. Soon, it was no longer "rare," and they camped in the living room for their usual Vietnamese program of dance and song. We learned from their shows, and they from ours. Only one Armed Forces and a Vietnam station did not give us a large selection, but it certainly passed the long evenings under curfew faster. Too, it was a feeling of security when we were all under the same roof….knowing a sniper was not in the courtyard and slashing the throats of our maids as they had done at the villa down the street. They were safe inside and didn't hesitate to come in when in fear. I owe our lives to them for waking us up more than once when there was trouble in our block, many times they led us all to the safety of the bunker when we had slept through their sneaky noises on the rooftop; we owed them our lives. Chi Hia would giggle when Lon and Kim were laughing and enjoying something funny on TV, as any mother would snicker when her girls were idolizing a handsome leading man. They entertained us by allowing us to watch them, and many times, a happy evening was spent trying to understand what made them laugh.

They appreciated us, they appreciated their job with us, and we appreciated them. It was a mutual love….not gone forever, but with lingering memories of devoted employees and friends long ago. They were so happy to be able to share their lives with us.

Lon would sway with anticipation of a lover nearby when a certain American cowboy came on the tube, she would chatter in Vietnamese as fast as she could so that we could not pick it up, but Kim and Chi Hia would catch it and laugh till they were sick. I suspect she was saying of the tall, handsome yank with chaps and side shooters: "Why don't you come to my bed tonight for a little fun?" The context of her thinking had to be along these lines, as Chi Hia would scold her in her monkey chatter voice, all the while, Lon would blush. They were having their own fun in a war of pure hell, not too much fun to be taken in this country in the late 1960s….Take what you can get, and smile when you can, as tomorrow there may be no laughter, or even breath. During all of this, the rains were depressing, downpours that lasted for weeks didn't do much to lift the spirits of war and death. The Vietnamese were used to it, and it never slowed down the bicycles or scooters, yet the traffic never slowed, and I always wondered where everyone was going. Everyone had a product to get into town, provided they got past the jungle snipers along the roadside. It seemed like they were everywhere, and all the time.

It was necessary to get crops to market so the 3 million in Saigon could have vegetables and rice, and roots and sweet potatoes. Sweet potatoes were a big crop in South Vietnam, boil one sweet potato and it made a whole meal. Being a staple of survival for many starving families; the unfortunate victims of this Police Action. And yet all I could think was how I ate top sirloin steaks and pork chops till they were running out my ears, so I often wondered if I would ever be able to eat another steak, ungrateful at the time for the cases of choice beef from the officers on the base….or rather for the monotony of variety, or lack of it. A hot dog with mustard and chili sure would have been good during the summertime, as Chi Hia and/or the Big Indian would char the steaks to death in the inner courtyard, except during the Monsoon season; then they used the second and most outer kitchen, as smoke could drift out either end of the kitchen with its open walls. The aroma must have made a lot of Viet Cong swim the river….maybe we drew them into the city; who knows? We had a big kettle- type grill and fired it up almost every evening, weather permitting. No wonder the G.I.'s from the base used to love to come in; whenever they were overnight guests of the Allens, they all had choice meals, super service by the three maids, and a family to visit with. It was about as close to "home" as they could hope for in the middle of this war. Sometimes….we just sat around and talked all evening with the Big Indian and I and our guests, letting them "spill their sorrows and homesickness" as much as they wanted to, getting it "all out." Many touching evenings were spent in that villa, and oh, if the walls could just talk, what stories they would tell. Grown men crying over a buddy lost days prior….or fear of the next bivouac in the jungle, wondering if they would come back alive, or how about a secret attack by Charlie. Huh?

Stories of torture, admissions of the slaughter of innocent civilians, peasants killed because they were ordered to do so….sometimes because of that certain awesome suspicion they may be Viet Cong, thus, the certain death for the old people. Stories of the burning of entire villages….the guys had these things all cooped up within themselves and found an outlet for emotions at our place. They were carrying fears and guilt around with them and needed these long evenings playing a quiet game of cribbage or chess with the kids and then relaxing with a sticker over the rocks and a lot of good talk. More importantly, they needed good listeners. I felt like a Priest at Confession….but how I managed to absorb their fears, sins and guilt as though my own. We shared it was the only way to survive. We made many beautiful friendships and tucked away our memories no one can ever take from us. The rains flooded the lawns and street like a river, and businessmen merely rolled up their pants legs to the knee, grabbed their briefcase, carried their shoes and "off to business as usual." They were natives, but I never adapted to the constant pounding sound of hard rains on the roof, just another annoying noise of war. Rain brought all the mosquitoes inside…they seemed to grow as the months went by.

The Vietnamese were generous with politeness, and they revered their tone of voice and manners. It was as though "do not speak until you are spoken to," and sometimes, you wondered if the maids were even around the villa or not. They could be observed going about their duties, almost tip-toeing, as though in a temple or church. The only outburst I ever heard was when Danny and his concubine mistress were fighting over her sewing machine, or his being drunk. She was insanely jealous, and rightfully so. He was tall and handsome, and a catch for any young Vietnamese girl wanting to escape to a better world. I couldn't blame any of them for wanting a ticket out of the country; after all, many had the G.I.'s children and no future of security when the troops pulled out. All Vietnamese girls tried desperately to hang on to their lovers…. in desperation for a better life. It was like Vietnam's culture was being blown to bits, its libraries burned, its theaters bombed, and the art reduced to ashes. The country would never be the same. Danny often told me how the girls pleaded for G.I.'s to impregnate their bodies, as they were hoping to have something to cling to; a "tool" to use against them when the time came to say "goodbye Yanks." Another Maria being made every second of the war but left behind to suffer and grow into little nothing's, never to know the wonders of a mother or father, or to climb upon their knees. God, wouldn't it have been better to have required vasectomies of all soldiers, that way these little children would not have to know a life of suffering? I wish I could bring them with me stateside….each and every one of them. I feel we owe this to all the little half-white or half-black, and half-Vietnamese waifs, little American-Asian outcasts who are so hated in Vietnam.

When the Big Indian told me I had to leave Saigon, he knew I didn't want to return to the States without him, insisting the children and I should "get out while there is still time." The fighting was fierce throughout the country, and Saigon was beginning to look like Europe of World War II, with devastation and death everywhere. Benny had advised us of captured evidence confirming a large-scale escalation within the next few weeks, and the Big Indian was determined to get us on a plane. I cried, and I begged, saying, "Please don't make me leave you, because I know I'll never see you again." It was a premonition of pain and loneliness that would stay with me for many years to come. I pleaded with him, "Please don't make me go." He assured me we could not stay there, and he made the necessary arrangements for the flight. He brought the tickets home….4 thick books. I just stared at them, afraid to read them, and I felt a tear in the corner of my eye. But Doug had one, too, in each eye. He would miss the children very much. He said, "Read them. At least you'll have a nice tour of Asia on your way home." I was reluctant to open the cover for fear the final page of the multi-page tickets would be the destination, the U.S.A., home; and it was…. The Big Indian hugged me and said, "It's the only way, honey, let's get these kids out of this damned place while we still can."

I was pleased he had booked us through so many countries going back to the States. He said we should see as much of Asia as possible while we were in the East, and I agreed. The educational aspects of visiting many countries would be advantageous in future school years, and I've always believed seeing history and geographical locations beat just reading about it. Doug dried my tears and laughingly said, "Well, hon, look at it this way: as long as you have to leave Vietnam…. leave it in style!" And we did! Mama and the siblings were going "tripping around the world" on a leisurely, luxurious tour of many nations, leaving our Big Indian and the war far behind us. There was a lot of packing to be done, and little time to do it in. We were to fly the day after tomorrow; less than 48 hours away. The maids and children were really wonderful to pitch in, and within 24 hours of the first sighting of our tickets in Doug's hand, we securely taped the final box. We had the same 8 big pieces of American Tourister and the same 4 green flight bags that flew over with us, and everyone was busily packing their own luggage….The kids were real pros at packing by now after all the experience they had prepared for the flight to South Vietnam. Now we had accumulated more, so we shipped some in the large boxes addressed to the folks and gave some items to the maids. We even packed a bunch of nick-nacks in our suitcases in lieu of our clothes, as we had so many of them that we wanted to make sure they got home with us.

The atmosphere was one of sadness, yet the anticipation just to be air-born was killing me. As long as the situation in Saigon made it necessary for the Big Indian to evacuate his family to safer shores, then the mutual feeling was, "Let's get this show on the road." So much to be done. I couldn't hide the tears as I packed, leaving nothing there but bare necessities behind for the Big Indian's survival. We even crated up the big Sansui 3000 to ship it halfway around the world. The Big Indian knew we were fighting a no-win war, and he said, "There's no way I'm leaving that for the Viet Cong to latch onto!" Doug had his personal papers and clothes, his razor, a few cooking essentials, 3 maids, a big empty villa, and Can Tho…. the kids' dog. He would later dispose of his Honda and the family 4-door Toyota; he and his briefcase would somehow survive without his wife and kids. Somewhere deep in the night, I already knew that he would eventually end up back with Kim, somehow, I just knew it. Only time would tell though, but if I was going to bet on it, then I was going all-in. The whole "caboodle" as they say. Well, sometimes. But it was a bet that I knew I'd win, no matter what….

He booked us on a fantastic route, and I mean fantastic; we were scheduled to spend three days each in Singapore, Singapore; Sydney, Australia; Kuala Lumpur, Malaysia; Bangkok, Thailand; Hong Kong, China; and Tokyo, Japan. He had already made all the advance reservations and handed me an itinerary naming each hotel, dates and times we would arrive and depart, advance payment of our rooms, and even names of whom we should contact in each country, and at each hotel in case of illness or any unforeseen troubles during our travels. As I thumbed through our individual airline ticket books, I counted the take-offs and landings we would endure….well over a dozen, including a Pacific Island stop for refueling, and then a touchdown at Frisco! I thought, "Now we'll really need God's hand on our shoulders, good flying weather and lots of prayers." The Big Indian had cabled mom and dad back in St. Joseph, and they said they would be at Kansas City International Airport to greet us on that certain date, but for me to check in with them before I left my final destination; San Francisco, California…. Somehow, the anticipation overshadowed our grief about leaving the Big Indian…

After a sad goodbye with the maids, and an even sadder goodbye with our little dog Can Thu, which involved forcibly removing him from the Toyota to come get me again, we drove through the massive gate that held so many memories. It was our final trip down Vo Than Street and on to Tu Do Street, where we showed our I.D.'s one last time, and we were allowed to pass beyond the guard station one more time. Then on across town to the Tan Son Nhut Air Force base, and with ever-loving Nigh riding shotgun; the last time we'll ever see him again….

On my last day there in Vietnam, Doug was pensive and quiet, and our departure time had an effect on him, too. Doug and Nigh checked our luggage, and we headed to the currency window to exchange my Vietnamese money for American "green," as we were not allowed to take M.P.C., or dongs, or pilasters out of the country. The Vietnamese had all kinds of rules. The airport employee in charge of exchanging monies balked at our request to change dong and pilasters into $1,200.00 "green," as the limit was $300.00 per person, and that's all they wanted to exchange, just $300.00, "I guess my 3 children aren't considered as people, huh?" he said with authority as they looked at each other…. They entered into a gibberish argument as to how many American dollars I would be allowed to take out of the country, and soon their heads turned as the yelling got louder and louder. The Big Indian won (as usual), and they allowed my requested amount of $1,200.00 for the four of us. I wasn't too concerned one way or another, as I had my spending money hidden in my bra, but I chuckled as he winked at me in victory….he had won his mini-war, and I had all my green that was already on my body, as he had previously slipped me $3,000.00 green, so I had no lack of spendable cash for our trip.

Doug explained thoroughly the process I must go through upon both entering and departing each country, and to temporarily exchange my "green" for the currency of that particular country. What I had not spent locally, I would change back into green upon departure at the airport, repeating this process each leg of the trip. This way, through the proper rate of exchange, I would have local money for tipping, limousine, taxi and shopping. I felt like a Queen, and I thought, "Wow! A big stash of green for shopping, a 15-day tour of the Far East, and a final destination of K.C.I. and my folks!" I felt happy….yet sad; I didn't want to say my final goodbye to the Big Indian. Yes, my Big Indian had thought of everything, and he was sincere in encouraging us to enjoy ourselves and put the war behind us. But we never forgot we had left him behind in a bloody, miserable war. I hated to leave Saigon. I hated leaving him behind in the war, yet he reassured me that he would be careful and how he would be following us to the States in just a few short weeks. He said, "Please don't cry, Juni, you must go. It's too dangerous for you and the kids to stay here, and I'm winding up on this job site anyway." I believed him. It hurt getting on that plane….a lot. That was our official last goodbye, a sad goodbye, to say the least. A goodbye that could be heard around the world.

We spent the next 18 days on the vacation of a lifetime, or so it seemed….We saw giant turtles in Singapore, Singapore; Koala bears in Sydney, Australia; water buffalo in Kuala Lumpur, Malaysia; Asian elephants in

Bangkok, Thailand; Chinese dolphins in Hong Kong, China; and Japanese black bears in Tokyo, Japan. And that's just the beginning of the list, as we visited a zoo in each and every country. It was so interesting to see all the different animals in each country. It was like a new, but old chapter, and everywhere we went. We went to see museums in a few countries, we saw the harbors in a few countries, we saw mountains in other countries, and we saw people of all different shapes, sizes, and especially origins like you wouldn't believe. But believe me….we did! We saw the back streets of some towns, and the main streets of others. We went out to eat in every country, every day in fact. We went to fancy restaurants sometimes, and to a burger joint the next. We saw tall buildings, short buildings, old buildings and new, and even some that you couldn't even believe that someone lived there. It was a sight that you wouldn't believe, whether good or bad, but we saw it. It seemed to go on and on and on. Day after day, we saw something new, yet something the same; it was just built differently. It seemed like a life of luxury, but yet it didn't, and it wasn't….we knew that we had to go home one day, eventually….

Chapter 17

Once we were finally home on American soil, the months seemed to be flying by, one by one, and the kids and I were making it as well as could be expected. We were still holding our heads high, but there were times we wanted to just let them droop down in a worried state, because we still feared for Doug's life and the unknown. We had to have faith and keep waiting, and my attitude had to be positive for their sake. I continued writing letters, and I inquired of each new lead I could get my hands on, never giving up, yet always wondering. It was there, constantly clawing at me, the unknown. Newspapers told of thousands captured and being held prisoner….I cried on my pillow that night, along with many other nights after tucking the kids in bed. I could often hear them as they cried, too. The kids' birthday parties rolled around all too quickly, not to mention the Christmas holiday that passed, the most difficult time of the year for all of us. There are too many bad memories of the one Christmas that daddy forgot to come home.

The children bestowed a lot of love on Figgi, the pup that nobody else had wanted when the litter was born on a moving day in February of 1969. "Figaro Allen" was her official name. She was a cute, short-haired tan and black critter built close to the ground. As I watched the children hug and play and hold Figgi, I soon realized the dog was a great emotional outlet for them. Figgi was getting all the love they would normally have had for their daddy. She was spoiled, and the kids would dance around her as they clapped their hands and sang a song they wrote for her as they spelled it out; "F – I – G-G-I'…'F-I-G- G-I'…all together now…"F – I – G-G-I"… "F-I-G-G-I." The dog was a nervous wreck hearing her name in this crazy verse, and she would turn complete circles chasing her tail, then crawl on her stomach with all four legs outstretched, inching along on her belly with her stub tail going from left to right. She got so excited, and the kids would roar with laughter at her antics. She was a lovable pup and a good friend. She never barked, and she never saw a stranger. Her diet consisted of leftovers mainly; she loved spaghetti and meat sauce or Rice Krispies and milk, but her greatest delight was ice cream, or bread and gravy. She had big cowl eyes that looked sad all the time, but her tail told us otherwise….She must have been sent from heaven to fill an empty space in our hearts. She accepted the love the kids offered, never whimpering, never saying no when they wanted to play. She never sulked behind the couch, or ran away from them, and she was always there to be their friend and play their crazy games. She was one of the family, and I don't think the children could have made it all those years without her. As the years passed, she soon learned to accept their moods of depression over the loss of their father and would sit for hours quietly on their laps, or lay beside them as they stretched across the bed, not caring whether they stroked her fur, or ignored her. Either way, she was loving and understanding of their daily moods. And the cats, a Siamese named Chi Hia, and a Burmese named Lon, named after our maids back in Vietnam, and Figgi the dog; they showered the kids with love. They rounded out our family with an equivalent score of 1 pet per kid!

Many days were spent just being alone, as each of us had to have our private thoughts and our cries. It was especially hard on the kids; they were so young and tender. Understanding the situation on their part was harder on them in their youthful years; the years they had been deprived of a father's love and help, their growing years. I was older, wiser and tougher, and I knew just how cruel this old world could be at times. They were learning, though, learning at much too young an age. They suffered so much hurt within them, and I thought, "If the Big Indian only knew…. If he could only see their tears, and their moments of silent loneliness." But it didn't bring him home or make the situation any better. A year had passed since our return to the States, and without the Big Indian. I had adjusted to a change of jobs. Life was so messed up, I couldn't get totally comfortable in any employment situation, and it was a restless 24-hours a day. Savings were quickly being used up, prices had increased, and wages had not. My car fell apart, and I found it necessary to fork over for a newer van. Children's clothing was expensive as they outgrew it so fast, too….There were child illnesses, and stitches from playing football, rashes that they got from something, and a whole bunch of other stuff. Soon, I was having a rough time surviving. I wondered how many years a wife should wait for her husband? Funds were still tied up, and a presumptive filing of Death was impossible to get signed. I needed a career position because it looked like long, hard years ahead without my Big Indian. "Oh God, please let him come home," I said in the dark, and I would later wake up, hearing him in the carport calling my name. I was going crazy.

The fugitive kids enlarged their Sherman Avenue tree house to two rooms….complete with wall-to-wall carpet (used), and my best feather-down pillows. They slept there on cool summer evenings; as they, too, needed a retreat where they could hide, think and ponder their past years of confusion. It was a neighborhood hang-out, even to the point that the bitchy R.N. who lived across the street tried to make a mountain out of a molehill, claiming to police and neighbors it was a "den of iniquity." By this time, though, I had been working for the Senator for several years, and she had the gall to call him….she threaten to cut off her political contributions, and the pledges of some of her friends if he did not investigate the actions of his secretary's children. What a bitch, with a capital "B." I doubt if she ever had a "piece", or ever wanted a piece, for that matter. She was indeed a crabby old maid and disliked by the entire neighborhood. She tried to make life miserable for us, and was continually spying from behind her curtains, a miserable old witch of a neighbor. The children were growing into young men, and Cid into a young lady by this time….nearly 5 years had passed since we returned from Vietnam. The boys were calling on Cid, hanging around to get a glimpse of her and her girlfriends sunbathing on the carport, or sipping cokes on the patio. Traffic was heavy up and down the grassy knoll that led up the back lawn, and it kept the bitch neighbor really busy spying on who was coming and going. I think it finally got the best of her, as she sure didn't say anything anymore!

Once, unknown to me, we housed a fugitive child in the tree house; actually, hiding him from the police. Seems he was a runaway and needed a meal and a place to sleep. Steve and Jeff, thinking no differently than any human, offered him shelter, complete with electric lights, blankets, and my feather-down pillows. Meals were snuck out the back door, and their breakfast scraps were carefully scraped from their dinner plates and onto paper plates, so that's how I finally caught them and their prisoner. Life was not simple raising 2 boys and a girl, yet they were good kids 99% of the time. But oh, that 1% of the time….That 1% of the time, the cops were bringing them home by the nape of their necks for snowballing cars, and once for siphoning a quarter's worth of gas from a nearby gas station. It seems their cycles were empty, and so were their pockets. But that's the extent of the trouble they caused me, and I was so grateful to have gained as much respect as I had from both of them. And Cid, well she was in her "wandering" years, or was it her "wondering" years? I couldn't decide….She wondered whether to fall in love with this guy or that guy, whether to finish high school or drop out, whether to sell cheese at the local deli or venture out to the West Coast with a friend. "God help me," I used to pray; raising boys is easier anyway than raising a girl during her mid to late teens. She went to California and spent her wad, but then phoned me back within a few short months for a return ticket home. Now, Cid was wiser and realized the need to finish her education. She had her ups and downs in growing up and adjusting to her world of "friends with built-in fathers," more of an adjustment than either of the boys had….Or perhaps she showed it more and soon became a despondent; an unloved and unwanted child, or so she thought. We had rough times and good times in between, and she turned out to be a dashing coed skipping across campuses from Missouri Western to the Kansas City Art Institute, desperately trying to find herself, partly the blame of her Big Indian father jar of "tigers milk who forgot to come home….She had needed him so badly during the formative years, his disappearance had been tough on all three children.

When Steve and Jeff were bored and fed up with the world, they went to Stew's house; or Stewart Wyeth, a big estate at the end of our block protected by high walls and a gatekeeper with a winding drive through acres, and acres of garden-like lawns leading to a mansion atop the hill. They liked his Grandpa Wyeth's estate, and they passed the time away over there riding up and down the stairs on Grandpa's electric lift-chair elevator, totally aggravating the family butler. They dined often with Stew's family, and they gloried as they told of the maid serving them the "best, biggest juiciest steaks in Missouri." They practically lived in Wyeth's pool… and often returned wrinkled and waterlogged from a fun day at Stew's. They admired Mr. Wyeth, Stewart's dad, and they thought of him as a father-figure and a buddy who looked forward to each visit to the estate. Stew would let them sneak their motorcycles through the back gates of the estate, and the three of them hit the private Wyeth gas supply. Steve had a Honda 70, and Jeff had a Yamaha 80, so I guess they rode for days, maybe weeks, before Mr. Wyeth put a stop to it. Sometimes, when they couldn't find anything else to do, Stew would come to the house to get them to go to the woods for a "picnic" as they called it. Now what that "picnic" really was, I couldn't tell you, so your guess is as good as mine….The Wyeth maid had already prepared them a picnic, complete with a can of beans, a small pan of sterna meat, and to top it off, a jar of "tigers milk" each, as Stew never came without his Tigers Milk. Sometimes, he had a can of the ever-so-good chocolate-covered ants or grasshoppers from the pantry, or prepared hors d'oeuvres meant to be served at Mrs. Wyeth's afternoon bridge game. He was a good friend to the kids, as were all their buddies. Never an evening without Mark, Shawn and Ronnie either, and a dozen others for that matter clustered around the TV, or out in the tree house….or ganging up on the front porch to "girl watch" and plot their next move.

The children would be 13, 15 and 17 before they would lay eyes on their father again. The letter finally came, as I pulled the assortment of daily mail from the box, it caught my eye. I knew it was the word I had been waiting for, even though the handwriting was almost illegible, and the Cancellation circle was smudged with Asian chicken tracks and symbols, and the smear indicated it had traveled a long journey. The envelope was thick, but it told me it was one of the Air Mail envelopes we had used in Saigon. My heart pounded….could it be from Doug? There was no return address, no revealing secrets on the outside, and I would have to read and reread its inner contents to satisfy my years of wondering. I held the airmail envelope close to my heart and cried, "He's alive, he's alive." But no one heard me, and I was alone. And even if I hadn't been there by myself, I still wanted to read it first before saying anything to the kids that may give them false hopes. Not after what their little hearts and minds had suffered these past few years; no way….No, not after Christmas of 1968. This envelope, bulging with its contents, hopefully held the answer to the past, it would hopefully tell me where he was, how he was and why he didn't come home. But did I dare open it? Where had he been?

Where was he sitting as he wrote this letter? Did I really want to know? My hands trembled as tears gently slid down my face. I ran to my bedroom and fell across the bed, sobbing at the letter close to my cheeks. My pillow was wet, my nerves were breaking down, and I had the good cry I had wanted to have for years. I must have laid there for an hour, afraid to open it, I knew one thing though: I had to have a drink, and I had to be alone to absorb this vital, long-awaited information, whatever the consequences. I had watched the mailbox month after month, year after year, now my heart was beating so hard I didn't know if I would live long enough to read it. Was I having a coronary? God, please help me; I shouldn't die without knowing the answer; it would be so unfair.

"The Park….That's it; I'll go to the park…." I had made up my mind that I'll go to the park where there will be no telephones, no cars, no children or interruptions. Cid was at her friend Cindy DeVine's; her best friend who lived with us for a year later on in time, and the boys were at Stew's estate and weren't due home for another hour. I left them a note stating I would be back soon, and I climbed into my white Dodge van and headed a few short blocks to the most desolate corner of the park. I found a bench that appeared to be lonely and in need of a sitter, and that's where I sat down and cried. "Thank you, God," I muttered to myself and to the trees….I held the unopened letter to my heart, still afraid to read it. I was afraid of it, and my body really shook uncontrollably, and the tears continued to fall. I was afraid it would say, "I'm coming home in just a few short weeks," just like the last letter. I didn't think I could ever go through that again. I questioned God why it took so long to reach me, and I was fearful I would know if I opened it. As long as it was sealed, then I could still dream, hope and wish, but once I lifted the sealed flap, and whether I liked its contents or not, the enclosed news would be final.

I couldn't open it. The letter was again tucked carefully into my purse when I got back in the front seat; still unopened. I drove off thinking I just couldn't cheat the kids out of this, the news they, too, had so eagerly awaited all these years, and I changed my mind. I took it home, put on a pot of coffee and reached for the Brandy, I wanted the courage to open it. When the kids came in, I announced that we should gather the clan at the dining room table, the Italian Provincial carved of solid cherry, the table now worn where elbows had rested, and tears had fallen during these past few years. Our private conference table was where we shared good and bad news together with the whole family. Well, most of the family, as the Big Indian was still missing. We had each other, if nothing else….a special closeness. And to think, an hour ago I was going to selfishly absorb this news alone. I had made a wise decision to share its contents, and we mutually agreed that whatever was in the letter, good or bad, it could be best accepted while being shared. Anticipation welled in their eyes, and their little chests heaved from heavy breathing and excitement. No one said a word as I opened it ever-so-gently….careful so as not to shred any vital clues on the envelope.

And there it was:

"Dear Juni, Cindee, Steve and Jeff, I am sorry it has been so long since I last wrote to you…."

My heart swelled, and my throat almost closed as the lump grew bigger. I thought, "Dear God, he is alive, and our prayers have been answered." I couldn't read anymore; the tears had obscured any vision and courage I may have had when we first sat at our conference table. We went to pieces, each hugging and kissing and crying out loud. We weren't four….we were one.

Finally, I managed to read another part of its contents, although other parts of the letter had not been meant for them.

It went on;

"I've been busy, and I'm still here in Vietnam. The war has gotten worse, so they still require my capabilities. I don't mean to let you down, but I honestly don't actually know when I'll be back to the States. Hopefully, soon. I've got to …… and ……."

The letter went on to say a bunch of other stuff that I'd rather not repeat. There was a lot of "business" discussed that they did not deserve to know about, as it would only hurt them more than they deserved. They had suffered so much already. Then came the ending; he had signed it: "I love you and miss all of you so much. Kiss the kids for me. Love, Doug"

Beautiful words….and I continued staring at his handwriting, and I ran my fingers over the words and traced each letter in black and white to see if it was really there. It was. He was alive and well, and it was his handwriting; I knew it. I traced the letters again: "Love, Doug"

Thank you, God. We talked into the middle of the night, as no one could sleep, and I heard footsteps and refrigerator doors in the early morning hours. A cold drink and a Kleenex to blow their nose on was the order of the day. I let them stay home from school…. and I checked in at the office; no one could concentrate on classes or business today. We studied the letter, and I reread the "good parts" over and over to them. It was the middle of the letter that upset me. He had told of his villa robbery and how "they" broke into it, and how "they" had stolen his personal papers and documents, his canceled checks, his tapes, all the communication and letters he had received, paperwork he had even prior to our joining him in Saigon in 1968….And then he told of his concern for our safety. "Our safety?" I read on. He indicated either Viet Cong or political forces had ransacked his villa; they had drawn weapons and held him and Chi Hia, the eldest maid, at gunpoint. He said they took a lot of personal items, and they denoted an air of suspicion as to his "employment" with no other explanation….

He was "concerned for our safety?" which bothered me greatly, and these words verified my fears of him being into something secret, or underhanded. Could it be that he was involved with the CIA somehow? And at the same time, he assured me he was not a prisoner. At least not at the time he wrote the letter he wasn't. Perhaps somewhere down the line he had been a prisoner, but not now. The enclosures in the letter scared me….checks, dozens of checks, and a list of names and phone numbers in varied states, and a note of explanation that these guys were back in the states now. It went on to say, "Would you please try to collect some of these checks owed to me, I think it would well be worth your time." He didn't go into any detail, nor did he explain the enormous amounts, but one glance indicated to me that they covered gambling on a very, very large scale. Each of the two dozen checks was in the thousands, or tens of thousands of dollars bracket…. could it have been one hell of a poker game? Bull shit. I wondered how so many people could owe him so much money, and what was the money for, and why didn't he deposit them in one of his many bank accounts in Asia and Hawaii? Or why had he not instructed me to deposit them in our joint account in Missouri? And the names; some of them I recognized. There was the base Chaplain, and Gen. Westmorland and his gang; they had secretly owned and operated a whore house and bar off Tu Do Street. And there was the Sargent from the MAC-V motor pool, and other officers whom I had never met on the base. They must have all been partners in something, because the majority of the checks were dated within a few days period. I didn't like it….It scared me even more than I had already been.

The Big Indian was asking me to make contact and collect what I could. No explanation, no details as to where he had been all these years, no reasoning as to why he never made it home on Christmas of 1968. There was just this letter saying he was sorry he had not written to us, that he missed us, and for me to do what I could with the money I could collect. But there was more, he had gone on to say he actually feared for our lives, and for me to be on the watch for anyone suspicious people around the neighborhood, not to let any strangers into the house, and went on to say he thought perhaps someone would try to kill us….He suggested the kids stay inside behind drawn drapes and locked doors. What in hell had possessed him to scare me to death? What was he mixed up in? He had put the fear of God in me, so I called the kids together again at our crowing table and was a bit more honest this time about "daddy's letter." They had to know, lest some stranger attempted to pick them up on the street or after classes….I had to warn them of strange people, though I could not explain the situation more fully. Hell, it hadn't even been explained to me, just a warning that we may be killed. All it did was petrify us so that we would walk glancing over our shoulders now and then, and not sleep with the lights on, jumping at each ring of the phone and with every knock on the front door. We kept the drapes drawn closely, and the kids went back on curfew again, just like in Saigon, accounting more explicitly for their comings and goings. Time schedules and a nightly report at the big table as to everything they had observed during the day, any suspicious people or calls or automobiles on our street; we became even closer than before. We were reliving the war again; our nerves and fears gripped us. The only difference was we didn't know who to look out for…. maybe an unknown enemy here in Missouri? I thought of the Mafia, and of gangsters and Communists, not knowing what they would look like if I saw one in our neighborhood. Any strange noises in the night brought them quietly sneaking into my bedroom to warn me, and together, we would check it out. If he was CIA, was the KGB after us?

The most miserable situation was wanting to share with our loved ones, and our friends the good news that daddy was alive and that we had received a letter. But knowing my mother would want to "read it" out of genuine concern, and my best girlfriends would also be interested, so it was kept a secret, I couldn't allow anyone to actually read the letter or see the checks. What do you say to a friend who has suffered with you all these years? Someone who shared a thousand and one pots of coffee, who listened while you talked of your missing husband, friends who consoled you on lonely evenings? This conjured conversation is like what was said with neighbors and best friends, co-workers, family and school chums when we finally mentioned the letter: "We had a letter from daddy, and he is alive. Isn't it wonderful!" They replied, "That's wonderful….where is he?" I said, "I don't know." They kept badgering me, "What do you mean you don't know? You're talking to him, aren't you?" All I could say was, "I just don't know, he didn't say." How could I not share the joyous news that I had a letter, and he is alive and evidently well? But the letter left me knowing less than before, confusing me more and more. People couldn't possibly understand. I know they couldn't, hell, I didn't even understand.

So, life went on in the Allen household, and it was a worse situation than before. Only my long-time friend and trusted attorney knew of the checks and had read the letter's contents. To everyone else, it was just a simple "I don't know" when we were questioned about the details of the letter. I made some calls regarding the checks, but even as of today's date, I can't disclose any information, as a pending file lies in a distant office. I knew the checks had something to do with the years of his disappearance, and I knew they had something to do with his being afraid for our lives….so they took the place of honor in hiding them with all the other correspondence. They were gathering dust till the right time when they would be introduced as evidence in a courtroom once again. I had only had them filed in my home office for two nights when I got to thinking, if anyone came to my house, as I surely didn't want them to find the checks, especially if he was afraid for our safety. So, the checks and letters made it across town to a place of safekeeping and guarded under lock and key, and I was free of evidence of any wrongdoings, monies legal or illegal, and I began to sleep better. I started my letter campaign again; I was determined to find him and know his manner of life if he was still alive. I wondered….There were too many pieces to the puzzle, and I couldn't fit them together. I registered another letter halfway around the world to my old villa address on Vo Than. Another returned letter stamped clear across both sides of the envelope, the same double versioned, double-red rubber smeared stamped from Vietnam that was totally illegible. Again, the foremost translator and friend deciphered it as saying, "No longer at this address" and "Return to Sender."

Months passed without another message from the Big Indian, and I know he feared for his life. I now presumed "they" had got him, and I went to the "presumable finding of Death Certificate" again, and again and again to no avail. Either the officials did not even bother to return the forms to me at all, or they were returned with a vague note attached stating they had no information on one "Mr. Douglas Eugene Allen." It was the same old story, yet he had been well known in Saigon, in all walks and phases of the military, political, social and street life. He had been well known from the men at Tan Son Nhut Air Force Base, and all the way down through the money exchangers of the street, the dock workers on the river and to the bar girls of Tu Do Street. And explicitly, Westmoreland's place. Dear man, what a farce he was to take monies from the G.I.'s and give to the prostitutes in the form of a cut on the Saigon Teas he sold at his house of ill repute. God, forgive me for what I think of him and his Vietnamese lady friend. Some money came into our joint account…. we had "experimented" and ran a few of the checks through my local bank to see what would happen. A few checks were good, but more were not honored, and so I found myself knee-deep dealing with irate, even mad, yet cooperative bankers who had never experienced this sort of thing before. This sucked just thinking about it.

My attorney was more interested in the case as the months went by, and he promised to assist with an investigation of his own. He checked into foreign banks, Asian banks where engineers, construction people, civil service and G.I.'s alike were known to make large deposits for various reasons, legal and some not so legal, rather than to send all their monies to wives and/or stateside accounts. He hit the jackpot and located several accounts. One bank account in Hawaii had over

$500,000 in it, and I wanted that money, at least Doug's part. I wanted it for the children's future security, so we proceeded to slap a lien against the accounts, tying them up for years. Too, we drained the local account and stashed a small fortune away; if I couldn't have my Big Indian, or be assured of his love for us, I would at least have his money. I became bitter….and slowly, I came to realize this was not a game like children play. This was espionage of a sort, a war game with rules of which I was not fully aware. I couldn't have cared less; he was over there, and I was here in Missouri, and I realized it was now or never to secure our future. I sure as hell wasn't getting anywhere with our investigation of the Big Indian's whereabouts, and I now felt certain our good officials were definitely keeping info from me. They had lied to me; they had known he was still in the country….and they knew it. So, something was up, but what? I couldn't find out the truth no matter how hard I searched, and it got to me, bad. I knew there was an answer out there somewhere, but where? Where would, or could I look?

The kids were all fine, polite teenagers coping awkwardly and inwardly as best they could with our situation. Life had to go on, and we had birthday parties and baseball games to attend, nights at the bowling alley, Thanksgiving at my sister's Kansas farm, and, naturally, Christmas at home-sweet-home. I especially remember one of Cid's birthday parties, it was difficult enough to plan and carry out events of supposed happiness when you are sad inside, but I was determined to make this party the best ever, just the way she ordered it. On the other side of the county, 60 miles away, across the bluffs of the muddy Missouri River and the Kansas plains, was the destination she had chosen for her party. A quiet country resort, complete with 2 spring-fed pools and grassy picnic areas, and simply named "Sun Springs." There was only one problem: she had a November 9th birthday….and November in Northwestern Missouri is cold, sometimes really cold; hardly a time for pools and picnics. But they had a skating rink, and she decided we would transport around a dozen close school chums to have a wiener roast over there, complete with hot chocolate to warm us from the brisk temperatures of winter, and that's exactly what we did. We were all standing around an open fire, huddling close together from the cold, munching on hot dogs and chili and sipping hot chocolate to stay warm. Bundled warmly in wool hats and mittens, knitted scarves of bright colors wrapped snugly around our necks, and blowing with the winds. What a party!!! But the kids managed to have a good time and we soon went into the enclosed skating rink… These joys we shared without a father, although he should have been a part of growing up. I even recall the Thanksgiving prayer Jeff wrote, and how proud I was when he announced he had been asked to read it at the Thanksgiving Program at school. And I remember the letter he wrote to President Nixon asking for help in finding his father. It was touching…I laughed, I cried, and it broke my heart. He was a tender child, and along with Cid and little Doug, he never fully understood what had happened to his dad.

Chapter 18

The time came when I thought I should quit the real estate office and go on to greener and more private pastures. It was becoming increasingly more difficult to concentrate on a boring job, and for the Senator, Senator Truman E. Wilson of Missouri as soon as he called. I had done a lot of campaign typing in my home office, so when he won his Senatorial election and offered me a permanent job as his private secretary, I was elated, to say the least! I assured him I would do my very best, and I remember his kind words as he said, "Well, Juni, that's about all I can expect of you. If everyone always gave his best, then we sure would have a grand world." Knowing he had said that, I knew right then and there that he was one of the finest men I ever had the pleasure of knowing, and/or working with to this day. Hell, I was scared to death the first morning… .I was actually afraid of the job, but he assured me I would learn quickly, and he would be patient with me while I was learning. The Senator was an insurance executive and had the District Senate office, as well as his insurance company, so I soon learned everything from Legislation to Credit Life and Keogh Plans. He employed several good men on his staff, and they were all cooperative and helpful as I learned the business of insurance, but the senator himself taught me everything I know about legislation and politics.

At first, I had a lack of confidence and fear and total fright of being at his side 8 hours a day; this intelligent, kind, brilliant, wonderful person was so far above me in a God-like manner. I had actually put him on a pedestal and worshipped him for his fine qualities. The job scared me, but he soon assured me that he had more confidence in me than I had in myself, he said he knew that I could, and would do a good job, so I did. I had started with him when he leased small offices on the south side of a local bank, but we soon moved to larger offices out on the Belt Highway there in St. Joseph. It was plush, yet comfortable; efficient, yet relaxed; it had an atmosphere in which to work. My co-workers were wonderful….always ready to lend a hand or take the time to show me something, or answer my questions. I soon picked it up and was hammering out credit life policies by the dozens, handling all incoming calls, both senate and insurance-related, reassuring his constituents and finding time to handle claims. As time went by, he gave me more and more Senatorial duties, and soon, he took me from the Insurance payroll and made me Senatorial 6th District Secretary, a real title. This meant a nice pay raise and better state benefits, including state credit union and retirement….of which I was very proud.

I was happy working for him as he was a sweet, tender boss-man whom I greatly admired. He ran for re-election; another battle, and we geared up the campaign for a big win. Later, he ran for Congress, but we lost that one, yet we learned a lot from the campaign, and we cried together when the results came in. But it had been exposure, and we agreed he would do battle for a Congressional seat at some future date, perhaps using the Governorship as a steppingstone. He was top material. I used to tell him when he went to Washington that I wanted to go along, and he assured me I would, as his private secretary….we had big plans. The Senator had taught me a lot, and he had compassion for my missing husband. He was interested and very helpful with my matters concerning government officials….he advised me to the best of his abilities, and yet listened when I just wanted to talk. He respected me for fighting all the red tape, and for being insistent when I hit brick walls and dead alleys. He always encouraged me to continue and to not give up hope for my Big Indian's return. But I longed for an affair, one I could live with without an abundance of shame or remorse, one that I could handle comfortably. My body got wracked with loneliness; I was starved for love, tenderness and affection. The Senator knew I had a close friendship with Lucky, the Representative from the eastern part of the state. I suspected he was a real-life Mafia man, and he was tall, handsome, balding, sexy….and Italian. I cherished the trips I made to the capital on business and the nights he put me up in the Governor's suite, or in his friend's trailer across town, as we always managed to have our privacy and fulfillment in love. We danced at the legislative hang out, drank it up at the Rathskeller, and he prided himself in my company, just as I did in his. He would introduce me to other politicians, but never share me, and soon, I was spoken of as "Lucky's girl," and I loved it.

Lucky was soft and gentle with me, and often, we would talk about the Big Indian all night. He was more than a lover; he was indeed my very best friend during those years. He found all the numerous business reasons so he could journey to the District Senate Office, and I loved it when he called and softly said, "Hi Baby, can I have tonight?" We dined elegantly and often, always with business associates and politicians, but we always had just each other for the remainder of the night. We made passionate love most nights; some nights, we just held each other tight, knowing it would be gone when daylight cracked through the drapes….Our feelings were mutual, and we grabbed every chance that came along for us to be together. Several hundred miles separated us, but the distance seemed short when one of us was traveling to be with the other. I flew commuter planes, commercial planes, and limousines with the chauffeur; but sometimes, I drove my own car. I often commuted with other legislators, never turning down a chance to spend time with Lucky. But most of the time, he came to me. He snagged an inspection of the same State Hospital where I had bad job memories; that was an excuse to spend a lot of time in my hometown. And I loved it, and we were more than lovers; we shared closeness only good friends could possibly know. Our sex was soft yet explosive, stolen yet gifted from one to another, wholly and completely. I found and shared love in his bed like no other love I had ever known.…I felt I could put an end to this pursuit of the Big Indian's missing status and go into another world with Lucky, but he had his family tucked away in the suburbs of his north-eastern Missouri city. Never wanting to intentionally embarrass the children, or the family, I learned to cover my tracks well. I fell into a State Representative's outstretched arms for temporary security and satisfaction, seeking what I had lost in the dark-skinned arms of my Big Indian. I was a normal human-being trying to survive, and without the robust sex life I had been used to with this one-time love of my life. In the affair I was having with Lucky, it was more serious than I had bargained for: not only was he a man, but a tender person and a good listener. This God-like man thrust upon me in my loneliness.…He allowed me to talk, and cry, both before and after the lovemaking, and he understood my need for a shoulder to lean on. He heard me when I spoke; he cared when I was there. We had something beautiful, though I imagine my talking about the Big Indian was my way of apologizing for being there with him, and I was there often. I accepted this substitute when the pain was unbearable, and I could no longer stand the isolation.…But I could not get my mind off of Doug, his thoughts hindered me day and day out, even when I was in the presence of Lucky. And that hurt; being with one man, all the while thinking and dreaming about another. Deep down inside, I knew that I really did love my Big Indian so much, and so being with Lucky was only for the passing times. It began to really bug me though, being around Lucky so often, so I started my trek of ending a relationship, if that was even possible….

Doug finally wrote to me. His letter arrived mid-December of 1974, assuring us he would land stateside in time to celebrate Christmas Day with us, and although it was 6 years later after we had left, I was still looking forward to a Missouri holiday with him. Knowing he would land before the 25th made me the happiest woman on earth as I read his letter, and the children were jubilant and fought over the telephone so they could spread the good news to all their friends. I cried when I heard them say, "My daddy is coming home for Christmas!" and we all had a good, hard cry. It was reassuring, good news. They had finally gotten back into the class routine, but now school would soon be out for a 2-week Christmas holiday, and they were looking forward to the vacation to play in the deep snows that covered the ground daily. That winter, the ground stayed so clean, as we had fresh snow almost daily, and it never had time to get dirty….I hastened my last-minute shopping and wrapping, being careful to hide the gifts in a secret place, except for the large ones that would go under the tree. I decorated the front porch with bows of evergreen and holly. This was to be a super holiday! And I was elated that he was leaving the war, and that we would have 30 days of official R & R to forge the horrors of the Vietnam War.

I was thinking how wonderful it would be as a family again, and their daddy would be there to give them their good night hugs and kisses, followed by an evening cocktail and long conversations in front of the fireplace. With 30 days of togetherness, I was already anticipating the flight to the next job site, we would be heading to Heidelberg, Germany, amidst the castles and forests of the River Rhine. This time though, we would be flying to a peaceful, beautiful country. I had experienced enough war, and I was given the grand tour of Asia; from the King-Of-Siam's now-turned-hotel in Bangkok, Thailand, to the beautiful cherry blossom trees of Japan, and everywhere in between on our trip back home. But this time….the forests in the Rhine would be relaxing, serene and educational, compared to the street fighting of Vietnam. I could already taste Germany's famous dark beer and visualize colorful clothing, street dancing, and robust bodies enjoying life. There would be no more starving children and dead bodies to count on the way to the office. There would be gaiety and beauty, unlike Vietnam. Laughter would ring out in joy. There would be no more hiding as we were forced to do in Saigon. The language of German would be easier for the children to learn, my father being of Dutch ancestry, and my Mother German

Jewish. I could already speak the language minimally, and I was anxious to hear the kids speak it fluently. It had to be easier than learning Vietnamese….or at least it seemed. What a chore that was. The trip would be one of culture and history, which would broaden their now war-torn minds, and it would enable them to take history courses later in High School and College. They had learned so much in Asia from the textbooks my parents had sent, that the lack of a formal classroom had not hurt them. I had been assured of a fine educational system in Heidelberg, so I was anxious for them to be enrolled. We had so much to look forward to, and nothing to be afraid of, like the last trip we went on….

So, I made up my mind to really enjoy the Big Indian over the holidays, as shortly after, we would be packing and traveling again headed to Europe. He was coming home for Christmas! We said our nightly prayers even louder, prayers of thanks. His letter said he was taking a small crew "upcountry" to check out radar towers, and he assured me after this brief run, he would be returning to Saigon to catch his flight home to the States. He said he was looking forward to an old-fashioned Christmas in the Midwest. A "real Missouri Christmas," as he put it, complete with Santa's visit, mince and pumpkin pies, turkey and Yankee oyster, celery, mushroom and sage stuffing, snow and sleds, toboggans and ice-skates, fat snowmen melting on the front lawn, the carrot noses withering with afternoon sunshine….Even mom and dad were just about as happy as they've ever been, having the grandchildren back home safely from the war, so having Doug joining us within the next few days made them doubly happy. After he arrived, I knew he would call his mother to fly up from Little Rock….it would be a fun, wonderful 30 days before it was time to travel again. I was pondering whether to replace the old star on the Christmas tree, and that's when Cid suggested we make a pretty gold one from heavy foil and trim it in lace. As I thought this over in my mind, I recalled a temple we had toured in Asia, a most beautiful, glistening temple full of solid gold statues, fat-bellied Buddha, and God-like creations with jeweled eyes and belly-buttons, based at the foot of a magnificent creature. But Asia was behind me now….I had a new world ahead of me and with my Big Indian. I wanted this very special Christmas tree to revel in the same temple-like splendor, so Cid and I started without a pattern and finished with a fantastic tree-top star. We carefully cut it out of cardboard, covered it with heavy gold foil, edging it in lace and sprinkled glitter on small daubs of glue, and we centered a hold for the twinkling gold bulb that would take the place of honor to show off its entire beauty. The twinkling light would enhance the glitter; it was lovely, and we were so proud of it. We carefully laid it in a shoebox full of crushed tissue so daddy could have the honor of securing it to the top of the tree….the honor of finalizing the tree decorating. It was customary after the last decoration went on to settle down for a cozy cup of eggnog, symbolizing the beginning of the actual holiday. Cid and I were convinced, and we knew daddy would secure it firmly atop our big, long needle pine tree. We anticipated his arrival, and the "topping of the tree" would be the certainty that Christmas was indeed here, and that daddy was finally home.

Doug had sounded so anxious in his December letter that he said, "I'll be there for Christmas, and I have shipped my men and equipment to other Asian job sites. And after this brief trip up-country, I will be returning to Saigon for my flight home." He told Steve, "You are the man of the house, so take care of Jeff and your sister, and help Mama out with whatever you can." It was touching advice to the eldest son, the son whom so many people called Little Doug. It was going to be a grand finale to my year of war and suffering. I was going to end the year in style, with my Big Indian home from the war, as this was the answer to my prayers. Our separation had been painful and long….there would be no more tears or goodbyes. We would be a family once again. I busied myself with cleaning, wrapping and baking, trying hard to control the excitement in my voice, the lumps in my throat and the knots in my stomach. We waited in suspenseful, but anxious anticipation, yet not aware of the exact landing date. His letter had ended: "I love you, Juni, and I can't wait to get home." Memories of the past year were creeping into my thoughts, so I settled cozily on the couch with a glass of wine. I remembered all the ups and downs the

Big Indian and I had over the past dozen years. I recalled the nights of fear, as well as the evenings of fun….I remembered the hundreds of friends we had made, the Stingers over the rocks, and my 36th birthday bash and pig roast. I remembered the Vietnamese children's swollen bellies on Saigon's streets, and the mamason's selling their bodies so a hungry child could have rice that day. God awful war. And most of all, I remembered Kim and my insane jealousy of her, and wondering if she was aware that her "Mr. Doug" was indeed leaving her city and coming home to his American wife. God it hurt….

We had the house in shape, and you could see your reflection on the hardwood floors. The windows were so clean you could gaze across the boulevard's lamp post and count each and every snowflake as it fell. Yes, we were open for business, and we could hardly wait to hear its walls ring with laughter. We were filled with the holiday spirit; we busied ourselves with whatever last-minute chores we could find, but as the time drew nearer to the 25th, we found it increasingly difficult to do anything but sit by the phone. We were anticipating that final call giving us a precise landing date and time. Would it be the 22nd? The 23rd? Or would it be Christmas Eve? It was hard to make any plans with the family to set up any dinner dates, or family get-together gatherings until I actually knew when he would land… .I would not have missed that call for anything. I was elated. The Big Indian coming home for Christmas was

God's greatest gift to us. We would start over again, and everything would be clean, pure and fresh, like the blanket of snow covering the entire city. It had been over six years since we had departed Saigon, yet it seemed like it was only a year. It was a war in this tearful goodbye at Tan Son Nhut Air Force Base.

Our star never made it to the top of the tree….

Little did I know at that time, but the Big Indian's routine would turn into 7 long years of waiting, 7 difficult years. He never made it home, and as far as that goes, I wouldn't see him again until 1975. He was probably in Kim's arms, making plans for his Christmas over there. For a long time, I couldn't even talk about it, and no one could possibly understand how I felt when his phone call didn't come. Christmas came, and Christmas went, and the kids and I had little to say to each other, each grieving and asking, "Why?" He hadn't called…. Our last contact with him had been the letter in mid-December assuring us he would be there in time for Christmas. The gold star never made it to the top of the tree. The guests never arrived because I had asked them not to come. The kids and I wanted to be alone to try to understand what had happened, as the pain we felt was almost too heavy to endure in the coming days ahead….And back at school, their classmates had too many prying questions, although asked in total innocence, they scarred their hearts a little deeper. I felt so sorry for them. What were they to say when their friends asked, "Did your daddy make it for Christmas Eve? Is he coming to school to talk to our class?" This was the Christmas we had never celebrated. It was like it didn't even happen....

Mounds of gifts were unopened and set on the closet shelf to gather dust. Neat stacks of linens were never unfolded, and prepared holiday foods soon went by way of the garbage disposal and down the pipe. Friends and family called and offered sincere concern and comfort, but we were unable to discuss the situation; we were dazed with total hurt. I was worried, then embarrassed. His letters ceased and having no explanation for the situation soon sent me into a psycho retreat. We had no idea if he was a prisoner, if the mission "up country" trip had been fulfilled, and if he had actually stayed behind to be with Ms. Kim....My mind was reeling with total confusion. I cried for days. The kids and I huddled close together, silently understanding each other's thoughts and not speaking a word. We had each other, and we became closer than ever before, making a new world and forbidding everyone else to step into it, lest they would disturb our thoughts. January passed, February and soon spring. The kids were doing remarkably well in school, considering they, too, were burdened with their father's disappearance. Was he alive, or was he dead? Was he missing, or in prison? Where was he? Oh God, if I had asked that question once, I would have prayed to God a million times....He was gone, and that's all I knew.

He had not returned home for Christmas as he had promised. There were no 30 days of R & R together. There was no new jobsite assignment in Germany. The severeness of the disappearance overtook me, and I continued crying and became even more hurt. It was hard to work, even harder to answer the kid's questions. Oh, how it broke my heart to see their little faces with tears streaming down as we gathered around the television for the evening war news. How they suffered, the Christmas tree stayed up until the needles started to fall off. I couldn't bring myself to take it down. It never twinkled because we mutually agreed not to light it till daddy came home. But by mid-January….it was too painful to look at any longer, and the boys drug it out to the alley for the trash pickup. The tree that was to hold so much joy, now held bad memories of a Christmas that never was. By summer, I had written a thousand letters, and made a thousand calls. I desperately sorted ideas in my mind, ideas of his capture….and his torture, then I played with the idea of his remaining in Saigon willingly. I wondered if he was doing CIA, mainly because he was so secretive and he carried a lot inside of him with his top security clearance, or if he couldn't bear to leave Kim? And had he fathered her a second child, a girl child….perhaps he did have a good reason to stay in Vietnam? Or had he somehow gotten mixed up in the street and dock rackets and flourished so openly in Saigon? No, not my Big Indian. He wouldn't steal from the government or armed forces. Then I thought perhaps he had gotten into the lucrative money exchange rackets that flourished in Saigon, and where he had made millionaires out of paupers over there. Or had his company sent him to another area within Vietnam, and it had happened so suddenly that there was no time to call me? Dumb thinking on my part, for certainly I would have been notified, I think. Wouldn't I….?

I had to know if he was still in South Vietnam. I intensified my search and my letter campaign to the Department of Defense, to the Department of War, to the President and local politicians. To Teddy Adawag's home address in the Philippines, to Tan Son Nhut Air Force Base in Saigon, to his parent company; Page Communications in Washington D.C. where he had originally worked. My thirst for information was desperate, and I begged for the truth. I received nothing concrete to go on, and I wrote to find out if passport and visa records showed him departing South Vietnam. I wrote Doug himself at the old address…. hoping it will be forwarded. When the registered mail came back unopened, I did not give up; I followed up each letter with another letter. Our own United States government and military officials were of little help or consolation….and all of their replies read the very same: "We are sorry to inform you, but we have no word on the disappearance of your husband. We suggest you write 'such and such." And I did. Some nights, I sat at my typewriter half of the night and mounds of paperwork.

All the while, my anger grew into bitterness untold. I even put tracers on my mail. I wrote the President, I casually threatened him if he didn't send a search party into Saigon to look for Doug....then I was going to sue him, and for what, I did not know. Well, that didn't even work, or even scare him, I think? Damn, God, wasn't I entitled to know if he was dead or alive? I made threats to other government officials, and I presume that's when my name went on the blacklist in Washington, D.C., alongside names of possible assassins, but I really didn't give a damn. I had to know where, when and why my Big Indian was missing....

We needed a change of scenery, and as it was just a couple blocks off the boulevard where we had been living and awaiting his holiday arrival, and where we still shared the same friends and neighbors. The children could finish their year at the same school, and they sure didn't need any more major disruptions in their young lives. The letters all said the same thing: a big nothing. I was assured they had no records of a 'Mr. Douglas Eugene Allen' leaving the country, and yet they had no documented proof of him being Missing in Action or a Prisoner of War, and no proof he was even still in the country. They lied to me. I was crazy about the unknown. I became possessed with a desire for knowledge I did not have. I stayed up nights writing letters, but the only thing I gained was typing speed.... We fought over the front page of the newspaper, and jockeyed for prime viewing seats in front of the TV at news time. We watched the news for views of prisoners, and occasionally caught a glimpse of a tattered prisoner being marched down a road, or of a prisoner being indoctrinated in a dim room. We saw men in cages in prison yards. We saw them shackled and crawling in the dirt, and we strained to see if any of these desolate men could be our Big Indian. I knew he was alive, but where? I felt it. I wondered if he knew I was crying during the night, and I turned my pillow over to the dry side. "Oh god, help me," I had prayed 24 hours a day, 7 days a week….My letters of inquiry as to his disappearance became more hostile as the months went by. One particular government official had asked me if I could get a "Presumptive Finding of Death" form signed by an official of the Saigon city government, a Saigon funeral director, an official of the Army or Air Force on Tan Son Nhut Air Force Base, or a Saigon physician to sign the form, They said that they would then, and only then, presume Mr. Douglas Allen to be legally and truly dead for purposes of banking records.

I mailed "Presumptive Finding of Death" forms to each of the above authorities, but no one wanted to put their "John Henry" on a line attesting that Mr. Allen was indeed dead. I even mailed the form with a plea letter to the base chaplain in Saigon, and all of his replies were identical. "I am sorry to inform you, but I cannot sign this form attesting to Mr. Douglas Allen's death, as I am not certain, and have not, as of today's date viewed a body. Nor can I produce records of death or burial in this country." And they went on to say they were sorry they could not help me, and blah, blah, blah. Another dead-end alley…. it seemed no one was able or willing to help, and here I was, writing halfway around the world trying to get some answers. I stared out the windows as I sat in darkness at my desk, and I used to "see" the Big Indian. He would be approaching the house from the boulevard in the distance, and I would cry convulsively and say to myself, "There comes Doug, he is coming, God, I thank you." And I believed it, I really did. I could see him as he neared the grassy rise beyond the backyard, making his way closer. Sometimes, he would be running, and I knew he was in a hurry to get there.

Then, I would crawl into bed and let the swollen eyes rest, hoping they would open in the morning so I could go to work. What a miserable period I endured. The unknown; I was bewildered as to his thoughts. Was he chained in a prison camp, crying out for me in pain? Was he being tortured? Was he thinking of getting home to his kids? Or was he there on his own, by his own choice and hiding out? Had he made a new life with Kim? Or had our government, the same government that refused to cooperate with me regarding his status in this world, been lying to me about where he really was? But, somehow I managed to raise the kids and keep my sanity to some degree….and until someone proved to me that he was dead, I consoled myself by thinking, "he will be home someday." I contacted other

MIA and POW families, and I attended conventions and rallies in support of our missing men. I distributed bumper stickers and window decals, typed envelopes for tens of thousands of mailouts, and grabbed every chance that came my way to speak to small groups detailing the plight of our missing men and POW's and relating I worked closely with other parents and wives who wondered "where" and "what" regarding their own particular case. Each had lost a loved one and needed the closeness and moral support of our groups. I proudly wore a MIA bracelet for a "Capt. Michael Johnson," I envied the ones whose congressman had actually contacted them with some definite information as to the status of their man, as at least they knew something. Some knew the dates of capture, the site of the prison, or where they had confirmation of witnessing their husband's abduction. Whether or not it was any easier on them having some details….I never knew. Sometimes, I thought it best not to have details because information could only force your mind to conjure up a picture of the abduction or capture that would haunt you 24 hours a day. Maybe it was best not to know, but regardless, we waited, and life went on. It was just another sad day for tens of thousands of us, and it hurt….

My home office was piled high, and I had found it necessary to purchase another file cabinet before things got too out of hand. I worked days in the work office, and nights in the home office, keeping myself busy so I didn't have a lot of time to be alone. But just before retiring for the night, that was the most difficult time of all when I would stare out the windows and across the lawn, only to "see" him running towards me. But I hung in there, and somehow managed to be a half-assed mother to the kids, as they needed some type of parental control in their life, I fed them, though sometimes the meals were not exactly what they should have been; all it depended on my mood….I clothed them, though I could not really get into shopping, and I shuttled them back and forth to school and scouts, and to ball games like a robot. But one thing is for sure; I never fell down on my love and devotion for them, and they knew it. There was never any question or doubt of our love for each other. We continued searching the newspapers and evening television newscasts for any shred of information that might give us a clue. We secretly prayed for a glimpse of him in some of the downtown Saigon street scenes in the news film, and once, I thought I saw him? An American civilian in a white car….we had owned a white Toyota in 1968. The sighting haunted me, and I tucked the image under my pillow and slept with it for years to come. Perhaps, he was indeed alive. He had told me so many times during our talks that we were not fighting this war to win…. and to this day, I believe him in those words.

About the only thing I really did right all those days was to visit my folks, and often. My folks, the most wonderful people on this Earth, oh, how I loved them.

They were real, down-to-earth, fine folk, and most of all, they were always there when I needed them. They were a pillar of strength to Cindee during her four years of college….they gave her reason to survive just by being there, and too, they never said "no" to her needs when emergencies arose. Steve and Jeff were happily building go-carts from parts they could scrounge, and to this day, I swear they traded their radios and trains that Santa brought them for some bigger wheels and tools that did something. But what? I'll never know.

Chapter 19

Cam Tu wrote of seeing my Big Indian. She told me, "I observed Mr. Doug when he walked to the next teller window, and I am very certain it was him." I had no reason to doubt her sighting, as he had always been easy to spot in a crowd; his weathered skin stretched over the high cheekbones and topped by wavy brown and silver hair. Also, there were not many American Cherokee Indians in downtown Saigon. So, he was banking at the Bank of America. He is alive! She had penned this information so I would not give up hope, knowing if there was any shred of evidence to keep me going, I would not give up my search. I pursued the matter and made the information available to government officials....but they wrote they could not launch a search for him as I had requested, even though I had proof he was still in Vietnam. I had begged them to launch a search party....hell, they could afford it! I was grateful for any clues denoting his status, and her letter gave me hope, knowing he was alive. But as I read on, she said she spoke to him, and he turned and walked out of the Bank of America without even completing his banking transaction. She had met Mr. Doug many times so it was now apparent he did not want to be recognized by any of my friends. Apparently afraid they would notify me of his whereabouts, or at least he thought so. But why? How could he do this to the children? Didn't he know the pain and suffering he had caused us?

On two later occasions, Cam Tu said he was seen elsewhere within the city, and co-workers of Cam Tu's had spotted him in restaurants and bars…. these sightings were within a couple of years after I had returned to the States and I was so desperate for any bit of information. She had tried hard at playing "super spy," and it was actually very dangerous for her own welfare and that of her children. You just don't "screw around" spying if you are a civilian. In Saigon, the Commies are always on your left and over your shoulder, incognito and ready to jump to report your "actions." So, asking questions was risky for Cam Tu.…and "snitching" on someone who is deliberately hiding within a war could well mean your life by not knowing precisely just what his work may be. Yet she took these chances and informed me as best she could. Her info was never 100% absolute, so it was difficult as I pieced together the puzzle of his disappearance and surmised, he might be involved in something I didn't like or understand.

Good News: It came in the form of a limp, well-traveled envelope bearing a strange return address reading "Manama, Bahrain." It was a long-awaited answer to my letter of inquiry and was from Doug's ex-employee and our friend, Teddy Adaway. I thought, "Where in the hell is Bahrain, South America?" My years of education failed me as I recalled the mystery of another faraway place years ago….when the Big Indian first announced he was taking an overseas job in Saigon, South Vietnam. That had been over 10 years ago, as he first went to S.E. Asia in the early 60's to make his engineering fortune on the coast of the South China Sea. Teddy explained his loyalty to both of us: his ex-boss, and his family…. Like friends of his, and the letter is worthy of quoting as it held valuable information that would answer the 7-year-old question: "Was the Big Indian alive? Was he still in Vietnam? What did Teddy know about his whereabouts and the well-being of Doug?" Teddy's letter was dated early February of 1975, only a few short months before the Americans pulled out of Vietnam in defeat….and just before the Marines pulled our people over the Embassy wall.

The heading was:

Teddy Adaway

Brown & Root - Wimpey Middle East S.A. Engineers - Constructors

P.O. Box 780

Manama, Bahrain

And It was dated February 8, 1975.

Teddy wrote he was sad after reading what he felt was Mr. Doug's lack of interest in caring about the situation and concern of for his family back in the U.S.A. He even wrote his brother in Vietnam and hoped to later advise me of Mr. Doug's location, home address and working location. Teddy told me that after I left Saigon in late '68, the Big Indian had a "big villa and a sort of restaurant/casino" near Tan Son Nhut air base. At that time, he was not satisfied with his cook, and he asks asked Teddy to provide him with a good one. It so happened that he knew somebody, and just an hour after learning of his need, he was able to get him an expert cook. Before he had this place near Tan Son Nhut Air Base, your information was correct: Doug had remained by choice instead of flying home for Christmas of '68. He was working with Philco-Ford/Motorola, and during that time, he had a little restaurant on top of the Monterey Building, which happened to be sort of BBQ of U.S.A.I.D. As to why he had totally turned his back on you and his children is something which I don't know, for when the topic comes to discussing his family, he tries to shift the conversation to a different topic, so I cannot give any idea as to why as you had said he had forgotten all of you.

"Yes ma'am, to me, who was a close friend of Mr. Allen, I cannot fathom the depth of his reasoning why he didn't even try to inform you as to, ma'am. To me, who was a close friend of Mr. Allen's, I cannot fathom the depth of his reasoning as to why he didn't even try to inform you of his whereabouts for the past years. It seems that he wants to stay forever as a married bachelor, and without responsibility and obligation whatsoever. I feel guilty in writing such words about a man whom I had considered as a great friend, but in your letter, I could feel the deep and great need of for the presence of your husband, Mr. Allen. On regarding your question about his being a bigamist and 'married' a Vietnamese, I can say that he had not done it, yet most of the time I knew that he visits the bars along Tu Do Street, and I know that he has some 'girl friends', but not a steady one. Ma'am, I know the hardships of bringing up a family, especially in your case. All of your children are going to school. I would like to help, even a little bit. Will it be alright with you, Ma'am? I am a friend to you, and to Mr. Allen, and to us Filipinos, we help our friends if there is something we can do to help without expecting anything in return. I hope you will not misunderstand this offer that I am making, and I just want to help and nothing more… Well, Ma'am, I will be closing this letter now, and I will be waiting for your next letter and any news that I'll receive from my brother in Saigon. I will let you know whatever it is. Regards to Cindy, Stephen and to my buddy, the one and only Jeff Lee Allen.

Your friend, Teddy Adawag"

Talk about a good man, there is one right there. He offered to help me, knowing full-well that our paths would never cross. Bless you, Teddy, bless you….

In 1975, the Communists began their victory drive in Saigon…. there were too many people and too few planes for Americans to get out. Saigon itself was cut off. Bribes were offered to get on choppers and planes. People were killed, many trampled as others pushed towards waiting aircraft, not wanting to be left behind in the hands of communist victors now patrolling their streets. Choppers were flying from Saigon to ships in the sea…and as they landed, their choppers were pushed off into the sea to clear the landing pad for other choppers hovering above, waiting for their turn to land. Hundreds were shoved into the sea….save the pilots who had flown to the American naval ships for asylum, but no room for helicopters, so off they went. Whoosh….the chopper hit the water and settled calmly on the bottom of the China Sea. Some say the ocean floor is lined with Gold, meaning the amount of money in choppers that lays there today. Over the wall in April of '75….the communists began a victory drive further south, the main target: Saigon. I remember watching the dramatic escape on TV, as did everyone in the world, especially in the United States. Too many people and planes for the Americans to get out. Cam Tu and her party were of the unfortunate who had seats and promises of boarding a plane with the Bank of

America, but somehow, her boss managed to sell her seats to others, perhaps wealthier South Vietnamese? We'll never know.

Cam Tu's older brother Kien was a helicopter pilot for the South Vietnamese Air Force, so when the American Embassy was stormed by the Viet Cong, all he could think about was getting Cam Tu and as many members of his family out of the country as possible. They had set a time and location for a rendezvous, and Kien was to land his chopper, take them aboard, and head to the safety of a waiting American ship. This second attempt to escape Vietnam didn't work out. Cam Tu and family were waiting at the appointed spot, but Kien found it impossible to land in the designated area and had to abandon all rescue efforts at the last minute….Either that, or get shot down by the Viet Cong. The gunfire was heavy on that spring day in 1975 when he flew across rough seas to set his chopper down on a USS carrier ship, leaving his family far behind. It was a "flight of survival" for Kien, getting out from under the very conquerors that would capture him and send him to "The school of love, the school of indoctrination" to change his way of thinking. He landed safely on the pad, and American sailors were yelling at him to jump, and as soon as his feet touched the deck….he was amazed to see dozens of sailors shoving and heaving his beloved machine into the sea to a watery grave. And just like his chopper, many more were hovering above behind him, all awaiting the clearance notice of the pad so they, too, could land. It was their only hope to escape the Communist takeover of their country; make it to a waiting ship or ditch it in the sea. It was difficult for Kien to see his chopper under the motion of rough waves, now churned by the blades in the water as they quit turning. It was one machine after another being pushed over-side in order to clear the decks and make room for people, a much more valuable cargo than the choppers. So many choppers were shoved over the edge, all the while hundreds of lives were saved as these helicopters sank slowly to the floor of the South China Sea for their final resting spot; a rusty graveyard….

Prior to this, in 1973, Nixon had announced a plan, a cease-fire agreement to the world, an agreement that "would end the war and bring America a peace with honor." In January of this year, Le Duc Toe and Henry Kissinger supposedly had this agreement: a cease-fire. But the American public decided they had again been taken. They would not see a cease-fire, no more than they would see and partake in an honorable end to the war. It was a ploy, another lie by politicians to the public. We were losing in the worst way, lives being snuffed out by the thousands even as Nixon spoke. There was no cease-fire and no peace. There was, instead….Watergate: a shameful and later withdrawal of American forces in Vietnam, and a loss to chalk up to remind Americans we were not the great nation we had once been. We lost a war that was never meant to be won, and we paid for it with blood. It has been said and seen on TV that the North Viet Cong, was rambunctious in a victorious takeover of the Presidential palace in Saigon in '75 hurriedly raised their flag of giant proportions above the palace, but neglected to remove the South Vietnamese flag….So, for a while, both flags ruled and waved as though they were still at war, even when it had ended. The tanks were circling the grounds, the gates were crunched, and the victors, many boy soldiers, danced with the excitement of a victory ill-gotten. It had been the blood bath to end all bloodbaths….a war to end all wars….and our troops were cheated out of a victory they so badly wanted and so deservedly fought for. Damn war.

Teddy's news had demolished me. I was crushed at the thought we had waited 7 years, cried, watched thousands of news casts, written tons of letters of inquiry as to his missing status, and wrestled with the presumptive finding of death forms. We had waited while he ran a casino and restaurant, and had lots of girlfriend's in the heart of Saigon. But was he alive now? That was the last time Teddy had heard, and the war was fierce now, it was to come to an abrupt end in a few short weeks. South Vietnam was losing the war. Teddy was in South America on a new "site," and the Big Indian had remained willingly there. So, I continued waiting; I felt remorse, and hatred, yet still had the old concern and fear of the unknown.

Then they broke the news….it was all over. America had given up, we lost the war, and the Communists had stormed the Embassy. We lost our Police Action type war, and at the last minute, Marines had lent a hand to pull our people over the wall during the final escape to freedom. Had he made it out? Washington called me at my Senate District office, where I heard these words: "Mr. Douglas Allen got out; He and his briefcase were pulled over the wall. He is fine. He is on a ship and headed to Manila. He should be stateside within 15 days." My stomach turned, my eyes teared up, and I found myself saying, "Thank you, God." He is alive…. and he did get out. I was happy for the children. As for me, I didn't know if I wanted to see him or not. But we had this closeness, I knew he would come home, and it would be a meeting of mixed reactions. Could we handle it properly? After all, we were not sure what all he actually had gone through, he hadn't stayed intentionally to hurt us, or had he? Did I want him home? Would the kids be happy to see him, or were they still full of questions as to why he had not fathered them this past 7 years? How would they accept him? Would it be hugs and kisses and tears at our reunion, the kind of homecoming we had dreamed and prayed for during these long 7 years? My head was spinning, and I couldn't believe the call. He was out of it now…. and with his trusty briefcase full of secrets. Or was it full of money? I wanted to think it was filled with the love of my letters and the children's photographs, but I was only kidding myself....

From late '68 to mid-'75, he didn't pine over us, so why expect it now? But my thoughts were just exactly that: my thoughts, and I was entitled to them. My thoughts, hopes and dreams had been my husband for the past 7 long years, and now he was coming home. I had been alone for years before joining him in 1968. He had first accepted an overseas assignment in the early '60's, so marriage to an Indian with the main ingredient of Asia was a lonely partnership. What would our marriage be like now that he was headed home? Did we have a future together, and could I accept whatever reason he would give me for his absence? I worried about his health and wondered about his employment status for the future. Could he find sufficient peace within himself to be the husband and father that he was before Vietnam? I'm not sure anymore....

I lived in a vacuum. I went through a denial period. I couldn't talk about it; I couldn't say my husband had been missing, but I grieved over his disappearance greatly. Total depression and hopelessness. The children were young, and we couldn't talk about him being missing or in prison at first....the subject was just too deep. It was especially frightening for me because I had been in touch with American and Vietnamese officials, and I knew more than the kids knew. I didn't want them to know. I discussed my meeting with the

Senator, and he, too, was in a state of shock that the Big Indian had returned to the mainland. Mixed feelings of detest, happiness and bewilderment. What would my future hold?

Chapter 20

In May of 1975, a taxi brought him to our door. On closer observation, he turned out to be tough, shrewd, but intelligent. It was a summer evening, and the door was open, and there, through the screen, I saw the silver headed Doug pay the driver and remove his luggage. "Oh God," I was thinking, "this really is him." The children were hastily summoned and told, "He's here!" His greeting seemed sincere enough, complete with hugs and kisses and smiles and tears. It was a wonderful reunion, yet one of distance and bewilderment. He never told me where he had been or what he had been doing for 7 years, yet I was overjoyed in his embrace, and neither did I question him….It wasn't the right time to delve into such a deep subject. A full 7 long years had been a long time for all of us, and it would all come out when the time was right. But not now, this was a happy evening, one I had prayed for all that time. He sat with us and we drank thousands of cups of coffee; or at least it smelled like it. Small talk was made with his children, like "You've really grown" and "Have you been good, and did you help your Mother?" It made me happy, but on the other hand, it almost made me sick. Especially after all this time.

I thought, "How can a man just disappear off the face of the earth for 7 years, not knowing if we were dead or alive in Missouri, or New Jersey, and then walk into a homecoming and expect love and respect? Did he not know we waited and shed a thousand times a thousand tears? Did he not know how deeply he had scared the children? Did he not give a damn during those long, lonely years? Had he been a prisoner part of the time….or had he been there willingly, running his casino, gambling as we waited for news that would tell us if he was dead or alive? How could this man be smiling, when in the background he didn't even give a damn what happened to us the past 7 years?" I had no way of knowing, but soon, I was feeling the excitement and longing any wife would feel over her husband's 7-year homecoming. Total happiness enveloped my body, my Big Indian was home, and that's all that mattered….The day I had waited for was an end to 7 years of the God-awful unknown. He suggested we go to dinner and for us to get reacquainted, and so we did just that: out to dinner it was. Boom! We were a family of 5; a father, mother and 3 children really out to dinner. Appearing to be any normal family and showing no visible signs of 7-year distant separations, we entered the local restaurant and he had requested a corner table so we could have privacy. If anyone could eat more than a couple of bites, I don't recall; our nerves were jangled, and the kids were aghast because it had all happened so fast. Their chit-chat and small talk soon renewed the kids' adoration for their dad. It was great having a man to discuss bikes and boyfriends, motorcycles and makeup, camping and cartoons once again. For Cid, it was a little more difficult as Doug chided her about having gained weight, and it broke her heart, and understandably so….Wouldn't you think a father, one who hadn't seen his own daughter for 7 years, could find something in his heart to say to her other than his "fat" remarks? He was cruel, and it hurt her badly. But we smoothed it over. and eventually returned to the house for an after-dinner drink, and he invited me to dance. I called a neighbor to sit with the kids, as I knew I wouldn't be returning for hours, maybe days. I had waited too long for this togetherness. My Big Indian was home, and I deserved whatever time necessary to find out where we stood after waiting for so damned long.

The next evening, we went to a local club and ordered a drink; that's where it seemed like the whole town spotted him and soon swarmed around us, although it was actually only several people. Friends and his old buddies couldn't believe their eyes, and were saying things like, "Well, I'll be damned. Is that really you, Doug?" and "It's Doug Allen! We knew you'd make it home. Hell, you're too ornery to die." So, during that portion of the evening, I shared him with others, and rightfully so, but begrudgingly so. I still couldn't think of anything to say, all I could get out was, "Where have you been? Why did you do this to me? Do you know how we suffered not knowing if you were dead or alive?" But these answers, too, would have to wait, at least for now. We danced a little bit, and he held me close, sometimes too close. We knew what we wanted, and we remembered how good it had been, but when? Finally, the bar was closing, so we drove to a motel and checked in. We didn't talk on the way….the silence had created a bigger distance between us than inches and feet, both of us having our private thoughts about the other one. We slid between the sheets where he took me in his arms and kissed me, the kiss I had waited for years to have. No words were exchanged; we touched and held each other tight as we both cried silently. It was the only explanation I ever got, but I knew he was telling me how sorry he was that he had done us the way he had….If he wouldn't talk now, then he probably would later. We made love late into the night and later woke to sunshine and the birds chirping. The morning was different. No, actually, I felt dirty with him in a motel, more so than I would have with a stranger, but this absolute privacy had been so necessary. We were close, yet distant. Our words were short, yet sweet, but still, I could feel the distance between us….

Actually, I felt wrong being there with him. We were strangers after 7 years, and while the lovemaking was beautiful as it had always been, we had forgotten what it was like to be casual and be comfortable with each other. The words just weren't there, so we got up and dressed, and eventually drove our way back home.

The both of us fixed a leisurely weekend breakfast; scrambled eggs and bacon for the kids, all the while we stared at each other over our cups of steaming coffee, not quite finding the words that we should have found. He told me he loved me, he told the kids he missed them….but he never told us why he had not come home for all of those 7 years. We still didn't ask. The boys led him out to the patio to see their dirt bikes, and that's where I overheard their stories of how well they could hill-climb at the campground. Then they ventured to the basement to show off their workbench they had built… it was their make-do repair shop for the neighborhood. Later that afternoon, he suddenly announced quickly and matter-of-factly that he was flying to Little Rock to visit his mom….Well, that sounded logical, having not seen her for all these long years, and he asked if kids could drive with him to the K.C. airport to catch a flight and so they did. It was during that short reunion, and that's when I realized his mother certainly deserved his love, so driving him down there was his second wish-come-true for the holidays. Had he not invited me to make the trip to see him off on the trip to Arkansas, then I'm not sure how I would have handled his taking off in the middle of our first time together in over 7 years. They finally had their dad back…and boy, it was a nice feeling. The past few days seemed to be an eternity, literally raising their eyebrows every time they spoke to him, and with pure enlightenment. We dropped him off in the front of the airport, acting like it was just another day, and only on a few days' trip. We had our goodbyes, and they were really no different than any husband going off to the office; A hug. A kiss. And a "I'll be back in a few days…." But daddy never came back; he had somehow disappeared into the sky. Now, I had lost the Big Indian again; I could feel when he went to Arkansas that he was pulling a fast one. Once again, it made me wonder, "Why wouldn't he want his wife and kids to visit Grandma?"

I was later told he had hit the States with two Vietnamese women, so I presume they were pulled over the Embassy wall and made the voyage to freedom via the Philippines, so I supposed he was going to set them up in business in the States. The kids waited for his call, but it never came, and they were crushed when he made no more contact with them. Then they became bitter all over again, but this was a different bitterness. There were no mixed emotions like before, the tears and worry over his disappearance this time was too much to take. He had actually shafted them, and they fully understood his future intentions when he didn't call. He had lied…. They were hurt beyond belief this time, and their broken hearts were too heavily burdened to carry the hurt around. Heavier than during the other 7 years, he had once again promised and not kept his word. How can a dad do this? They couldn't understand it, they had already suffered the first 7 years without him, and so now, why had he done it again?

Their hearts were broken, and sometimes I wondered if they were literally broken....

So, he was gone, and we still didn't know what had kept him in Vietnam all those years. We really didn't care anymore, and we hardly talked about it, and I mean hardly. Many months went by, and then my attorney called and said the bastard had filed a custody case for them. He especially wanted Steve, as he had been somewhat partial to him, the one we often called Little Doug, his spitting image. But he had filed a custody case wanting all the kids, and my God, my world was falling down around me. How in hell could a man leave his kids for 7 years, not be concerned if they were dead or alive while he cajoled around the China Coast, and then all of a sudden he would turn-up and try to take them away from me? Was he crazy? Had the war done this to him? Any reasonable, intelligent person would know you can't desert and ignore your children for 7 years.... and then all of a sudden try to "claim them." Hell, hadn't I been the one to raise them, tote them to school, help throw their paper route when it was below zero weather? Wasn't I the one who had nursed them through sicknesses and broken bones? Didn't I make a good meal every evening for them, or do the laundry all those late nights? It sure as hell wasn't him, he was missing for all those damned years. For over 7 years, he never called to see if they had been run over by a truck, or if they had a good report card. He hadn't given a damn, at least it seemed, and now he had filed for custody? This world was screwed up. He had to be out of his mind. No judge in his right mind would even hear such a case….

But we went to court, a gloomy, rainy day befitting of the mood I was in. I had been right; the Judge threw the custody case out, and the Big Indian threw his briefcase across the courtroom. The judge cautioned him, "One more outburst like that, and I'll fine you with Contempt of Court. Do you hear me?" Doug was sick; he had to be. Here we were again: Cid, Steve, Jeff….and me, our little fatherless family. We managed to hide the hate and remorse we felt for dad's actions, and we were hurt to think our 7 years of waiting had ended this way. Yes, he needed counseling and medical help. He had a problem. We blamed it on the war and forgave him. At least we didn't talk about him in a bad way. My job with the Senate kept me busy, and the kids were old enough to chase the opposite sex. Life went on, and I legally ended our marriage, while Steve married Karen, and they gifted me with a beautiful granddaughter. He and his bride Karen had gone together for over a year…. and now, with a child on the way. He had to give up his last year of high school to make a living for the new arrival, so it wasn't the ideal circumstance to start a life together. The high school romance and the baby coming, all the while he worked outside in the weather as a carpenter-in-training, rain or snow, or even better, the sunshine. But he and Karen had tried their best raising a new baby; he had a whole new life in front of himself.

By now, I had met a man, Les Ellis, that I fell in love with, again….It was a year and a half with he and I, and we were settling in as a new couple, yet it only seemed like a few months. He was nice, a "gentle giant" as I liked to refer to him as. He had his own restaurant, a really nice place at that, and it was called "Les's Steakhouse" and located out on the southern end of the Belt Highway. As time went by though, times became rougher and tougher, so he decided to sell some shares of the stock in his business to some closely associated contractor friends. Les had thought nothing of the sale, as it was to two of his very best friends, but boy, was he wrong. That was the biggest mistake from hell he could ever imagine. Each of the three men held 33.3% of the stock, and things were going well for Les, or so he thought. The other two had different ideas; they were going to sell the property to a bank that wanted it. And sure enough, they did. Although each of the three owners got their fair share, Les was now out of a job, and out on the streets, so to say. It had saddened him a lot, a whole lot. He felt cheated out of a business he had owned for a few decades; and it showed. It had been in his life for what seemed like forever, but not now.

Eventually, we moved to Texas, bringing Jeff along with us to finish his schooling, mainly because of his age, as he was only 15 at the time. He hated to leave Missouri and all his friends, but knew he was too young to live with Cindee, so he made the trek down south with me and my new husband. Jeff was busy at his new school, and Cid was living in Kansas City deciding if she wanted to go to college, or what she should do with her worldly life. About the same time, Steve walked into his home, and, well, it was quite a shock; he had found his new wife in bed with another man, and so Steve stormed out….In fact, he moved out the next day; lock, stock and barrel.

Steve called me from home with some kind of even stranger news, he said that his dad had called after all this time, and it kind of felt strange to him. Dad wanted him to come out and eventually go into business with him, that's if Steve even wanted to go down that route. Doug said that he would have to buy him a ticket, so let him know when a good time would be, especially because he would probably be out there for several days. Wouldn't you know it, amidst all his confusion and dejection and rejection, his father would pick this time in his life to call him? Strange….He convinced Steve he had a good job as an Engineer for one of the famous hotels, and he also said he had purchased an air conditioning business, complete with a fleet of trucks, and he could teach Steve the business if he wanted to move to Nevada, and that was a decision that only he could make. So, he did just that; he packed up whatever few belongings he had left and headed off to Las Vegas; the big "Sin City," the city full of "girls of the night," and gambling, everything he thought he had wanted.

So, the Big Indian fired the tickets off to Steve from Kansas City to Las Vegas. He did fine at first, or so Doug thought, but he was wrong. Steve was starting to go down the wrong path by doing just that: girls of the night and gambling, and it just kept going and going to the point that he had to leave. After just 6 short months, he again packed his belongings and got on a bus headed to Beaumont, Texas, a city that he knew nothing about. Steve left unannounced, except for a note left behind on the television saying, "It breaks my heart to see you ruining your life with your constant, daily drinking. I have gone to mom's in Texas….please forward my Income Tax check to the following address listed below in Texas. Love, Steve"

So, by then, the Big Indian knew I had remarried again, though I doubt if he gave a damn. Our love had been so real between him and I, or so it seemed. We had married first, then we fought, divorced, and remarried again, but we just couldn't live without one another back then. Like a magnet, we were continually attracted to each other through the ups and downs, but we always had a final "get back together" and loving it each and every time. But the reality finally set in after I had left Vietnam some 7 years ago, our love was apparently over, for good….Les and I discussed this future with Steve, and what all he intended to do with his marriage. What would happen to his tiny daughter if his marriage ended in divorce? What would happen to his wife if she continued seeing this crud of a lover after 6 months, and the possibility of the effects that such a man could have on baby Amber in the future? Steve was depressed when he arrived in Texas, and being short of funds, he had sold his bike and left Las Vegas in a hurry. He had sold it for a measly amount in a hurry to just "get out." He left his father with Vegas, and what was left of him. He took the money, from the quick sale of his bike, and hit the roads to the Gulf state. He had left the Big Indian behind in his life, and he told me how very hard it is to actually walk out on your father. It hurt him badly that his dad was in the condition he was in; the bottles of liquor had won, and Doug had lost his son….again. After a couple of weeks in Texas, Steve decided to follow up on his Income Tax check, as it was long overdue. He needed the $600.00, so he called his dad, but his dad was never home. He called his dad's favorite Vegas hang-out, and finally got to talk to him. His dad informed him he had received the check, endorsed it and deposited it in his bank, and solely because Steve had not repaired the damage to his company truck.

The damage was from when Steve exited a ramp on a rainy evening and ended up rear-ending a guy, so basically, Doug was right in keeping the money. Like Steve had said though: "The damned S.O.B. was wrong in cashing my government treasurer check, he even forged my signature." The next steps involved contacting the IRS in Houston and agreeing to prosecution for the theft of a government check.

The paperwork was filled out, and so the search was on. A replacement check came in the mail to Steve, and as for the Big Indian, the $600 no doubt bought a few more bottles before he departed Vegas for paths unknown. What a sad waste of a brilliant mind, the years of engineering and telephony were gone now, and I'll always think down deep in my heart that it's the war that still got to him….The Big Indian must have felt total disgrace and distaste for himself, or maybe his bottle comforted him. Regardless, he disappeared again. As late as 1993, I still got calls from the FBI and IRS inquiring about his whereabouts and wanting to know if he had made contact with me. I just tell all these Nevada and Washington D.C. agents that I have no idea where he is. Steve had a phone call last year, it told him that his dad was employed at a remote desert test site, but by then he didn't seem to care anymore. He may be a wanted man for reasons we don't understand. We don't know, and we really don't care.

Perhaps his lack of adjustment, and the loss of children triggered the now famous "Delayed Stress Response Syndrome," But, life goes on….Steve had already deserted his homestead in Vegas, especially because the happiness he so desperately searched for was not meant to be found. After he made his move to Texas earlier in the year, he got accepted to the local union as an apprentice carpenter, Carpenters Local Union #753, and for the next 4 years he attended his Apprenticeship there. Two years, and many, many thousands of dollars later, he lost his court battle for custody of Amber, his lovely little daughter. The old bastard of a Judge on the bench had finally reached his horrid decision, "I believe there is a good relationship between Amber and her mom." That was a statement made….I believe, in poor judgment by such a respected man. Each year though, she grows from a pudgy baby into a lovely young lady. Oh, how kids can change in a lifetime, but yet still be the same….

Chapter 21

Cam Tu remained a faithful friend throughout the years following my return to the States, and for all the years that followed Saigon's downfall. After I had returned to Missouri, I received her letters in broken English, informing me of action in Cholon and Saigon. She included the formal announcement of the birth of her first child; a daughter born two years after my departure from the horrors of war. She named her Dong Dieu and sent a photo of a beautiful child with dark, almond-shaped eyes and well-formed cheekbones. I knew she would be another Asian beauty just like her mother….Dong Dieu was born in late 1970 in a small hospital, followed by the birth of Cam Tu and Tran's son, Thanh Binh. Thanh was later born amidst total confusion and death in 1972, but he died in 1975 when all hell broke loose, and all of America pulled out of Saigon. Cam Tu has the courage of a G.I. in battle, and in fact, she has seen and been in the middle of many neighborhood skirmishes, so she knows when and where to hide the children for their safety. She was well aware of all the security precautions regarding one's own home and neighborhood. She explained, "You just learn these things in time of war…." And this most definitely was war. And the war was behind every tree, and around every corner.

Cam Tu was tall and slender, a beautiful Asian and proper in her dress, mannerisms and language. Her letters soon became perfect as her English improved, yet they were full of sadness as she told of her people's situation under communist rule. She told of atrocities being done to her people in smaller hamlets and villages north of Saigon. She had many brothers and sisters, parents and Grandparents still in the jungle, as did Tran, and they were barely surviving outside of Saigon proper. They were forced to sell off their pigs, rather than let the communists steal them almost daily. They survived on sweet potatoes, rice and vegetables such as greens in the early seventies, and worse since the take-over of Saigon in 1975, since then only a thin, watery soup as a daily ration. Yet, she somehow managed to give birth to a fine, healthy son, and work at the bank while planning her escape to freedom, as her biggest wish was to raise her children in the free world and away from the suppression of communism….Cam Tu and Tran anticipated their needs, and they accumulated funds to buy their route to freedom via a boat. They saved and scrimped on food, doing without many evenings, and others, only eating a small portion of soup so extra piasters could go into the secret hiding place. The hiding place that would provide the exorbitant amount of money necessary to purchase passage on one of the refugee boats that would carry them and their offspring to distant shores and freedom.

Her letters of the early 1970s were sad truths of life, pleadings for bare necessities because they had nothing, simply nothing on which to survive on. She wrote of the dire need for new or used clothing, antibiotics, painkillers, aspirin, makeup, dried or packaged foods and any medicinal products. They were desperate. And, too, she could always resell items from the Western world and turn that cash into more escape money. We took on a new project and spread the word to friends, knowing any Western apparel we accumulated would go on the Black Market. She was so appreciative of anything, and though these boxes were of no large monetary value, they meant a lot to her…. Many boxes never reached her, thanks to Saigon's fantastically stupid postal system, a department full of ignorant thieves. Those were the guys who were also responsible for a lot of the boxes I packed and shipped back stateside that never reached their destination back here in Missouri. It seemed Saigon's postal system consisted of a junkie or elderly person, or a dirty, hungry waif riding up on a dilapidated wobbly-wheeled rusty bicycle. No established routes, no uniforms, no actual "Mailman," only a system where you gave a kid a coin to take a letter or parcel to a certain address. Maybe he delivered it, and maybe he didn't, depending on his mood that particular day. That, or his hunger pains…. Sometimes, though, he sold its contents, as some letters had "green" money in them, and some even had documents that could be copied or forged, so taking someone else's mail could be very profitable.

The maids would giggle and sniff and hold their noses upon receiving a letter that had arrived, tucked neatly under a Saigon "Mailman's" sweaty armpit and smelling of the same. Receiving one of these stinky, hand-delivered arm-pit missives through the local postal service was the pits, yet amusing. I was thankful we had APO privileges through both VRE Headquarters, and the Big Indian's communications company on the base. Our letters from the USA usually arrived in Asia in 4 to 7 days: that's not too bad, especially coming from the other side of the world. Cam Tu had been a dedicated employee of VRE Headquarters since August 1967, where she was equally devoted to her duties and her peers, and where she performed her clerical translation duties to the best of her ability….She shuffled around the office quietly and businesslike, yet she found time to comfort and console those who had lost a friend or family member during the fortnight's skirmish. She was compassionate and sweet, beautiful and intelligent. Cam Tu was a favorite of all VRE and the armed forces personnel employed there, a menagerie of different color and race as her friends. Most of all, she was admired for her fortitude and guts, this sweet, tiny lady of oriental beauty. Guts that would lead her through jungle trails and dense forests in coming years….trails eventually leading to the South Coast to sail the sea to freedom in an overcrowded fishing boat on the China Sea. She could always see what was coming her way, and she sensed an American pullout.

Her woman's intuition told her that as early as a year and a half before the Embassy took over, so she left headquarters and accepted employment at the Bank of America as a teller in downtown Saigon. The VRE was having a reduction in forces, and she could foresee the termination of her position as a translator if Americans were preparing to go home…. and this proved true at the war's end in early 1975.

After the communists took over the city, she was appointed as a "collector" because of her past experience as a teller. She lived four and a half years of hell under the communist rule, collecting house to house. She was on foot, beating doors, and only because she was ordered to do so. Not asked. Not assigned, just told to do it. The conquering communists found the economy in bad shape, and times were hard for the local citizens, now under the watchful eyes of gun-wielding rulers. The new rulers of Saigon needed funds, and so they forced "collectors" such as Cam Tu to collect what monies were owed to the banks…. monies owed before the Communist's takeover. She was confronted with hostile actions as she performed her duties; she was under stressful orders, and at gunpoint. Ahh, life under the communist rule. She was also ordered to tell citizens of Saigon to deposit their monies "for the glory of the leader" to look upon them. She didn't ask them to save at the bank, but instead, she told them to save, and how much. By now, the Bank of America was closed, as were all banks in Saigon. Only one functioning bank had its doors open, and that was the Communist government bank. But it was a job….and it was either be a collector as she had been told to do, or dig in the fields and shovel in the streets. Too, as she was already out in the neighborhood "collecting," she could sneak by her house and check on her babysons.

Cam Tu and Tran should not have suffered those years after Americans pulled out; they were actually cheated out of the on-going escape in 1975 when the Bank of America evacuation plane left without them. The BOA issued and distributed every BOA employee and their direct relatives an I.D. card, and it was explained these I.D. cards were issued to board the coming evacuation plane that would take them away from their North Vietnamese captors. This followed the Viet Cong storming the Embassy wall and the total American pullout in the Vietnamese war. This plane was to carry only BOA personnel and families; the Americans and Vietnamese to freedom. Cam Tu was an employee in good standing, even a signed "Permanent Status" form with BOA….A Mr. Le Huu Luu and a Mr. Vo Van Than were in charge of the Bank of America evacuation staff entrusted to handle the assigning of the "BOA Identification Cards" that would entitle employees and their immediate families to board the plane to freedom. These very men had a big responsibility, and temptation crept into their souls when they accepted bribes as big as $10,000 per seat. Yes, they sold Cam Tu's seats before the plane even arrived that afternoon. Only those BOA personnel and staff who were in very close contact with these two gentlemen.

There was no evacuation for Cam Tu and her family, no compensation, no severance pay, and, worst, no escape to freedom. Only tears and fear of the new communists who had taken and secured her city. She endured pitiful attempts to escape, and she begged on the streets for food. And she was jailed for her attempted escape to a waiting boat, and she has endured the fact that her college-educated sister sells coffee on a Saigon street corner to this very day. She had led a degrading life due to losing her seats on the BOA plane, and she has since been forced to sell everything and live on just rice and beans. She's been imprisoned, and starved, all the while other BOA employees have enjoyed freedom, good working conditions and good wages in other countries. She and Tran were again forced to be captives in Saigon, the land of the Viet Cong; a dirty world, to say the least.…Cam Tu waved to the ship, the one she thought he had landed on, but he couldn't see her as she hid in the dense jungle just outside the city at their point of rendezvous. She wiped her tears, as there would be other opportunities. They were determined to keep on living, but deep down inside, it hurt. It hurt bad, so bad that she wanted to throw up, but she couldn't. Her stomach was already so empty that it didn't even realize it.

Her brother Kien would live again in the safety of the Western world, and hopefully, marry and have children to carry on the family name. At least one of the families was alive, and she was grateful. If only she and her family could get out of there, then, there would be no more leeches, monsoons, maggots in his food, no more shells ringing in his ears, and no more street murders to witness. He would be taken by the American Navy to a free world, this young, handsome pilot. But life was unbearable for Cam Tu in the weeks ahead….She realized what life was like under the communists when they took her father's farm and turned it into a commune, leaving him but a tiny patch of land on which to raise his vegetables. It was barely enough to feed his family on, as many children still remained at home. There are many people that now farm his land for the "Glorious leader," and leaving her father with a plot of earth no larger than about the size of an American bathroom. He raised a few sweet potatoes, a hearty staple of Vietnam, and a few potatoes and onions, a miserable way to live when your own God-given land is taken from you at gunpoint. But he kept his mouth shut so as to keep his life….he had a family to raise, and was determined to do so the very best way he knew how. Cam Tu's family was better off than Tran's family, as they had 13 kids and were much poorer, and with too many mouths to feed. It was made even more difficult by a failing rice crop several years in a row, and starvation went along with prostitution.

People survived as best they could, regardless of the morals involved.

Shortly after the Americans pulled out back in 1975, the Viet Cong rounded up all the trucks and automobiles in the Saigon area, and then lined them all up for a two-day processional convoy of vehicles headed north to Hanoi, the capital of the victorious communists. It seemed like all of the cars were forcefully taken from their owners and driven to the capital, but thankfully, not every single one of them. No monies were ever paid to the owners, nor was any consolation given: just a "we are taking your car for the glory of the people." Cam Tu must have been tired of hearing that expression, and she saved harder and scrimped more for her day….The day of escape. Meanwhile, the Communist victors were raping all the young girls, and the older ones who weren't married, were again taken and had no individual choice of husbands, or even lovers, for that matter. Forced love and forced labor dominated the city, but for fathers to object over the abduction, rape or marriage of a young daughter meant one of torture, and in full view of all family members. Or, sure death, miserable death. Luckily, the older women like Cam Tu were basically left alone. But, the daylight hours meant constant observation by heavily armed guards in every block. So, the evenings were cherished when Tran and herself could be with their children, partaking of a late meal of the normal watered-down soup or rice, but never meat, and rarely any vegetables….Behind locked doors, they felt secure, though they slept with open eyes and ears turned to the locked gate, forever fearful of the mysterious soldiers who continually demanded answers to questions, or papers to be shown. A constant and painful fear gripped them. A nagging swept deep within their hearts for their parents in the hamlet miles away.

They were caught, and jailed, during a third attempted escape, but they somehow kept their spirits up. So they eagerly planned a fourth escape by boat, as all they wanted was out. Out of the daily watchfulness of Charlie; the Viet Cong, they had planned their every move, both day, and night. Cam Tu knew she wanted to take her 16-year-old brother, Cuong, so that he, too, would have a life ahead of him, but passage on the refugee boat was exorbitant, and they didn't have enough money. Cam Tu and Tran decided to beg friends and family….She made the long bus trip through the jungle, many hours of riding hot, dusty roads, and only after she had been granted permission to travel and had filed a travel plan with the communist authorities. She finally found her family, downhearted and beaten, yet eager for her and her family to make this dangerous escape to freedom, and whenever they felt they could chance it. Villagers and friends donated small items to sell, and Cam Tu's father sold his last 2 pigs to cover Cuong's passage. He was a starving father who gave up his last livestock, and just so that his young son could buy his freedom. He said they would get by somehow, and some way. They had sweet potato soup, if nothing else, and the roots that he could dig from the ground would suffice, as would the greens they could pick from the lowlands.

So, the plans were laid out, and dates and times were set within the following weeks. Maps were secretly passed by underground messengers, and Cam Tu was drying foods that would enable the two small children to survive the boat trip. Not knowing if they would be at sea for weeks, or months, that was always preying on her mind, and so she was constantly worried. She prayed as she planned for the dark, moonless night, when they would get the signal. It was then, and only then, that they were to start their dangerous trek through the jungle to the southern shores of Vietnam. It was there that they were to rendezvous with the captain; a captain who had been well paid in advance for their precious passage to freedom. The children had no toys now that Saigon was "Ho Chi Minh City," nor did they have clothes or furniture. What the communists had not taken for themselves, Cam Tu had sold for the best price she could bargain for and secretly hid the money for her escape. They sold their television first, Cam Tu's pride of the 20th century….The Communist party controlled the station now, and so the viewing had changed from opera and theater, to now a communist preaching for the "Love of Labor," and she didn't want anything to do with her children being indoctrinated. She knew she would someday, somehow, raise them in

America, and didn't want them to have any more party indoctrination shoved down their throats than was necessary to survive. If they heard it on the street, that was one thing; but to turn it on and view it by choice, that was an entirely different matter. So, the TV, now unimportant in their new lifestyle, was the first to be sold.

The Communists held street dances for the young children, just another way of instilling the "Glory of the Party." But Cam Tu never let Dong Dieu or Binh go out to play, or dance; that was just too dangerous. They remained stationed within their little hut, never daring to disobey their parents. There was no school, only what Tran and her called "school," which consisted of a couple of hours each evening learning their numbers and the ABCs....All of the children's stories, and the news also, were read aloud under the glow of soft candlelight. Manners and religion were taught, and no child of Cam Tu and Tran's would ever grow up without knowing the "Please and Thank You's" that are so necessary in this world. These classes were often interrupted by incoming rockets and falling debris, and plaster, or a blood-curdling scream piercing the night like a sharp knife. Any night noises always brought the question, "Was it a neighbor?" or "Was it a friend?" God, war was awful.

Weeks passed, and Cam Tu's mother knew it was near time to go to Saigon and say goodbye to her family. As before, she had to report to the police and tell them she was making a trip to the city and fill out fourteen copies of papers to satisfy them, including her name, age, address, and the reason she wanted to travel to Saigon. The purpose of the visit was naturally a lie. The planned escape had to be kept a mutual secret by all involved, or the boat would never be allowed to leave the shores of the China Sea where all escapees would be shot and left to die in the sand. How long had she intended to stay….what mode of transportation she would be using. Then, when it was time to leave Saigon, Cam Tu had to tell the communist police that her mother was leaving again. She had to name what time and date it would occur, and what mode of transportation, and she had to file travel papers all over again, as well as a proposed "map" of her travel route back into the jungle. There were no secrets, and there was no individual freedom under the Communist party. Like prisoners, these people abided….as they had no choice. This was years of planning and selling, begging and borrowing had gone into this well-laid out plan.

Then, Cam Tu got word that her Captain had already sailed his ship without notifying her, also taking their passage monies to sea with him….How hard can one lady cry in one night, or every night? Surely, she and Tran filled a river with tears at the disappointment, for it meant starting all over again with barely enough clothing and no furniture to live with. It would be hard to round up enough items to sell for another try….let alone just the day-by-day living. Money was the answer, and somehow, they would get it; enough to buy payoffs to another captain of another ship. They would escape and they would survive, and all because Cam Tu's guts were showing again. Guts and determination filled these tiny people, as they had already begun a planned fifth exit from South Vietnam. She worked hard at buying some western clothes, as they were hard enough to buy in Vietnam for one price, and then resell them at another, but she did. Before any of the western items in the shops in Saigon sold out, she would bargain with the seller for a lower price…. Naturally though, anything and everything "western" was forbidden, so these pants were grabbed up fast, and then resold for a higher price. Prostitutes were mainly interested in the slacks they called "cow pants," so Cam Tu hated to part with them; she took a lot of pride in the few American clothes she had collected again. Yes, everyone was forced to wear the ugly standard black pajamas. Communism takes everything that you've got.

I wanted to send more boxes over the next few years, and I tried, but after the Americans pulled out, there was no way to get the mail through. The Communists allowed no parcels into Vietnam from the USA, as they were too busy indoctrinating their newly conquered people and didn't want them to have any contact with the free world. The mail was still allowed to enter from other Asian countries, but not from America. Many people from the USA could mail the package intended for a Vietnamese resident to the neighboring country, only to be rewrapped and readdressed, and then forwarded on to Vietnam…. It was a long time before parcels were allowed into Vietnam from America, so sending Cam Tu anything of value was "out" due to theft and lack of postal privileges from the other countries. In her earlier years, she had sent me lovely gifts, gifts that were native to her beloved country before the communist took over. My most cherished item is a wood carving of a village hut on high bamboo stilts; a tall, slender thatched hut, with a narrow entry ladder leading to the elevated safety of the hamlet jungle home. It's complete with a large rock under a small tree, and trimmed in bark for authenticity. It never fails to bring back memories of my year with the people of South Vietnam, I have been in these sparsely furnished huts, and seldom found more than a pot to boil rice and sleeping mats, yet always statues and an altar denoting strong religious beliefs….Hell, even Cam Tu never failed to get Christmas cards out of the country, even though mailing to the United States was illegal. She probably paid a pretty penny to see to it that I had "Best Wishes" during the holidays….as she would have done anything to get the mail through to me as I was her only link to freedom. I was her "Ba Juni," her American mom, her hope for the future.

It was very important to her to stay in touch with me as I was the final link in her escape plans, the one whose name she would give to the Red Cross if her escape materialized. I was an American citizen, so it was desperately necessary to finalize the papers so she could be released from the refugee camp and make the trip to the USA. I would be the contact that would take her from the squalor, stench and starvation she had endured for many war-torn years. Without a sponsor, the refugees were forced to stay years in the camp, so it was of the utmost importance to stay in touch with me and her brother, Kien, who was already here, and a helicopter pilot in Louisiana. We were her passport out of the refugee camp…. providing the next attempted escape was successful. All Cam Tu could think of was America, escaping the horrors of war and communism. Though it was difficult, no, extremely difficult to think of leaving her family and parents, and her homeland of traditions she had grown up with. But it was no place to raise her children, and she was more determined than ever to succeed in the next escape. She continued sneaking letters out of the country to me, right under the noses of her communist and rulers, risking going to jail again just to do so. And perhaps, even death….

I cherished each and every word she wrote, and I reread each and every postal mark itself, remembering the months and months it took some letters to arrive. I wonder how many people hid her letters under something, all in passing them on to the next person in the underground chain to smuggle them out of Vietnam. How many people guarded her letters with their lives, a precious letter so that she may, indeed, stay in touch with her American friend, a friend who someday may assist her with sponsorship and paperwork that would bring her into America? She did the impossible with her communications….

All of the cards that she snuck out were made of things like silk, satin, feathers, leaves, and mother-of-pearls, complete with sampans, fish, palm trees, and children, all so unlike our fat, jolly Santa's of an American Christmas wish. They continued a life of misery, life and suffering insurmountable at times. But she never gave up. With no medications available, and an improper diet to sustain life, they became weakened and thin, but still full of courage. They continued to plan and save for the big day…. The communists rationed rice in small amounts daily. They had no shoes all these years, only what they could manufacture by cutting rubber from old tires that were a part of the war's aftermath. Strips of rubber formed thongs that would cushion their trek through the jungle floors as they further planned the 5th escape. The thongs were hidden beneath a board on the floor, as shoes were at a premium. They could not afford for them to be ruined or stolen, especially just before they started down the path that would lead them to the China Sea.

Tran had taken such pride in his teaching, and he was allowed to continue teaching for a couple of hours each morning. He taught what he was told to teach, as there is no freedom of speech under the Commies. His teachings were those of his conqueror's beliefs, and afternoons, he was forced to labor with bare hands in the dirt as he built and rebuilt his hometown of Saigon. The devastations of many years of war were everywhere, and the once proud city had its ugly scars all over the place. Tran slave labored and dug ditches till his hands bled, and his back was almost broken, a miserable step down for a once-respected professor.... Cam Tu sold Kien's bicycle, the one that he had left behind when he joined the South Vietnamese Air Force. They hated to part with the bike, their only mode of transportation, but it brought $200, the equivalent to American money, towards the passage on another refugee boat. The shops were padlocked and boarded shut, and what items were already in the country when America pulled out was it. There would be no more luxury items or western apparel under Charlie and his enforcers. The next to go was Cam Tu's traditional Al dios, her traditional dresses. She cried when it was time to part with her long, sleek dresses slit up the side to show the matching long pants underneath, the traditional dress of her country. The dresses had been tenderly and carefully sewn by hand by her mother and grandmother. But they, too, understood that money was the answer to their freedom, and they would sell till there was nothing left to sell, except two items for each member of the family to be worn on the boat to freedom. Where these people get the courage to keep going, I have no idea....

Chapter 22

Cuong had been hidden at Cam Tu's house for two and a half months before they actually made their escape, as his name was on the draft for military service under the North Vietnamese captors. He was kept inside, not allowed to go out for fear of being picked up and sent off to war. Also, Dong Dieu and Binh were not allowed to go out. They lived most of the 4-1/2 years behind walls in the safety of their little home. The communist-held street dances were still going on, but "brain washings" actually would be a better name for them….And the children became quiet and withdrawn, obedient to the "Nth Degree," living with the fear of the world around them day-in and day-out. Yet they had the love of their parents, a gift that the North Vietnamese could never take away from Cam Tu's closely-knit family. They bonded together and planned for their freedom as they had done so many times in the past, never quarreling or uttering a cuss word. Everything was so clearly understood as to what each individual's role was in surviving this unique situation. The kids were taught not to speak to strangers, and if soldiers came to the house, the children never uttered a sound, as though they were deaf-mutes. They played their roles beautifully; it was a matter of pure survival.

They were too Americanized already, with Cuong, little Dong Dieu and Binh surviving the days pretty much alone, month after month, never seeing an outsider. Cam Tu checked in on them between her collecting, yet it was a hard, lonely life for the kids, for all of them. They played the role of the conquered by daylight, but night-time was a different story. They plotted and planned into the wee hours of the morning as they longed for a taste of freedom….The wealthier, older residents in Saigon, those who knew their health would never permit them to make the jungle trek to a waiting refugee boat, much less survive the weeks at sea, gave their monies to young people to buy passage. They knew if they kept their money, the communists would steal it, so rather than take a chance of their captors stealing it, these monies were given with love and "Good Wishes for a safe journey." Tears were shed, bundles of cash were handed over to the younger, stronger generation, all with the hopes of a better life elsewhere in the Western World….The elderly stayed behind in the horrid conditions, as they had no choice. All shops in Saigon were closed by now, as only one market was open, the Communist Government Market, and yet no one could afford to make any purchases anyway.

It was time to go, Cam Tu, her husband, son, daughter and her 17-year-old brother. From here on out, it was the jungle trails, traveling only at night. They took only what gold and jade they could stuff into their pockets, or wear on their fingers. They hoped that the gold would be bartering material at a later date, that's if they ever made it to the freedom of a refugee camp, or if the damn captain increased their fare at the last minute. They could wage a good battle with gold and meet any last minute demands he may make of them. They had a small bag of dried foods for the children, and each wore two complete sets of clothing, one over the other as protection from the sun and saltwater at sea, as if that even mattered…. They would set out in the darkness of the night, sneaking down the alleyways of Saigon, and then onto the jungle paths pre-routed for them. Along the way, the villagers were alerted as to what nights and what routes the escapees were traveling and often took advantage of them. Cam Tu had to purchase water along the way to drink, and she paid dearly for boiled water so as not to contaminate the children, as they couldn't afford any sickness before reaching the shores of the China Sea. She paid the equivalent of $3.00 for a pan of boiled water and $6.00 for a bowl of rice with a little pineapple and nuts, coconut and sugar in it for the children at breakfast time.

Cam Tu's father had made contact further down the trail, and he had prearranged a few huts for them to sleep in a couple of nights along the way. It was an empty hut, just a mat on the bare floor to rest on, and the bugs, oh, the bugs. The children were cautioned not to whimper, or even to talk as they stepped lightly down the trail. They never uttered a sound, even when frightened by the sounds of the dark jungle and the unknown. They had been well prepared, well trained after the escape failures of years before. This one was to be the final try….or give up. Human beings can tolerate only so much, and there was nothing left to sell or borrow. They had to make a go of this try, and so Cam Tu prayed, "Oh, please, God, lead us to the shore and let our boat be there, please." Through rice paddies and at every jungle clearing, keeping low, they were crawling like snakes when necessary, the children closely followed their father and were protected from the rear flank by Cam Tu and Cuong, their brother. Bravely bellying their way towards freedom, they often stopped to remove leeches, and to comfort the little ones. Cam Tu thought of her family as she crawled through the muck and mud, and she cried because she left her four sisters, and her mother and a father in the hands of the war's victors. Tran was from a family of 13 children, and he had left his parents and 12 brothers and sisters to rot in communism. He has 6 younger brothers already inducted into the communist army, and all fighting in Cambodia. And not because they wanted to fight for the communists, but because they were forced to. Tran cried, too, as he remembered the large, loving family back in the hamlets, now miles behind them.

There was never any doubt as to which of Cam Tu's family would make the escape with her and Tran. Her parents had sold what they could to help this only son remaining in Vietnam get out, as Cuong was the man of the family who could carry on, so he must have his freedom. Somehow, they survived the treacherous jungles, and they cried when they came out of the jungle and onto a sandy beach where they spotted the waiting boat. There was a group of them by now, along with a few stragglers who had joined them along the trail. They melted quietly into one as they went the last 75 yards south to the prearranged location to sail out of…. They soon began loading on-board, and there was no returning now. There was little drinking water aboard the boats, and only a bit of dried food for the children. The sun beat down on them, burning and charring their already dark skins till they writhed in pain. Salt water splashed aboard the deck of the 45' X 16' foot boat, hardly able to accommodate a couple of dozen people, which was nothing like the 260 refugees that were actually aboard. Again, they were clothed in double clothing. Children were lashed together to the boat, and the 260 or so people sat with knees up under their chins, and with someone at each elbow, in front and in back of each other…. they were in horrible, crowded conditions. Tran told of the day when the engine was broke on the boat trip, how high the swells of the sea were, and how the boat would rock like a cradle up high to the right, then off to the left. The boat rocked to the top of the wave, then back down to the bottom, only to rock high to the top again. It was miserable, but anything would beat being in Vietnam, and I mean anything. He said everyone was so sick, and he wondered what kept them from turning over at the top of the waves. These people are Buddhists….very religious, and very thankful to all Gods for their escape. They were heartbroken to think of families they had left behind. How sad to hear such a thing like that, yet they'd look at their brother and know he was there to help them, to save them.

They finally spotted land; The land of somewhere that there was peace. Somewhere they had only dreamt of….And when they were finally at the safety of the shore, they all bent down to kiss the land, almost in disbelief they were finally there, and no longer in Vietnam. A few days later, they were taken by truck to the Leamsing Refugee Camp, arriving on June 17th, 1979. It felt like heaven, although it was just a roughly made-up campground. But again, it wasn't Vietnam. At the time, it was all they could do but to rest, and doing their laundry in the camp was late at night, perhaps 1 or 2 AM….They wrapped kids in rags or a sheet given to them by the camp and headed to a well where they tied a string around clothes and sloshed them around, up and down, back and forth, up and down, back and forth in the well. In the camp, Cam Tu said they went out and picked greens and cooked them for food, and all the drinking water was hauled in. Although it was just the basics, they will be so eternally thankful to eventually be in America, and they promised God that they would make good citizens. After leaving the camp, it was 7 more days on a boat trip on to Hong Kong, China; an arrival port for the Vietnamese evacuees. Once there, they spent 10 days waiting for their passport to go to America, so they were sort of like prisoners for all those days.....

In the fall of 1979, they landed in the United States, where Mrs. Cam Tu looked as pretty with her long, raven black straight hair, and her sweet, natural beauty. Tran is small, and can't weigh over 140 lbs at the most. He is a brilliant person, and Les and I both enjoyed listening to him….he is very intelligent, interesting and a good conversationalist. And oh how we talked, we spoke for hours on end. The kids had their first taste of chocolate, and I even had some miniature Hershey bars on the coffee table where they ate their share, so I sent the rest of them home with them. The kids preferred water over Coke, as they had never had any Coke, and they thought it was yukkie! They are just content with rice and water, just what they have always lived on forever. So sad….But such lovely little kids, they have a beautiful smile from all of these happy people. Their journey is finally over. Only God knows their suffering during their boat trip across the China Sea, as that had to be the second worst thing they ever experienced, second only to the daily bombings back in Saigon. They spent the next 3 nights with us, each day with story after story of their trip over here. God, they must have gone through utter hell getting out of Vietnam, and not a day too late. Their stories of creeping through the jungle were enough to make a person cringe, and that trip went on for days on end. In the jungle one minute, and out the next….She said it was the worst part of the escape they had to go through, as everything else was out in an open field, or down the edge of a country road. I can only imagine what all they went through though, it could only be like being in hell, or worse.

I later received a letter from Cam Tu and Tran Ho dated March 22, 1980. They had settled down in San Jose, California;

"Dearest Mamason Juni,

We all believe everything is OK now here in our new home. We didn't pass by Beaumont to see you all on our trip back from seeing my aunt down in Louisiana. We were afraid of disturbing you while you were busily worrying about papa Les's hospitalization and the expenses of the care he was receiving. I know he was going through a bad time, so we just kept on going when we passed through town. Besides, Kien's working for a helicopter company in Phoenix, Arizona, made us in a haste, as he had only 48 hours to be in Phoenix, and this opportunity he had long enough been waiting for. We must be without delay, sorry. We left New Orleans that cold and windy morning, and emotionally, our hearts sank, for we began to love that French-tradition city. From 8 AM to 10 PM on the first day, we passed San Antonio and stopped for the night in a rest area. On the second day, we reached New Mexico State, and at 3 PM, the third day to Phoenix, Arizona, where Kien was accepted for his job, which would start on 3/17/80. The following day, we drove again from the early morning, and arrived at San Jose only at midnight. All through the journey, both Tran and Kien miraculously drove the car safely so we could enjoy our trip very much. It was our first experience across the continent of North America by car. Thank goodness, the two children were always in good health, and they had learned a precious lesson on the geography of the United States. Once back in San Jose, we had to spend almost half of a month to restart everything from the beginning. Renting an apartment here is something harder than passing an examination, both in price and in search of lodging. We stayed in a friend's home until 3/27/80 when, only at that time, we could find an apartment with two bedrooms at the price of $450.00 a month. God that's a lot of money for a small apartment. As soon as we came to San Jose, both Tran and I submitted our Basic Grants to Condie College, a private school in business and technology, for enrollment in an 18-month course in Electronic Technician Training. This course consists of 3 semesters and begins on 6/25/80. The aim of our move is to be something professional so that we can have a relatively stable living in the future. That's why registration for vocational training is the top priority. Duong and Dawg Pierce again continue their schooling near our home, and though Binh will be sent to a daycare center on Monday with the cost of $130 a month. Can you believe that? I cannot find this sum of money. Perhaps I must call for Kien's help. He has now returned to Phoenix for his "flying carrier." Poor him. He must be so lonely. I really don't want to be far from him after those four long years! He told us that when our training course in San Jose is completed, we could move to Houston and find jobs there. Houston is a big city now under development. They need electronic technicians. Anyway, we could be near you, my dearest Mamason Juni. We all want to be with you. We are alone among the immensity of the American environment, a new way of living, a new struggle for life. And we know without the love and moral support from a sentimental mother like you, we could hardly overcome. We need you, by our sides, the same way Cindi, Steve and Jeff do. And we understand so well that you always worry much about our first hard steps of living. Thank God almighty for leading us into your motherly arms! And we love you so much! Now again, we are trying to keep balance of our daily living full of difficulties. I hope it will only be a short time, 18 months of training, and then we could earn something better to support the children in a steady life of freedom and comfort. Everything is but at the beginning. Oh, will it be a long time, 18 month's worth!

How are Steve and Jeff doing? Cindi and your Grandparents are surely enjoying this beautiful sunny weather. I hope it won't hurt Grandpa and Grandma's rheumatism. How is papa Les now? We all love to read about him. Whenever Dong Drew and Thawhi Binks see a McDonald's Hamburger on TV, they always cry cheerfully, "Grandpa Les's hamburgers and the clown!" I must say goodbye for now, dearest Mamason Juni, there are so many things that need to be in order these days in a new home.

With our deep love and best wishes to you all, I remain.

Cam Tu

729 Menker Ave, #4

San Jose, Ca 95128

Chapter 23

In 1981, the Americans were visiting communist Vietnam. They are led on a tour to visit the War Remnants Museum, the Mekong Delta, and the sprawling Chinatown of Saigon (Cholon), where the "boat people fled." They were driven by Mercedes Benz, and their tours were guide-controlled and well-organized. They saw just what the communists wanted them to see. They visited a drug rehabilitation center, the former U.S. Embassy, which is unchanged since we deserted it in such a hurry in 1975….and they spend their monies which are badly needed in Ho Chi Minh City. They see the Mekong River Delta, the resort of Vung Tau, the G.I.'s resort for R & R during the war, and they see Cu' Chi where bloody battles took place. They are shown the elaborate tunnels used by communist forces for shelter, evasion and offensive strikes. "Why would Americans spend their money on our defeaters?"

A dear friend of mine made this trip against my better judgment and threw her money to the "Reds," and she told me the beggars still had outstretched hands, and actually forced their hands into her car window asking for a "dong." Even the Communists were overheard asking one tourist, "Why you prefer the capitalist-imperialist way of life?" in their broken English language. "Why you come here? You be Marxist comrades?" She reports a lack of luxuries on the ships, and young mothers pleading for help for their babies. Farmers were observed hoeing their fields, though they have had failing rice crops for several years only due to the drought. They were shown only the best sides of the old Saigon. Tourists were not allowed to film the ragged peasants whose homes were built of black cloth anchored to a fence…. only supported by two bamboo poles on a downtown street. They were shown the "Museum of U.S. Puppet Atrocities," they discussed the communist outlook on the world, and as they think it should be. Thank you, God, for letting me be an American. In the case of Vietnam, the United States Government supported the repressive government with economic and military aid, and advisors for the betterment of the country. These few advisors began our involvement in Vietnam. Our policy was often charged as a misguided pursuit of our own interest, as we were said to have collaborated with a terror-wielding junta to obstruct the legitimate aspirations of the people.

Vietnam should have been no more than a vital interest to the USA, and not a place for a false war to take place. We should have allowed them to work out their own problems, rather than intervening and causing domestic anguish and international disgrace, leading to the publics' cries of "No more Vietnam!" Why were we bogged down in a war we were not allowed to win?

Why were we supporting the government of a country that its own people did not support? Why was Russia supporting the North Vietnamese regular army units? Huh? It was these forces, and not the peasant forces of the back hill Viet Cong that captured Saigon back in 1975. In the early beginning of that year, these forces invaded the south, and they pushed across the demilitarized zone that separated North Vietnam from South Vietnam….We should have known, yet we let it happen. We should have learned something when the South Vietnamese people themselves did not rise and support the political and military during the North Vietnamese and Viet Cong general offensives in 1968, and again in 1972. Many stories show a constant, persistent flow of allegations of atrocities, and all the war crimes perpetrated by the South Vietnamese and the United States that supposedly took place.

Yet the headlines seldom blared of the tortures carried out, and of the massacres carried out by the Viet Cong. Nor did we often hear of their systematic assassination and mutilation of village chiefs….and only in an attempt to intimidate the populace. When the North Vietnamese and the Viet Cong slaughtered more than 20,000 civilians in Hue of 1968, little was said and/or written about its wrath on the country. Our news media made our enemy appear compassionate, even humanitarian when actually they were brutal and sadistic killers. There is a wide discrepancy between what actually occurred in Vietnam, and what all the home folks heard about it back in the States. No more Vietnams, as one was plenty….Monies were loaned to many foreign nations, especially to Asia. This money was lent for specific projects, such as irrigation, road construction and electrical power projects. Loans are interest-free, although the principal is to be repaid. Most of the aid goes to nations generally friendly to the United States, or where there is a strong U.S. interest, such as India. Although, a $50 million loan to Communist Vietnam in 1978 aroused the wrath of many members of Congress. Yet, the $50 million dollar loan was made three years after our Marines, Air Force, G.I.'s, civilian engineers, non-commissioned employees and contractors were pulled over the Embassy wall….and Saigon fell.

Three years later, we loaned them, the Communist, $50 million. Really? I'll never understand our government if I live to be 100 years old. Why did our boys bleed to death? Why did they endure neck-deep mud? Why did they even have to die? There was an immense, coercive persuasion, or brainwashing, and long sessions of interrogation. It has been said the standards of the Marine Corps deteriorated during the Vietnam era, all the while anti-war sentiment ate into the troop's morale. Our G.I.'s and Marines, the Air Force and the Swabbies all entered a world of drug-taking, and questionable behavior hastened these men's desire to get completely out of South Vietnam. Reports of assaults on officers by enlisted men were numerous….

Amnesty was extended to Marines and others who fled the country to avoid Vietnam service. Some Marines, like Garwood, were said to have disgraced the uniform, but I feel America disgraced itself by losing this war. There was never a desire or a plan to win amongst the strategists. Only a plan to be there to make our presence known and to keep our soldiers busy, regardless of the cost. There was a lot of disgrace and shade felt by veterans of the Vietnam War….perhaps that can explain why not one Vietnam battle name is commemorated on streets and buildings labeled with famous and obscure memories. The memories of wars like Korea, World War II and earlier wars. And not one date is listed on, of all places, the reverse side of the Marine War Monument at Arlington National Cemetery. Our young men are trying very hard to forget their Vietnamese experiences….they prefer it that way.

Our Marines bled freely in the jungles and ridgelines, and they were exposed to Charlie due to high command decisions forced on the Marines, as they were never allowed to win. It was a bloody, bogged-down stalemate when our first American troops set foot ashore in South Vietnam. Stories of torture, corruption and persuasion erupted from our vets who once hoped where they could speak freely of their feelings….Psychological warfare consisted of group indoctrination, solitary confinement during their beatings, starvation and inhuman acts of violence. Americans were never considered "war criminals," and they were not entitled to prisoner of war status and consideration. Where were the universal rules of the Geneva Convention, the rules of protection equally exchanged between countries? Why wouldn't a man break? Was my husband one of these Americans who knelt and mercilessly begged for his life, only to be promised the moon in exchange for cooperation? Is this where he spent his 7 years from late 1968 through mid-1975? I'll never know. Our Vietnam Vets never had a ticker tape parade, or confetti and 10 gun salutes of welcome, their reception of "Welcome home, Soldiers, a job well done!" never came.…

This was a war. A war that actually ended after the mass of troops had been flown home by the plane loads after we withdrew. The American public had no great day of celebration, just a contrasting view of why we had been there, no delight in a victory. These men made sacrifices, as did their families. The Vietnam vets had a bad reputation. Some were spit upon, some were mugged and beaten, and some were jeered. No one respected them, even though they, too, suffered wounds, both physical and psychological. Many were taken prisoner and spent years in captivity. More than 50,000 died in the war. That's about $1,000 per dead G.I. that we loaned Communist Vietnam in 1978.… and that was only 3 years after the war ended. A rather high price to pay, especially for as many men we had lost. The Vietnam warriors and veterans are known as the "tarnished soldiers," but yet, not because these men served under some of the harshest conditions known to man. They were our brave American citizens trying to defend the honor of our nation, but welcomed home like rats. There was one veterinarian killed in Vietnam; he should have been home tending to sick cows and lame horses, but he was over there doing his job, as did many, many others. He left his shop of tools and an old Mustang only to "do his bit" in preserving peace…. but he was not allowed to fight to win. He died in a losing war….

For 15 years, a period from 1945 to 1960, the United States reigned over the entire world like an arrogant emperor. All the other great powers of the world had been crippled by World War II. But, the United States, blessed with vast resources, technological know-how and military might, set up and knocked down governments, bossed around other nations, and otherwise reorganized the world, more or less, as we saw fit. True, we had one powerful competitor for the world's allegiance, but despite Cold War rhetoric, few Americans really believed that the Soviet Union could ever prove to be our match. The USA was simply too far ahead, we were out front and speeding away like the first-place car at the drag races. We believed Kennedy could do no wrong….he personified the American imperial spirit. He was cocky, bold, dashing, sophisticated and compassionate, a vital, fresh figure on a world stage otherwise largely populated by ancient, decaying leaders. Though predictable, that conviction that "we could do no wrong" beguiled us into making colossal mistakes….Possessed by the notion that we were somehow responsible for the destiny of the entire globe, we dumped millions of tons of bombs, billions of dollars, and tens of thousands of lives into a tiny Southeast Asia nation. At home, we squandered resources as if they were infinitely replenishable and instituted ambitious social programs that we couldn't afford. We never thought we might lose a war or run out of money. There was no bottom to the supposed "America the Bountiful" barrel.

In the 1970s, we learned to accommodate ourselves to some disenchantment; we were soured by Vietnam, and we abandoned our global goals. Soured by Nixon, we came to distrust all our leaders. The near bankruptcy of New York City, that was what persuaded us that there were absolute limits to what programs a society could afford. Despite these awful blows to our self-confidence, we never doubted the country's ability to provide citizens with an opportunity to lead a good life. A life full of hope and prosperity….

In the 1980s, our savings had eroded, and inflation appeared to be here to stay. We have other global problems; shouldn't we have learned a lesson from Vietnam? Reagan, hopefully, will not continue to do such stupid things, as his resurrecting the Vietnam War by branding that most bitter and divisive conflict as a "noble cause." He should have been there. He should have saw what I saw, and he should have walked where our soldiers walked….

Of course, I, too, showed confusion in the declaration of my mixed feelings regarding the Vietnam War. One day, I was sick to my stomach that we were not there at all, whereas the next day we were. I am proud that we did make an effort to win, even though we were not allowed to win. It was a game called a "POLICE ACTION," and heavy side-betting assured all the "game-keepers" that the victor would be North Vietnam, and not America and South Vietnam. The current U.S. main battle tank, the M60, first appeared in 1959. Its replacement, the new XM-1, now undergoing field testing, is vastly improved and revolutionary. The prestigious Defense Department claims in its engine, armor, fire-control system, and eventually, its gun, to be dominant in the intervening 20 years. Meanwhile, the Soviets have introduced four new tanks, each an improvement on some specifics of its predecessor. While the Soviets make turtlelike progress, the U.S. opts, at some risk, for a frog-like leap. But we do have the SR-71, the super spy plane, the one that carries high-resolution cameras and imaging radar that can make pictures in the dark and through clouds. It also carries eavesdropping equipment to monitor radio traffic and radar emissions. It has sensors that can look sideways, which clearly means the SR can fly outside a country's border, all the while peeping deep into the nation's interior. The SR can map 100,000 square miles in a single hour. It's the Ace photographer at his best!!!

The first operational Blackbird mission was flown in 1965, and it went directly into the most hostile anti-aircraft defense ever mounted, over Hanoi, the capital of North Vietnam, and a laboratory of the best missile, anti-aircraft guns and radar systems the Soviets could design. And yet, although SR's flew daily reconnaissance missions over North Vietnam during the remainder of the war, not one was ever touched. At one time in the 60s, Lockheed had some 9,000 workers on the SR-71 assembly line, but only around 40 aircraft were ever built. The exact number is a classified secret….The tools and dies, forms and melds were cut up and scrapped. I managed to get into the country with two 100-ounce silver bars; these were Engelhard silver at .9999+ fine silver with their individual serial numbers, but I never saw them again. What the Big Indian did with them, or traded them for on the local black market. I never could find out where or why. The money exchange rackets flourished daily over in Vietnam, and openly so, although there were the consequences untold if you got caught. The American "green" we carried in our wallets was not allowed in the country, and MPC, the standard military and Civil Service pay in Asia, did not buy as much as the "green." It was easy to trade green for 3-1/2 to 5 times its worth in exchange for money, so it was a very good deal….

Vietnam syndrome is considered similar to "shell shock" in WWI, or "combat fatigue" among WWII veterans. The emotional wounds of Vietnam ran deeper in their bones, and only because it was an unwanted war. They received the worst reception anyone could ever imagine, no pats on the back of "job well done." Much smuggling of marijuana and cocaine, hashish and cannabis goes on. Yet, today, and only because our Vietnam vets had a never-ending war from battle to home, it all happened too fast, and their total efforts in the war were unappreciated... They have a delayed stress reaction, which symptoms include nightmares, flashbacks, anxiety, depression, rage and jumpiness. They had unpredictable and aggressive behavior, guilt and distrust among each one of us. Researchers claim more than one-third of combat veterans from the Vietnam War suffer from this disorder. Many need, and are getting, psychiatric counseling. We need more programs and centers to assist these men who gave of themselves....and for us.

To alleviate any potential hiding places for Communist forces in Vietnam, the U.S. Defense Department used more than eleven million gallons of Agent Orange, as far as I know, to defoliate large areas. This highly toxic chemical, containing TCDD, strips plants and trees of leaves, thus eliminating foliage cover for the enemy, and it prevented sneak attacks along jungle trails. Exposure to Dioxin has been proven to cause cancer, respiratory problems, skin, nerve and liver diseases. Miscarriages by our veterans' wives, impotence, emotional disorders, genetic damage and several other illnesses associated with our most famous, undeclared war….The toxic herbicide was used widely in Vietnam, and the physical ailments and birth defects blamed on Agent Orange are becoming common. Many veterans' lawsuits are still pending, and that's years after the wars ended back in mid-1975. Agent Orange contaminated water and food, and it was consumed by almost all of the American ground forces and civilians alike. What was not unsuspectingly consumed….was inhaled. Everyone, including myself, and possibly my children, was contaminated to some degree just by routinely inhaling polluted air. This poison was all around us. This substance was used by the Air Force from 1962 to 1971, a nine-year period, and where eleven million gallons were sprayed to dispose of all protective umbrage. Substantial numbers of the millions of Vietnamese war veterans have been determined to be contaminated, and these numbers will just keep increasing as more birth defects and cancer show up in future examinations. Why? Why did all this happen? The Department of Defense turned up some astounding information following the pull-out in South Vietnam, and it showed over 90 different instances when airplanes dumped their chemical cargo in emergencies. Also, over 40 other instances in which Agent Orange, apparently, was dumped directly over, or near, the U.S. Air Bases and other military installations. Yes, the crews on spraying missions were forced to dump Agent Orange on our own men. Military records provide evidence of these spraying missions.

This dumping of the herbicide cargo near large groups of American troops and bases in the whole of Saigon, and it happened because of failing engines, or because the planes were under communist fire. An emergency that has endangered over 60,000 vets who have advised the Veterans Administration of their fear of impaired health.

And to think that my husband and I carried

on a true love affair during all of this….

Please, no more Vietnams' for God's sake;

This really was "True Love in a False War"

THE BIG INDIAN

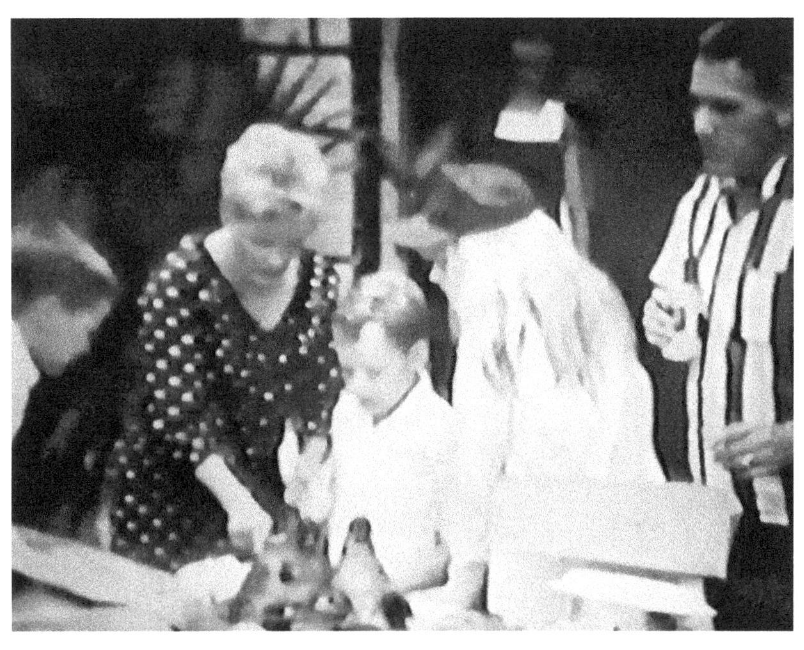

Juni's 36th birthday party pig roast in Saigon